THE FAERIE PLAGUE

DARK WORLD: THE FAERIE GAMES 5

MICHELLE MADOW

DREAMSCAPE PUBLISHING

CHARACTER LIST

Selena Pearce: Chosen champion of Jupiter, the king of the gods. Lightning magic. Half fae, half witch. Adopted daughter of Queen Annika Pearce (the Earth Angel), and Prince Jacen Pearce (vampire.) Biological daughter of Prince Devyn Kavanagh (fae gifted with omniscient sight) and Camelia Conrad (powerful witch.) Soulmate of Julian Kane. Lives in Avalon, but has been kidnapped to the Otherworld.

Julian Kane: Chosen champion of Mars, the god of war. Combat magic, and the ability to pull weapons from the ether. Half-blood fae, with unbound fae magic. Soulmate of Selena Pearce. Lives in the Otherworld.

Torrence Devereux: Powerful witch. Daughter of Amber Devereux (powerful light magic witch) and an unnamed father. Best friend of Selena Pearce. Lives in Avalon during the weekdays, and at the Devereux mansion in Beverly Hills on the weekends.

Reed Holloway: Mage. Younger brother of the triplet mages that helped found Avalon—Iris, Dahlia, and Violet Holloway. Has lived in the mage realm of Mystica for most of his life, and moved to Avalon a few weeks ago. He's betrothed to a princess in Mystica.

Thomas Bettencourt: Half vampire, half wolf shifter. Gifted with magic over technology. Leader of the Bettencourt vampire coven, which is based in a luxury hotel in Chicago. Mated with Sage Montgomery. Lives in Avalon.

Sage Montgomery: Half wolf shifter, half vampire. Alpha of the Montgomery wolf pack, which is based in Hollywood Hills, LA. Mated with Thomas Bettencourt. Lives part time in Avalon, and part time with the Montgomery pack.

Empress Sorcha: Empress of the Otherworld. Has a magical gift she calls *bliss*—the ability to mute magic and/or dull the mind.

Lavinia Foster: Powerful dark magic witch, with demon ancestors. Lilith (a greater demon) sent Lavinia to the Otherworld with Lilith's daughter, Fallon, so Lavinia and Fallon can exterminate the fae. Lavinia created a plague using Fallon's demon blood to do the dirty work for them.

Queen Gloriana: The First Queen of the Otherworld. She lives in Elysium and meets the chosen champions at the dock as they arrive, to ease them into the afterlife.

Bridget: Chosen champion of Minerva, the goddess of war strategy. Future sight magic. Killed in the second week of the Faerie Games, by Selena. After seeing Selena in Elysium, she chose to be reborn.

Cassia: Chosen champion of Ceres, the goddess of agriculture. Earth magic. Killed in the fourth week of the Faerie Games by Pierce, after an intense torture session by Octavia. Selena last saw Cassia in Elysium, where Cassia was unsure if she wanted to be reborn or not.

WHERE WE LAST LEFT EVERYONE:

Selena and Julian brought the Holy Wand back to the citadel, but refused to hand it over to Empress Sorcha. Prince Devyn revealed that the half-bloods who win the Faerie Games aren't free to return to Earth—he'd tricked Selena earlier with his words.

Fueled with anger, Selena tried using the Holy Wand to create her own portal back to Earth. But before she could finish, Julian threw knives through her palms to stop her, and she blacked out.

Torrence, Reed, Sage, and Thomas finally arrived in the Otherworld. They were immediately surrounded by zombies, and they used their holy weapons to turn the zombies into ash. They met with their contact in the Otherworld—Princess Ryanne—and the princess learned that the group disintegrated the zombies. No one has yet to be able to stop the zombies, so Princess Ryanne sent the group to the citadel so they can tell the Empress what they can do.

Will Torrence finally reunite with Selena? And most importantly, why did Julian turn on Selena when she

was seconds away from creating an escape portal to Earth?

Turn the page to find out...

SELENA

I FLOATED between that moment of being awake and asleep, not wanting to wake up. Because in my dreams, Julian was there. He held me in his arms and gazed down at me with his familiar ice-blue eyes, looking at me like I was the most important person in his world.

I love you, he said, his voice calm and soothing.

But then his eyes hardened. His expression twisted into anger, pain, and grief. He pulled away, like touching me disgusted him.

Pain shot through the centers of my palms and seared up my arms.

I woke with a gasp.

Sweat dampened the mattress and feather pillow beneath me. My muscles felt like molasses, and my mouth was paper dry, like I'd been walking in a desert for days.

A chandelier with vines and flowers wrapped around the glittering crystal hung overhead. Fae decor.

I was still in the Otherworld.

But the portal I'd created... I should have been home. In Avalon.

Julian's hard, distant eyes flashed through my mind again. The centers of my palms throbbed with stabbing pain.

He'd thrown daggers through them. He'd snuffed out my magic.

He'd stopped me from bringing us home.

Devastation hit so hard that it hurt to breathe.

My own soulmate had betrayed me.

Why?

Forcing past the heaviness in my body, I pushed myself up to sit in the bed. My breaths quickened from the effort. I collapsed back into the mound of pillows and rested my arms on top of the comforter covering my legs.

I stilled at what I saw.

Light brown henna tattoos swirled from my hands to my elbows. The skin around the lines was puffy and red. It tingled, like it had been scrubbed raw.

I traced a finger along them. They were raised, and sensitive to the touch.

It wasn't ink that had seeped into my skin.

These were scars.

Burning electricity searing up my arms.

I stared down at the lines in disbelief. It shouldn't have been possible... but my own magic had scarred me.

I raised my eyes and scanned the room. It was large, plush, and decorated in whimsical fae furniture. The windows looked out to fields and palaces that reminded me of Elysium.

Illusions. Or maybe not.

Panic pounded in my chest.

Am I dead?

The Holy Wand wasn't there. Julian wasn't there. The room was so silent that my ears rang from the lack of noise.

I needed to get out of there.

I tried to move my legs, but they wouldn't budge.

I knew this feeling. This sluggishness. It was like when Sorcha had touched me in the arena, when Octavia and Emmet had been murdering Molly, and she'd infused me with her magic to calm me down.

Arms wrapping around my waist. Calmness rushing through me, relaxing me so much that I couldn't stay conscious.

After Julian had snuffed out my magic, Sorcha must have used her gift on me. She'd *drugged* me.

She and Julian were working together. This plush room was some sort of prison.

But they couldn't trap me. I wouldn't let them.

So I called on my magic for protection. Dim light glowed from the scars wrapping around my arms, but my magic slipped past my fingers.

I was helpless.

No, I thought. *I'm one of the most powerful people in the Otherworld. Sorcha's magic is strong, but mine is stronger.*

I pushed the comforter off my body. Someone had dressed me in a white, silk nightgown fit for royalty.

I gathered as much strength as I could and swung my legs off the bed, pushing off with my hands to land on my bare feet.

My legs crumpled under me, and I collapsed to the floor with a resounding *thump.* The side of my head slammed against the hardwood. I cried out as pain ricocheted through my brain, and black dots danced across my vision.

The door creaked open, and crystal shoes that resembled Cinderella's glass slippers stepped inside.

I blinked the dots away and rolled my head slightly back to look up.

Empress Sorcha stared down at me with creepy blue

eyes that were so light they were nearly white. She wore a fluffy white ballgown and a tiara that must have been a foot high. Its diamonds matched the color of her wings. She held a breakfast platter with a tower of pastries in one hand, and the Holy Wand in the other.

My wand.

I opened my hand and pictured the wand flying out of her grip and landing in my palm.

Nothing happened.

She turned around and handed the wand to a half-blood guarding my room. "Return this to where I've been keeping it," she instructed, and just like that, the wand was gone.

She closed the door behind her and released sparkling diamond magic from her palm. It flowed into the doorknob, which clicked as it locked shut.

I dug deeper and called on my magic again. The twisting lines on my arms glowed dimly, but my magic still refused to answer my call.

I grunted in frustration, rolled onto my back, and pushed myself up so I leaned against the side of the bed. A few beads of sweat rolled down the sides of my face from the effort.

Sorcha walked over to the coffee table in front of the fireplace and set the breakfast tray down on it. "You've been asleep for nearly three days," she said, and alarm rushed through me at how much time had passed. No wonder I was so weak. "You must be hungry."

The sugary scent of warm pastries wafted through the air, and my stomach growled.

I tried to swallow, but my throat was so dry it hurt. "You drugged me with your magic," I said, although my tongue was so stiff that the words came out in a slurred mess.

She picked up a glass of cloudy white juice—lychee juice—and walked over to me. She kneeled down and sat, her dress mushrooming out in a perfect circle around her, and held the glass up to my lips. "Here," she said. "Drink."

I glared at her and pressed my lips together.

She pulled the glass back toward her. "It's just lychee juice," she said. "It's not drugged. All it will do is hydrate you."

If fae could lie, I wouldn't believe her. But fae *couldn't* lie. And I was dying of thirst.

She must have sensed my desperation, because she continued, "Would I have given you such comfortable accommodations if I wanted to hurt you?"

I bristled, since the villa where the chosen champions lived during the Faerie Games was fit for royalty, and they were sending all but one of us to our deaths.

"Just drink," she said. "I can't talk with you if you're so dehydrated that you can't speak."

We sat there in silence and stared each other down.

But it wasn't doing me any good to sit there powerless and thirsty. So I sighed and reached for the glass.

She moved it away from my hand. "You're too weak," she said. "You'll spill it. Let me." She held the rim of the glass to my lips, and the tantalizing scent of the juice teased me until I opened up and gulped it down.

It was sweet and delicious, and gone far too soon.

"That's better." She nodded, raised herself back up to her knees, and held out her other hand. "Come. Let me help you over to a chair."

I recoiled and snarled. "Don't touch me."

The sides of her lips curved up into a small smile. "There's the spirited little minx I remember. I knew she was still in there."

I reached for my magic again, but it was just as far away as it had been before. "You should know," I said. "Since you're the one who did this to me."

She placed the empty glass down next to me and lowered her hands into her lap. "I saved you from yourself," she said. "You should be grateful."

"You took away my magic."

"I temporarily muted your magic. All three types of it."

Crap.

I glanced over my shoulder to look at my wings. They were blue, silver, and violet. The glamour I'd been using to keep up the illusion that they were still only blue must have stopped working when Sorcha had muted my magic.

I needed an explanation—quickly. One that wouldn't reveal that I knew half-bloods had the same amount of magic as full fae when our magic wasn't bound.

"The wand unbound my magic the moment I touched it," I said. "It seems that since I'm half-fae and half-witch, my magic is stronger than a regular half-blood."

She eyed me curiously. "Much, much stronger," she said. "Once we've settled things between us, I look forward to seeing what else you're able to do with the wand."

I perked up instantly. "You're going to give it back to me?"

It was too good to be true. There had to be a catch.

"Perhaps." She smiled in that unnerving, calm way of hers. "The Holy Wand is no good in my hands, since it only answers to you."

What?

I froze, since I hadn't expected that.

"At least, it answers to you for now," she continued,

seemingly oblivious to my surprise. "Since its previous owner was dead and no one has risen to claim it, it became yours the moment you touched it. Now, you can choose to bequeath the wand to someone else, in which case, they'd be able to use it instead."

"No chance," I said.

"I thought as much," she said. "Unfortunately, there's only one other way to pass on the power. And that's if someone kills you and claims the wand for themselves."

2

SELENA

I SUCKED IN A SHARP BREATH, dizzy from more than just hunger.

She was going to kill me.

Or was she?

"I was unconscious for three days. You could easily have killed me and claimed the wand for yourself," I said, trying to remain as calm as possible. Sorcha was always calm, and I had a feeling she respected calmness from others, too. "So why am I still alive?"

"I value your father's guidance," she said simply. "It would hardly benefit me to kill his daughter. Plus, I might be able to use your help."

"So you want to make a deal with me."

"That would be my preference, yes," she said.

"Like how you made a deal with Julian?" My chest panged when I said his name.

"Julian would do anything for you," she said. "He loves you dearly."

No, he doesn't.

The cold way he'd looked at me before I'd lost consciousness flashed through my mind, and it felt like a piece of my soul had been ripped from my body.

She raised an eyebrow. "You doubt his love?"

"Never," I lied, and she sat back and frowned.

A second later, she was back to her normal serene self. But it didn't matter. I'd caught her by surprise, and it felt good.

Let her wonder if Julian was deceiving her instead of me. She deserved it.

"He's here, in my house, in a guest room similar to this one," she said, and my heart jumped at the realization that he could be on the other side of one of these walls. "He's been asking to see you."

"Bring me to him." Fear about what he might say clawed at my chest, but I pushed it down. I needed him to explain why he'd done what he'd done—even if that explanation broke my heart.

"First, come with me onto the balcony." She stood and straightened her skirts. "I need to show you something."

"You won't harm me out there?" I needed to make sure she didn't intend to throw me over the rail. "And you'll bring me to Julian right afterward?"

"I promise."

I tried to push myself up on my feet, but my muscles were jelly. They refused to listen to me.

The Empress's diamond wings sparkled as she observed my failed attempts.

Hatred surged through me. If I could access my magic, the entire floor would have combusted by now.

But Sorcha was a diplomat—not a fighter. And using my words to get what I wanted seemed to be working relatively well with her so far.

So I took a deep breath, imagining it as a wave of calm cooling my veins. *One, two, three,* I counted off in my head. Then, I returned my focus to her. "If you expect me to get up and walk, you need to stop using your gift on me."

"The magic I most recently used on you is muting your magic. It's not making you physically weak," she said. "That's the effect of you nearly depleting your magic when you attempted to create a portal to your realm, and then not eating for three days."

I wished I could accuse her of lying. But even if fae could lie, this wasn't the first time I'd nearly depleted my magic. It felt just like this.

And there was only one quick fix I knew about.

"There were two golden apples in the pack I flew in here with," I said. "We found them on our journey. I can eat one of those to regain my strength."

"I already found them," she said. "It was kind of the gods to gift them to you."

"Julian told you?" I held my breath, praying she'd deny it.

"He told me the entire story of how the two of you found the wand," she said, and another wave of pain hit me at the extent of his betrayal. "The gods, Sibyl, the Golden Bough, the Underworld, the Fomorians. All of it. The two of you had quite the adventure."

What about the Sanctuary?

I stared up at her and blinked, waiting for more.

Did Julian not mention the Sanctuary?

It didn't seem like it.

What was he playing at?

I didn't know, but if I paused any longer, Sorcha might get suspicious.

"Where are the apples?" I asked to get us back on subject.

"The gods must have decided you didn't need them anymore, because they were rotted and crawling with worms. But the pastries were baked with care by a fae gifted with healing magic." She walked over to the breakfast tray, picked it up, and placed it on the floor next to me. Then she sat down again and laid her skirts around herself like we were having a picnic. "The food will help you, not hurt you." She plucked a jelly doughnut from the top of the tower of sweets and tore it in half. "Choose one side. I'll take a bite of it, and you can decide what to do from there."

Her expression revealed no trickery. Of course it didn't. She had centuries of practice with deception.

But my bones were hollow with hunger, and my stomach was eating itself from the inside out. I wanted that doughnut. No—I wanted to devour every pastry on that platter.

What would Julian do?

"That side." I pointed to the one in her left hand.

She nodded, took a delicate bite of the doughnut, and swallowed it down. Then, she held the other half out to me.

I snatched the half she'd bitten out of and finished it off in two bites.

She smiled in approval.

We continued that way—with her tasting each pastry before I ate it—until reaching the bottom row. There were only a few pastries left when I sat back in defeat and wrapped my arms around my full stomach.

Arms that were covered in swirling scars.

They were hideous.

All right, maybe not *hideous.* The vine patterns themselves were pretty enough. But I hadn't chosen them. I didn't want them there.

They reminded me of Julian's betrayal, and of my failure to return home.

"How do you feel?" Sorcha asked.

My magic was as unreachable as before. But my head no longer felt light from hunger, and I was no longer leaning back on the bed for support to sit up.

"Better," I said, and I pushed myself up onto my feet. My legs didn't wobble, and while I wasn't in the shape to sword fight, at least I was able to stand.

Sorcha stood as well. She was shorter than me, but her diamond crown was so tall that it towered above my head. "I told you the food would help," she said.

She was so small. So frail. If I had my magic, I could easily take her down.

But I didn't have my magic. So to stay alive, I needed to continue pretending that I was considering helping her.

"Can you walk?" she asked.

I took a few trial steps toward the doors that led to the balcony. Like the other windows in the room, the glass panels looked out to an illusion of Elysium. Thankfully, I had no issues walking toward it.

Sorcha stayed by my side. We stopped at the door, she reached for the handle, and then she swung it open.

Dark, angry clouds covered the city in shadows. They growled with thunder, and bright red light flashed between them, tinting the marble buildings red.

Lightning.

Red lightning.

It was a scene straight from Hell.

Rain sounded overhead, although it didn't penetrate the dome. There was no wind, either. It was like being inside a glass house during a storm.

I walked over to the rail, rested my hands on it, and continued gazing up at the eerie red sky. A sharp sense of *wrongness* seeped through my skin and sank into my core.

"It started about an hour after you tried making that portal," Sorcha said from beside me. "They're calling it the Red Storm."

I tore my gaze away from the fiery sky to look at her.

She was watching the storm with an expression I never thought I'd see on her face.

Fear.

"I didn't cause it," I said.

"I know," she said. "The storm started after I muted

your magic. It would have been impossible for you to cause it."

"So why did you bring me out here?"

She looked at me, her eyes sharp. "Because you're the only known person in this realm who has lightning magic."

"I didn't do this," I repeated. "This magic isn't mine."

"Clearly. But I was hoping you might be able to stop it."

"*That's* why you didn't kill me for the wand," I realized. "You need my magic. And even the Holy Wand can't gift you with magic you don't already possess."

"I believe you can help save the Otherworld from both the Red Storm and the Wild Plague," she said. "So I don't want you dead. I want your loyalty. I want you fighting by my side. I want us to be allies—not enemies."

Anger rushed through me, and I tightened my grip on the railing. "You trapped me in the Otherworld," I said, and red lightning flashed between the clouds. "And now you want me to fight here with you instead of going back to Earth to help my family against the demons trying to claim *my* realm."

"Not necessarily," she said. "I want us to come to an agreement. A compromise."

We held each other's gazes, and more thunder rumbled overhead.

"Will this agreement involve unmuting my magic and allowing me to return home to Avalon?" I asked.

"I'm open to the idea," she said, and for the first time since waking up, hope rose in my chest. "But now that you've seen the storm, let's go back inside. Your soul-mate is in his room, and he's waiting to see you."

3

SELENA

SORCHA STOPPED in front of the doors that led out of my room. "Try anything against me, and I *will* use my gift on you again," she warned. "Right now, I'm only muting your magic. But as you've experienced before, I can also numb your body and mind. I'd prefer not to do that to you again, but I will if you force my hand."

"Understood."

"Good." She released an orb of her diamond magic toward the doorknob, the lock clicked, and she opened the door.

Two fae guards were stationed outside my room. Neither of them acknowledged us.

"Julian's room is at the end of the hall," she said. "Follow me."

We headed down the hall, and the guards followed quietly behind us. My heart pounded with each step that echoed on the marble floor.

How long has Julian been working with the Empress?

Will I ever be able to look at him the same way again?

Who can I trust if I can't trust my own soulmate?

Maybe I'd been stupid to trust him at all. Our relationship had started with deception, so I knew he was capable of it—and *good* at it. Julian's strategic mind was one of the reasons why Mars chose him as his champion.

But I'd believed our soulmate marks made me different in his eyes. I thought he saw me as someone he wanted to protect instead of deceive.

Apparently, I'd been wrong.

Sorcha stopped in front of the door at the end of the hall. Two guards flanked the sides of it, just like they had mine. She aimed her magic at the door, unlocking it, and for the second time that day, hope bloomed in my chest.

Why would she keep Julian guarded and locked inside if they were working together?

She leaned forward and rapped her knuckles on the door. "Julian," she called, continuing before he could say he was there. "Selena's awake and here to see you."

The silence was so heavy I couldn't breathe. I fidgeted in place, about to explode from anticipation.

Then, finally, he said, "Bring her in."

The closed door muffled his voice, but it didn't hide how stiff and formal he sounded. Like he was ready for some kind of business meeting.

Sorcha opened the door and motioned for me to enter first.

I swallowed down a lump in my throat and stepped inside.

Julian stood at the far side of the room. His back was turned away from us, his hands clasped behind his back as he looked out his window at the Red Storm raging overhead.

There was no trace of ice blue fae magic in his steel gray wings.

He was using glamour to hide it.

Sorcha followed me inside and clicked the door shut behind us. All four guards remained outside.

A shadow passed over the tips of Julian's wings, and he turned around to face us. His eyes drifted to my arms, and I quickly clasped my hands behind my back to hide the scars.

His jaw muscles tensed, although he showed no emotion beyond that.

Sorcha sat down on the chair near the fireplace and arranged her skirts perfectly around herself, like she was getting ready to watch a show.

But all of my focus was on Julian. And it was taking every effort to stop myself from running over into the comfort of his arms. The only thing holding me back was fear that he'd push me away.

Another rejection from him would break me into pieces.

"Selena," he finally said. "You look well."

Anger flared within me and heated the surface of my skin. "That's it? You shot daggers through my hands to stop me from bringing us home, and all you can say is *you look well?*"

"Creating your own portal to bring us to your realm was never part of the plan," he said.

"Going back to Avalon was *always* the plan!"

He looked away from me, pressed a finger to his temple, and met my gaze again. "Did you even think about my family?" he asked. "They *need* me. What would happen to them if we couldn't get back here?"

I lowered my eyes, because I should have thought of his family, but I hadn't. All I'd cared about was getting home. "If I could get us to Avalon, I could get us back here, too," I said. "You'd have been able to see your family again. I would have made sure of it."

"You can't know that," he said. "Our plan was to complete the quest, and get tokens so we could go back and forth from the Otherworld and Avalon as we pleased. You could see your family again, and I'd still be able to see mine."

"I'm sorry," I said. "I really am. But that plan failed. I needed to do *something*."

"So you pushed your magic so hard to create that portal that you would have *killed yourself* if I hadn't stopped you."

"I wasn't killing myself." I started toward him, but stopped halfway there. "I was bringing us home. And I was so close. All I needed was a few more seconds—"

"And you'd be dead!" he screamed so loudly that I flinched backward. "You should have seen yourself. Your magic was tearing your skin open. Beams of it were shooting through the cracks. You were screaming in pain. Your magic was breaking you apart."

"No, it wasn't."

"It was," he said. "Our souls are connected. I *felt* what you were doing to yourself. Your magic was destroying you from the inside. And you have the scars to prove it."

I glanced down at the scars and ran my fingers along them. "I was pushing myself more than ever before," I said, and I looked back up at him, standing strong. "But I had it under control."

"You didn't. And you were so consumed with your

magic—so determined to get to Avalon—that you didn't even realize it."

No. I shook my head, refusing to believe it. *It's not possible.*

But that wasn't true.

Because it was starting to sound awfully similar to what happened to a witch when she cast her Final Spell. A spell so far beyond her capabilities that she gave her own life in exchange for it.

The same type of spell my biological mother had used to bind my magic right after I was born.

I turned to Sorcha, since she couldn't lie. "It is true?" I asked. "Was my magic killing me?"

She pursed her lips, as if debating her words carefully. "Using more magic than we're used to can tax us and make us feel physically weak, similar to working out a muscle you haven't used in a while," she said. "But when we push our magic beyond our abilities, it warns us to stop by causing us pain. I couldn't see you clearly through the cyclone you'd created, but your soulmate claims you were in dire pain. Is he correct?"

Her words struck me like a knife to the heart. "Yes," I admitted, although that wasn't even the half of it. Because I'd never felt such awful pain in my life. Not even when the Minotaur had almost killed me.

"Julian and I saved your life," she said. "If he hadn't used his daggers to stop you from using your magic, and if I hadn't used my gift to relax your body enough so it could take the time it needed to heal, you'd be dead."

4

SELENA

I BLINKED AWAY tears and looked back at Julian.

He watched me with so much sadness. And despite whatever agreement he might have with the Empress, he'd saved my life. Just like he had so many times before.

I walked toward him, expecting him to scoop me into his arms and hold me close.

My heart dropped when he didn't.

There was only a foot between us, but it felt like a mile.

"I'm sorry," I said, needing him to believe me. "I was so angry when Prince Devyn said we couldn't go home. And I was so close to creating the portal. I could practically see Avalon. *Smell* it." I could also smell my burning flesh, but I left that part out. "You stopped me, and you looked so guilty..." I paused, since I needed to be careful about what I said with the Empress watching. "I thought you'd turned against me."

He stiffened, looking at war with himself.

Then he closed the space between us, wrapped his arms around me, and pulled me close. All of the tension left my body at once. He buried his face in my hair, and cool air brushed against my ear.

Fae magic.

A sound blocking spell, so Sorcha couldn't overhear his next words. He was using my hair to hide it.

"I know you don't like the Empress," he said quickly, and I frowned, because that was an understatement. "But I love you, and I'll do everything in my power to make sure you get safely back to Avalon. Right now that means working with her. I have this under control. Will you trust me and go along with it? Please?"

My lungs tightened. Because he was right. I hated the Empress. She was keeping me trapped in the Other-world. She was also binding the half-bloods' magic to keep them as slaves.

The half-bloods were my people. I could have easily been in their position if I hadn't been hidden by Avalon's magic. Julian *had* been in their position. So had Cassia and Bridget. And Julian's mother and sister—who were my family now, too—were still slaves living in a hovel apartment in the outskirts of the city.

I believed I could help the half-bloods. But I was in no position to do that from here.

So Julian was right.

To get to Avalon and still be able to return to the Otherworld so I could free the half-bloods, we needed to get on the good sides of the fae and strategize from within. Which would be exceptionally easy, since the Empress had just finished telling me she wanted to be allies.

Likely thanks to Julian, I realized. *He's had her ear for three days.*

He must have played a part in convincing her that I was better use to her alive than dead.

I couldn't believe I'd doubted him.

I'd let my anger control me. I'd let it stop me from thinking straight.

I wasn't going to do that again.

At least, I'd try to be aware of it if I was, so I could step back and see the situation from another perspective. If I wanted to be the queen that the half-bloods in the Sanctuary, Julian, Gloriana, Bridget, and apparently the Holy Wand wanted me to be, then I needed to stop acting on impulse, and think like a queen.

"I love you," I said, since I couldn't reach my magic to cast a sound blocking spell of my own. "I trust you."

The cool air of his sound barrier spell disappeared,

and he pulled away from me and took my hands in his. "I think you could be the key in beating this plague," he said. "The Empress agrees."

"I do," Sorcha chimed in. I spun to face her, and she straightened her skirts again. "Now that I've followed through on my promise to bring you to your soulmate, and your lovers quarrel seems to have ceased, are you ready to listen to my proposition?"

Not really.

But I plastered a smile on my face anyway.

"Yes," I said, and Julian relaxed his stance next to me. "I am."

"Wonderful." She motioned to the love seat across from her. "Please, take a seat. Both of you. I'll have the guards bring us refreshments, and then we'll talk."

A guard brought in a platter with a carafe of milky dragon fruit juice and three glasses. He served us, and let himself out.

Sorcha picked up her glass and raised it in a toast. So did Julian.

I made no such effort.

"You say you want us to trust each other," I said, my

gaze level on Sorcha's. "So before we talk, I want you to unblock my magic."

She lowered her glass slightly.

"Selena," Julian said slowly.

I didn't look at him. My eyes remained on Sorcha. "I won't use my magic against you," I continued. *At least, not yet.* "I'm just having trouble focusing with my magic dulled like this."

"I dulled your magic, not your mind," she said. "I won't consider unblocking your magic until after we discuss my proposition."

Tricky, tricky words.

She wouldn't *consider* unblocking my magic until then.

It didn't mean she would.

I narrowed my eyes, ready to rail into her for it.

But Julian pressed his thigh firmly against mine. "The Empress's request is sensible," he said. "You have no need of your magic at the present moment. I have full access to my magic, and am more than capable of protecting us both if the need should arise. Which it won't."

Sorcha gave him a satisfied smile. "You should listen to your soulmate," she said. "He's quite smart."

And I'm not?

I was a straight-A student at Avalon Academy.

But my grades were proving pretty irrelevant in the real world.

Julian had far more real-world experience than I did. Plus, he *could* protect both of us with his magic. He could pull a sword out of the ether for me, and I didn't need magic to fight with a blade.

"Fine." I grabbed my glass and raised it.

Julian did the same, and the juice inside sloshed around slightly.

His hand was shaking.

Is he nervous?

I'd never know it from his calm expression—so calm that it competed with Sorcha's. But I'd also rarely seen him nervous. In fact, I didn't think I'd *ever* seen him nervous. Not even before each time he'd entered the arena in the Games to fight for his life.

What had he been up to for the past three days?

I couldn't wait until we were alone together so he could catch me up. But for now, I needed to focus on every little nuance of each word the Empress said.

"To a possible alliance," she said.

Julian and I repeated her words, and then we drank. The dragon fruit juice was bursting with sweet, delicious flavor, and the milk added a certain amount of comfort to it.

Julian set his glass down on the coffee table and

rested his arms by his sides. Sorcha placed hers back down as well.

I held onto mine. I needed something to do with my hands, plus, the drink was delicious.

"The domes around the city and villas are strong, but the afflicted are growing in numbers," Sorcha started. "And we can't live in domes forever. So we must figure out a way to save the Otherworld."

"I can't kill the afflicted," I said. "I've already tried."

She waved it off. "Don't worry about that. I've already made progress on killing the afflicted."

"What kind of progress?"

Her eyes sharpened. "That's on a need-to-know basis," she said. "Right now, I'm concerned about those who have been bitten and have yet to fully succumb to the plague."

"You mean the ones who haven't become full-blown zombies."

"Yes." She nodded. "Julian told me of this name you call them. Zombies. From what we know so far, there's an incubation period between when a person gets bitten, and when they become a zombie. The length of this period varies from person to person."

Julian rested a hand on mine, and warmth traveled through my body. "We're curious to see if you can cure someone in the incubation period." He sounded steady, yet doubtful at the same time.

"I'm not sure," I said, and then I refocused on the Empress. "I haven't come across anyone in that state. So I haven't had the opportunity to try."

"Then you're in luck," she said. "Because I have. And she's safely locked away, anxiously waiting to meet you."

5

SELENA

A YELLOW-WINGED GUARD brought us average clothes worn by regular fae—colorful, cotton garments with decorative stitching throughout. Sorcha left to change in her quarters. The guard remained in the room with Julian and me as we changed, so we couldn't speak freely.

The Empress returned relatively quickly. Her hair was down, and she wore a common light blue dress with purple and silver stitching.

The colors of my magic. She was goading me. But I pressed my lips together, saying nothing as she used glamour to change her irises from milky blue to bright green, her hair from blonde to brown, and her wings from diamond to topaz.

She was barely recognizable.

"Do I have permission to glamour your wings so they appear only light blue?" she asked me. "No fae have wings with more than one color, and we don't want any unwanted attention."

"You do," I said, and when I glanced back over my shoulder, the purple and silver were gone.

"Perfect." She smiled, and looked to the guard. "Tell the servants to prepare Aeliana's carriage. Then go fetch the Holy Wand. Conceal its true form with glamour, and wait with it outside the door."

He bowed his head. "Your Highness," he said, and he left the room.

She glanced at the hearth and then back to me. "There's something important you should know before I unmute your magic and hand you the wand," she said, and she looked to Julian. "Should I tell her, or shall you?"

He shifted uncomfortably and cleared his throat. "I will," he said, and when he looked back at me, he was as serious and intense as he'd been when I'd first entered the room. "While you were sleeping, I spent time with my mom and sister."

"That's wonderful," I said with a smile.

He didn't return it. "The empress has generously allowed them to live in a guest suite here in her house," he continued. "They're only a few rooms away."

He should have sounded happy about it.

But he didn't.

"They'll remain here as my guests until this mess with the plague is sorted out," Sorcha told me. "Once I unmute your magic and return the wand to you, I urge you not to try anything against me or my people. I'd have no choice but to retaliate, and we wouldn't want anything unfortunate to happen to my guests, would we?"

I stilled, shocked. "You're threatening them," I said.

"I've been providing them with the luxury of being guests in my home," she replied. "What you choose to do with your magic will determine if that experience continues."

I glanced over at Julian. He held my gaze, his eyes hard.

I have this under control, his words from earlier echoed in my mind.

I'd never do anything to purposefully hurt Julian or his family. The Empress knew this, and she was using it against me.

As much as I hated to admit it, it was a smart move on her part.

"I understand," I said, and she smiled.

"I knew you would. Now, let's be on our way." She led the way out of the room, where the yellow-winged guard stood next to the door, holding a long sword with a gemmed handle. He balanced the point on the ground.

It had to be the Holy Wand.

I narrowed my eyes to see through the glamour. But with my fae magic muted, the sword remained the same.

"You might as well give me my magic back now," I said to Sorcha. "Since you've ensured that I'll only use it as you please, you don't have to worry about me using it against you."

"Very well," she nodded, and she reached for my arm.

I flinched backward.

"I can't unmute your magic without touching you," she said. "Do you want it back, or not?"

"Of course I want it back."

"As I thought." She rested her fingers on top of the scars on my right forearm, and this time, I didn't pull away. Her touch tingled, and a wave of release crashed outward through my body. The wave reached my toes, and Sorcha lifted her fingers from my arm and stepped back.

The scars on my arms glowed blue, purple, and silver, and I sighed as my magic ignited back to life. I reached for it, held up my palms, and created purple and silver orbs that hovered above each of them. Lightning crackled around them.

I glanced back at the sword and narrowed my eyes.

The air around it shimmered, and a ghostlike image of the Holy Wand appeared in its place.

The orbs in my hands disintegrated, and I moved forward to take the wand. But Sorcha stepped in front of me, stopping me.

"I'll give you the wand once we reach our destination." She took it from the guard and held it inches away from me.

Electricity crackled at my fingertips. Every muscle in my body screamed at me to shoot lightning at Sorcha's heart and paralyze her. Julian and I could easily take down the guards, find his mother and sister, and get out of there.

But Julian had told me to trust his plan. And the last time I'd gone against our plan, I'd nearly killed myself and then woken up with my magic muted.

So I'd do things his way.

For now.

Sorcha nodded. Then she spun around and started down the hall, and Julian and I followed her out to the waiting carriage.

6

SELENA

THE GLASS CARRIAGE was drawn by a regular horse instead of a pegasus. Sorcha and the yellow-winged guard sat facing front. Julian and I had to ride backward. The Empress kept her hand on the wand, and her eyes locked on me.

The warm aura of the wand kept brushing against my skin, trying to pull me closer.

Resisting it was nearly torture.

The ride along the stone roads was bumpy, but it provided me a different view of the city than I'd previously gotten from above. The marble buildings stood strong and proud. I'd seen photos of the ruins of ancient Rome, but it was incredible to see what the buildings would have looked like at the peak of the Empire.

Fae with wings of different colors walked from shop

to shop. Some of them traveled by litters carried by half-blood servants. They all wore gloves, they kept a fair amount of distance between each other, and many eyed one another suspiciously.

"The citizens are on edge because of the plague," Sorcha said. "I've postponed the ball to celebrate your victory in the Games until the city is in better spirits."

"That makes sense," I said, since a ball in my honor was one of the last things I wanted to do right now.

She nodded and stared absentmindedly out of the carriage.

Eventually, we stopped in front of a modestly sized house covered with green vines that bloomed with bright pink flowers. The house sat at the edge of the city's inner circle, right before the gate that separated the shiny, luxurious fae quarters from the drab, crooked insula apartments that housed the half-bloods.

"This is the safe location I mentioned earlier," Sorcha said. "Your trainers for the Games—Bryan and Finn—live here."

"I thought we were going to a prison?" I asked.

"We don't have prisons in the Otherworld," she said. "When a fae is being investigated for a crime, I mute their strength and magic with my gift. They're then put under house arrest until their sentence is decided."

"And the half-bloods?"

"Half-bloods are dealt with justly and swiftly."

Julian tensed. He didn't need to say a word for me to understand that the half-bloods weren't dealt with "justly." Sorcha clearly believed so, since she wouldn't have been able to say it otherwise, but *her* truth wasn't necessarily *the* truth.

"This situation, however, is different," she continued. "It's too risky to keep an afflicted fae in my house, as people may find out and talk. And Finn and Bryan are the two best fighters in the city. It made sense to put them in charge of this unique case."

Our driver came around and opened the door, ending the conversation.

Sorcha lifted her skirt as to not trip on the hem, and exited first. "Follow me inside," she said once she was out of the carriage. "Finn and Bryan are expecting you."

Bryan and Finn pounced on me the moment I stepped inside, enveloping me in a group hug. They only let go once I feared I might suffocate.

Bryan was decked out in a shimmery purple tunic and breeches, and he'd dyed his hair the same bright pink as his wings. Finn wasn't wearing a shirt, and his breeches hung low to show off his chiseled abs that cut into a defined V down his hips.

"You did fabulously well in the Faerie Games." Bryan beamed and pranced around me. "All thanks to your wonderful trainers, of course." He twirled so pink sparkles swirled around him, and then they twinkled out. "And your soulmate is quite the hottie, if I may say so myself." He winked at Julian.

Julian's cheeks turned red, and his eyes darted around the room, like he didn't know where to look.

I stepped to Julian's side and smiled up at him. "He most certainly is."

Sorcha tapped the end of the wand—which was still glamoured to look like a sword—to the marble floor with a *thud*, and all eyes went to her. "A touching reunion," she said, and then she dropped her glamour.

Bryan froze and lowered his gaze. "Your Highness," he said.

Finn straightened and bowed his head respectfully. "Your Highness," he said as well.

"Bryan." Sorcha nodded at him. "Finn. I trust every-thing has been under control here?"

"It has been." Finn glanced at the wand in Sorcha's hand, then looked to me. "I see you chose to give the Holy Wand to the Empress, after all?"

Right—the orbs had stopped broadcasting our

arrival back to the city after Juno had left. That was before I'd tried creating the portal home. The citizens of the citadel were clueless about what had happened after Bacchus had announced that Julian and I were the official winners of this year's Games.

And with Sorcha holding Julian's family under house arrest, I didn't want to say anything that might anger her or be construed as an attack on her character.

"She didn't," Sorcha said before I could speak. "I'm simply holding onto the wand for safekeeping for now."

Finn glanced at me, suspicion in his sharp gaze. "Understood," he said.

Bryan brought his hands together and smiled—likely an attempt to diffuse the obvious awkwardness in the room. "Would you all care for a refreshment?" he asked. "Some plum wine, perhaps?"

"I'll take you up on that another time," Sorcha said. "I assume she's where I last left her?"

"She is," Finn said, and Sorcha breezed past him without a second glance.

She stopped in front of a tall bookshelf in the parlor. Bryan and Finn aimed their magic at it together—a beautiful mix of pink and green—and the bookshelf creaked open, revealing steps so narrow that we had to walk down them in a single-file line.

The steps took us to a large basement. Cement

bricks lined the walls and ceiling, keeping it mildly cool, and the room housed about ten wooden barrels full of what smelled like sweet wine. Weapons and shields decorated the walls like artwork on display in a museum.

At the very end of the room, a girl with golden blonde hair who appeared to be around my age lay on a twin bed inside of a small, diamond colored dome. Her dim, ash gray wings darkened at the edges.

Sorcha hurried to the dome and pressed her hand against it. "Kyla," she said, her voice strangled with far more emotion than I'd ever heard from her. "I brought someone here to help you."

Kyla slowly pushed herself up in bed and leaned back against the pillows. "The Holy Wand," she said, light and dreamlike. "You found it."

"It's here. As is its owner." Sorcha dropped her arm back down to her side and looked at me over her shoulder. "Selena. Come forward and meet my daughter."

7

SELENA

I WALKED to Sorcha's side. Julian stopped a few feet back, to stand with Bryan and Finn.

Kyla's big blue eyes had purple bruises beneath them, and her skin was so papery thin that it was nearly transparent. But somehow, she smiled at me anyway. "I watched you in the Faerie Games," she said. "I was hoping you'd win."

"Thanks." I shifted uneasily, since by winning, so many others had died.

"Kyla," Sorcha said, and the girl's smile disappeared. "As you know, this is Selena, the chosen champion of Jupiter, and one of the winners of this year's Faerie Games. Selena, this is my daughter, Princess Kyla."

I lowered my eyes in the expected display of respect for the Empress's daughter. "Princess," I said.

"Call me Kyla," she said, far more brightly than I'd expect from someone in her condition.

"Kyla," I repeated. "It's nice to meet you."

She beamed like she'd just befriended a celebrity. "You, too," she said, and then she added, "I'm sorry for how awful I must look."

"You don't look awful."

She frowned, since we both knew that wasn't true.

Not knowing what else to say to her, I turned to face Sorcha. "Why are you keeping her trapped in this thing?" I asked. "She's hardly in a condition to hurt anyone."

"It's unknown when the afflicted will fully succumb," she said. "If it happens here—which, hopefully with your help, it won't—the dome will keep the plague contained."

The plague.

Not her daughter.

She sounded so cold and clinical.

Kyla's lower lip trembled. She took a shaky breath inward and brushed away a tear.

"I'll try my hardest to help you," I told her. "I promise."

"Thank you." She sounded so full of hope.

I prayed I wouldn't let her down.

Sorcha cleared her throat, although I wasn't sure

whether it was to get our attention or to control her emotions. "We have no time to waste," she said. "Kyla, show Selena the wound."

Kyla removed her right hand from under the covers. It was covered in black, veiny lines. With her other hand, she pulled the sleeve of her white nightgown up to her elbow. A strip of rough, tan fabric—the same material of the clothes worn by the half-blood servants—was wrapped multiple times around her forearm. She unwrapped it and revealed a deep, bite-shaped wound leaking black, bloody puss. Black veins snaked out of it in all directions.

My stomach rolled.

Julian stepped forward, his eyes locked on the wound. "How far up does it go?" he asked, speaking just as clinically as Sorcha.

"It covers my whole arm," Kyla said. "It's on part of my chest, too."

"Does it hurt?" I asked, even though from looking at her, the answer was clearly yes.

She glanced at Finn and Bryan. "They've been giving me medicine that's helping with the pain."

"Boswellia?" Julian asked.

"Willow bark," she said. "I've been chewing on the bark, and drinking it in my tea."

Julian eyed her curiously. "And has it slowed the spreading?"

"We're unsure, since we have nothing to compare this to," Sorcha said. "But the infection is approaching her heart, and I fear what will happen once it gets there. The Holy Wand is our only hope."

I zeroed in on the wand. "Like I said, I'll do my best," I said, and I reached forward to take it.

She stepped back and held the wand to her chest. "I'll bring you inside the dome, and then return it to you."

"And you'll give me full, permanent access to enter and exit the dome as I please?" I asked. "And you'll allow me to keep the wand afterward?"

"I'll bring you back out of the dome after you use the wand to attempt to cure Kyla," she said. "And you can keep the wand so long as you don't use it against me or my people."

I balked at her huge request. "If I need to defend myself with the wand, I will."

Then I realized—I had the power in this bargain. Sorcha was desperate to save her daughter. I needed to use that desperation in my favor.

But I also wanted Sorcha to feel safe enough around me to start granting me leniency. That was how I could eventually get back home. So I needed to tread carefully.

"I won't use the wand against you, as long as you

don't use your gift on me or try to attack me," I said. "For my own safety, I can't agree to anything more."

Sorcha turned away from me and looked at Kyla.

Is she going to say no?

I held my breath, waiting.

"Fine," she said, and she held out the hand that wasn't wrapped around the wand.

I took her hand, and we walked inside the dome. A tingly, icy coldness travelled through me as I passed through.

The inside of the dome smelled slightly of rot and decay, assumedly from Kyla's open wound. A hint of that smell had been following me ever since Julian and I had crossed the Eastern Mountains and fought the horde of zombies. I'd never smelled anything so awful and suffocating in my life. The Otherworld was so infected with zombies that their stench must have been permeating the entire realm.

Sorcha held the wand out to me. "As you requested," she said, and I snatched it from her hand.

Magic hummed from the wand and coursed through me. Electricity crackled along my arms and lit up my scars. Purple and silver magic poured out of my palms and twisted around the wand, and a breeze of fresh air blew through the dome.

If having my magic unmuted felt freeing, having the Holy Wand back in my hand felt ten times as powerful.

I was never going to let anyone take it from me again.

Kyla watched me in amazement. "Wow," she said. "Your wings."

I glanced over my shoulder, and sure enough, my wings were blue, violet, and silver.

"Damn, girl," someone said from outside the dome. Bryan. "That's hot."

My wings sparkled in the corner of my eye. "Thanks." I smiled, and then I refocused on Kyla. "This might hurt," I warned her. "I'm sorry about that."

"You said you haven't tried this before," Sorcha said.

Memories of when I'd freed the half-bloods from the tattoos that bound their magic flashed through my mind. They'd screamed and arched back in pain at the start, although according to Julian, the relief once the poison was out of his system was like nothing he'd ever felt before.

But I couldn't tell them about freeing the half-bloods.

"I'll be trying to use my magic to suck the poison from her body," I said instead. "So yes, it will likely hurt."

"Just do it," Kyla said, and she straightened as much

as she could. "I'm ready." She held her gaze steady with mine, her face set in determination.

I stepped up to the foot of her bed, raised the wand, and dug inside myself for my magic. *This can't be much different from freeing the half-bloods*, I thought. *Just like with the half-bloods, I'm removing a poison. I succeeded with them, so I can succeed with Kyla.*

My magic swirled through me, and the wand's light blue crystals pulsed with energy. I gathered as much magic as I could, and then channeled it through the top crystal, toward Kyla.

The scars on my arms lit up. The magic surrounded her in a glowing orb, and tendrils of it slithered toward her. The tips of their tentacles pierced her skin and buried themselves deep inside.

Kyla sank into her pillows, gripped the covers, and let out a soft cry. Her sleeve fell back down to her wrist, covering her wound.

Now, I thought, and then I reversed the flow of my magic to suction the poison out of her. With the half-bloods, this had sucked the dots of red—the poison inked on them by the fae—out of their systems.

Nothing of the sort happened with Kyla.

I braced myself and pulled harder, grunting from the effort. The crystals on the wand glowed brighter. It hummed louder and louder, like a lightbulb about to burst.

Pain seared my palm, like I'd touched a hot stove.

I screamed and dropped my hold on the magic. The tendrils snapped out of Kyla's skin, and the orb surrounding her dimmed out of existence.

I wiped a bead of sweat from my brow, switched the wand to my other hand, and studied my palm. It was red, but the pain was already fading.

Julian rushed inside the dome and was by my side in a second. He grabbed my palm and examined it. "You pushed your magic too far," he said.

"I stopped in time." My muscles ached slightly, and I was a bit more tired, but I'd recover. "I'm already feeling better."

"You sure?"

"Yes," I said. "I'm sure. But you shouldn't have come inside the dome." I glanced at the Empress, who was kneeling by her daughter's side.

Kyla's face had a healthier flush to it, and the bruises under her eyes had lightened. But black sludge stained her sleeve, right above the wound.

The Empress hovered her hands over it.

"It's okay to touch," I said. "Julian and I were splattered with their blood when we tried to fight them, and we're totally fine."

Julian stiffened and focused on the Empress. "Contact with the blood doesn't seem to cause infection."

"I've heard this from many sources," Sorcha said. "However, as the Empress, I need to keep myself safe." She stood and took a step back from Kyla. "I'm already putting myself at risk by being inside of this dome, but it's worth it to see my daughter well again."

I lowered my eyes, since I knew in my heart that I hadn't cured Kyla.

"Kyla," the Empress said steadily. "Pull up your sleeve."

Kyla did as instructed, and I gasped.

The veiny, black lines no longer covered the majority of her arm. They only surrounded the outer edges of the puss-filled wound.

But the wound was still there, as angry as ever.

"How do you feel?" I asked.

"Better," she said, and she gave me a grateful smile. "Like I did right after getting bitten, before the poison spread."

"But the poison's still inside of you."

"Yes," she verified what I already knew.

"I'm sorry," I said. "I tried my hardest. But my magic..." I looked back down at my palm, where the bright red was already fading to a lighter pink.

"It was turning on you," she said softly. "I understand."

Sorcha spun to face me, and I braced myself for a verbal attack. "You were right to listen to your magic's warning," she said instead. "We need you alive."

I stared at her, speechless.

"Why so surprised?" she asked. "I meant it when I said I wanted us to work together. We can't do that if you push your magic too far and kill yourself."

"Even if it means I can't cure Kyla?"

"You may not have cured her, but you seem to have reversed the poison's progress," she said. "Perhaps you'll have better luck now that she isn't as sick. So you'll try again tomorrow, once your magic is fully rejuvenated."

"Of course," I said, since I was going to suggest it, anyway.

"Very well," she said, and then she said goodbye to Kyla.

Kyla finished saying goodbye to her mother, and then turned to me. "I'll see you tomorrow," she said brightly.

"Yes." I smiled. "See you tomorrow."

Sorcha nodded, took my and Julian's hands, and escorted us out of the dome. She made no mention about how she hadn't promised to let him back out as well, and I didn't question it. Once we were outside of the dome, she focused on Finn and Bryan. "Continue taking good care of her," she said.

"We will," Bryan said, and Finn echoed the sentiment.

"I know." She gave Kyla a final hopeful smile, and turned back to me. "Now, we need to be getting back to my house. Put the glamour back on your wings and the wand."

I did as she instructed, amazed by how naturally the use of glamour came to me. It was supposedly that way for most fae. But after so many years with no magic, it was going to take some time for me to get used to—if I ever got used to it at all.

Sorcha also restored her glamour disguise.

Finn and Bryan led us back up the stairs. We said goodbye, and then headed out. The carriage was in front of the house, and the Red Storm raged just as strongly overhead.

Goosebumps prickled along my arms, and my chest tightened at the red, ominous glow.

Sorcha led the way toward the carriage, as nonplussed by the storm as ever. I followed behind her, although I continued to glance up as I walked.

Julian stayed where he was.

"Are you coming?" I asked him.

"I'm going to find my own way back," he said. "We're

close to my apartment, and there are some friends I want to check up on."

Friends?

In the weeks I'd known him, he'd never mentioned any friends. He'd only talked about his mom and sister.

But obviously he had to have friends.

"I'll come with you," I said, and I made my way over to join him.

"No." His answer stopped me in my tracks.

"Why not?"

He paused, and the question hung heavily in the air between us. Then he walked over to me and took my still-pink hand in his. He cradled it, and his eyes met mine, soft and caring. "You just used a lot of magic," he said. "Go back and rest. I'll see you soon."

"Are you sure?" I asked.

"I'm sure." He let go of my hand, but didn't move away. "Go."

"All right," I said. "You'll be back soon?"

Sorcha came to stand beside me. "You'll be back by sunset," she said to Julian—a statement, not a question.

"Yes, ma'am."

"Very well." She lifted her chin slightly in approval. "Selena, come with me. There are four people waiting for you in my house that I know you'll be happy to see."

My parents? Did they find their way here, after all?

"Who?" My voice nearly caught in my throat.

She smiled knowingly. "Come with me, and find out," she said. "And Julian?"

"Yes?"

"Take this." She removed a diamond ring from her index finger and handed it to him. "It's worth a fair amount, and we can't have you wandering the streets without any coins."

He stared at the ring, although he didn't move to take it. "That's very generous, Your Highness," he said. "But I can manage on my own."

"I'm sure you can," she said. "But the Empire owes you compensation for winning the Games, and you've yet to receive it. I *am* the Empire, and I'm giving you the first bit of your reward. This isn't a gift. It's something you've earned. Take it."

"Very well." He took the ring and placed it deep in his pocket.

Unease flitted in my chest at the thought of being away from him, even for a few hours.

He can protect himself, I reminded myself. *And maybe this is part of the plan.*

He told me to trust him, and trust his plan.

So that was what I was going to do.

"I'll see you soon." I stood on my tiptoes and pressed a soft kiss against his lips.

He pulled me close and kissed me back with far more intensity than I'd expected, given that we had an audience. It was only a few seconds, but when we parted, my breathing was shallow and my face was warm.

"Go," he said. "I'll see you soon."

I nodded—still spellbound from his kiss—followed Sorcha into the carriage, and didn't look away from Julian until we turned the corner and he was out of my sight.

8

SELENA

ONCE BACK AT HER HOUSE, Sorcha led me down the
guest hall to a room at the end with larger double doors
than the room where Julian and I were staying.

She unlocked the doors with her magic and flung
them open.

Inside, lounging in the chairs and on the bed, were
Torrence, Reed, Sage, and Thomas. Aiden—my cousin
with the orange wings—was there, too.

Shock hit me in a wave.

Is this glamour? Is Sorcha doing this to trick me?

Torrence ran toward me, flung her arms around me,
and gave me the biggest, most welcoming hug ever.

This wasn't glamour.

They were real.

I buried my head in her shoulder and cried. Chest heaving, tears flowing, full-blown crying. The wand made the hug slightly uncomfortable, but I didn't care.

"Get inside," Sorcha said. "No one can know they're here."

She nudged us inside, forcing Torrence and me to pull away from each other. The door clicked shut behind us.

"You're here." I stared into Torrence's familiar green eyes in disbelief and wiped the tears off my cheeks. "How?"

"Of course I'm here." She smiled. "I'm the one who got you stuck in this place. No way was I sitting back and doing nothing to get you back."

"It's not your fault," I said. "You didn't force me to drink that transformation potion. I did it myself."

"You wouldn't have done it if I hadn't brewed it."

"Maybe. Or maybe not." I shrugged, hardly able to focus. Being with my best friend again was so surreal. "But how did you get here?"

Sorcha cleared her throat in the most melodic throat clearing ever. "Now that your reunion is complete, I have other matters to attend to," she said, and then she looked at Torrence. "I'll be back by sunset with the items you requested." She left and shut the doors. Diamond magic shimmered along them, sank into them, and disappeared.

"She locked us in," I said.

"She's kept us locked in here since we arrived." Sage sneered. "Apparently the fae like trapping people places. Just like they did to your dad and to Bella."

Fear pierced my bones, and I stilled. "What did they do to my dad?"

"He's safe," Thomas said, and I let out a breath of relief. "He and Bella went to the Crossroads to speak to the fae to bargain to get you home, but the fae refused to hear them out. They created a dome that trapped them there."

"What have the fae been doing to them in there?" I held my breath, bracing for the worst.

"They're giving them food and water, and keeping them comfortable," he said. "They haven't been harmed. But fae magic is strong. We haven't been able to break through the dome."

"And my mom?" I asked.

"She's bound to Avalon and can't leave the island, as you already know," Sage said. "Which is where the four of us came into play."

"I see," I said, and I turned to Torrence. "What 'items' did you request from the Empress?"

"We'll get to that in a bit. But first…" She stepped back and stared at my wings. "Aiden and his family told us about the Faerie Games. It sounds…"

"Awful," I finished for her. "But I survived. And I have magic now." I removed the glamour on my wings, showing them the mix of blue, purple, and silver. "Not just Jupiter's magic. I have my fae and witch magic, too." I raised my hand that wasn't holding onto the wand, created an orb of tri-colored magic, and let it float up to the ceiling.

"Wow." Torrence's mouth opened in amazement, and her eyes followed the orb until it popped out of existence.

"I know." I flexed my fist and dropped my arm back down to my side.

"We have a lot to tell you, too," Torrence said. "Let's sit down." She took my hand and walked with me to the sitting area around the hearth.

Aiden stayed sprawled out on the bed. Sage and Thomas were cuddled up on a loveseat near the fireplace, and Reed sat on an armchair across from them. He leaned back, as broody and silent as ever as he stared at us with dark, haunted eyes.

No—he was staring at *Torrence*.

He couldn't take his eyes off of her.

Interesting.

But Torrence was oblivious to him as she and I made ourselves comfortable on the loveseat perpendicular to Sage and Thomas's. A platter of crustless sandwiches sat on the coffee table, my stomach growled, and I reached forward to take one. My attempt to cure Kyla had left me famished.

None of the others reached for food.

I stopped after my first bite, embarrassed at how quickly I'd rushed to stuff my face.

"The Empress warned us you were going to be hungry," Thomas said. "Sit back and enjoy, because she and Aiden have already caught us up on everything. Including how you got that wand." He eyed the Holy Wand by my side.

I nodded, even though the Empress couldn't have caught them up on everything, since she didn't know about the Sanctuary.

But I couldn't tell them about the Sanctuary while we were in her home. Who knew who could be listening?

"We'll fill you in on how we got here, what we discovered when we arrived, and the item the Empress is bringing us," he continued. "From there, we'll strategize on how to team up and where to go from here."

"Does that 'strategizing' include getting back home?" I asked.

"We didn't come all the way here to leave without you," Torrence said. "And we came a *long* way. It all started with a message from the prophetess, and a visit to the Haven."

9

SELENA

"AFTER ALL OF THAT, King Devin finally gave us the tokens," Torrence said. "We tossed them into his fountain, and portaled to the Otherworld."

I stared at the four of them, mind-blown by all they'd told me. "So you got Charybdis to eat Scylla," I said, just to make sure we'd covered everything until now. "You stole Circe's staff from under her nose while she was sleeping. You fought and slayed the Nemean Lion. *And* you killed a cyclops."

"Not just a regular cyclops," Torrence said proudly. "*The* cyclops. Polyphemus. The one from the *Odyssey.*"

"You mean the book you never read?" I teased.

"Hey." She raised her chin in the pretense of being offended. "I've read the children's version of it now. And it was way more interesting than the real thing. Not nearly as wordy and boring."

"I missed you," I said.

"I missed you, too."

My eyes watered, and I rubbed them to stop from crying.

"Enough with the mushiness," Aiden said from where he was still sprawled on the bed. "We're just getting to the good part."

Reed glared at him. "You mean the part where you showed up?"

"Whoa." Aiden held his hands up in defense. "Didn't mean to anger the mage."

Reed's eyes flashed black, he ripped his gaze away from Aiden's, and stared into the hearth with his hands curled into fists.

Torrence rolled her eyes and gave Aiden an encouraging smile. "Don't worry—it wasn't you," she said. "He's like that all the time."

"No, I'm not," Reed said, his eyes back to normal now.

"Yes, you are."

The two of them stared each other down, both as stubborn as ever.

What's going on between them? And how did his eyes flash black like that?

Sage looked back and forth between them, sat forward, and crossed her legs. "It sounds like I should take over from here," she said, and she continued on to tell me about the zombies they'd fought when they'd arrived at Princess Ryanne's villa.

"You should have seen them turn the afflicted to ash," Aiden said once she was finished. "It was just like what you can do with your lightning."

"My lightning can't do that to the zombies," I said. "But from what you're saying, the holy weapons can."

"Yep," Sage said. "And the holy weapons turn zombies to ash in the *exact* same way that they turn demons to ash."

"I get that. The question is, how?"

"We've been wondering that ourselves," Thomas said. "Especially because the zombie blood had a bit of a smoky smell to it. It was hard to distinguish under the rot and decay, but it was there."

"Only Thomas and I can smell it," Sage added. "Thanks to our wolf sides strengthening our sense of smell."

"But only demons have a smoky smell to them," I said, and they nodded. "So are you saying that you think the demons are related to the zombies?"

"Practically sure of it," she said. "And the items the Empress is bringing to us are going to help us prove it."

10

SELENA

THEY EXPLAINED THE PLAN, and as we continued sharing more about our journeys, the sky that was already dark from the Red Storm grew darker.

Sorcha returned right before sunset. She was back in her white, poofy empress dress, and she held a satchel of items on one side.

Julian stood at the other.

I stood and rushed into his arms, holding him tight.

He gazed down at me and brushed his thumb over my cheek. "Did you think I wasn't coming back?" he asked with a slightly teasing smile.

"Did you find your friends?" I asked in return.

"I found what I was looking for," he said. "But my friends aren't the important ones here. Don't you want to introduce me to yours?"

"Yes." I nearly jumped up in excitement, and proceeded to introduce him to Torrence, Sage, Thomas, and Reed.

Torrence waggled her eyebrows and winked in approval when Julian wasn't watching.

When I looked back at Julian—who was getting along remarkably well with Thomas—my heart was so full that it was about to burst.

I didn't think I'd feel any happier until I was back on Avalon and my mom and dad were there, too.

Reed wasn't particularly warm while meeting Julian. It didn't surprise me, since it was the same way he'd been toward me. Apparently, that was just his personality.

Sage's eyes kept darting in Julian's direction, full of suspicion.

She doesn't like him.

But why?

I didn't know her well, but wolf shifters were territorial. She was probably always cautious around people who weren't from Avalon, or who weren't members of her pack.

Hopefully she'd warm up to him soon.

Sorcha had a guard take the empty tray of food and replenish the carafes of juice. "Would anyone prefer wine?" she asked.

"Yes," Aiden said, at the same time as the rest of us said, "No."

Once the guard left, Sorcha used her magic to lock the door. Then, she placed the satchel on the coffee table next to the juice and wine. "Everything you requested is in here," she said.

Torrence opened it and looked inside. She nodded approvingly, brought the bag over to an empty spot on the floor, and settled herself down on her knees so she was sitting on her heels. We all moved to stand around her, and she removed the objects one by one.

A green candle, a red candle, a blue candle, and a yellow candle. Then she reached to the bottom of the satchel and pulled out a slim, leather-bound book. The parchment inside was thick and uneven, and it smelled like dust.

She opened it, flipped through the pages, and frowned. "There isn't much detail in these."

"We don't keep many maps in the Otherworld." Sorcha straightened and raised her chin slightly. "Fae travel by our innate connection with nature. This was the best I could find."

"All right," Torrence said. "I suppose it'll have to do."

She opened the book to a map of the Otherworld. But it wasn't the *entire* Otherworld. The top of the

North was cut off. An arrow with the word *Hypernia* underneath it pointed upward.

I shivered at the memory of the arctic tundra.

"There are no maps of Hypernia?" Torrence asked Sorcha.

"Hypernia's a cursed, icy wasteland," the Empress replied. "Fae can't survive up there, so we haven't been able to map it."

"Hopefully the demons won't be up there," Sage said.

"They won't be," Thomas said. "Demons are from Hell. They hate the cold. If Hypernia freezes out the fae, it should freeze out the demons, too. In theory."

"Right," Sage said. "In *theory.*"

"We'll find out when I do the spell," Torrence said, and she placed the candles around the book. Each color represented an element, and each element correlated to a direction. The green one—earth—was above the book, the red one—fire—was below, the yellow one—air—was to the right, and the blue one—water—was to the left. North, South, East, and West.

I'd learned all of this at Avalon Academy.

And now…

"Maybe I can help," I said. "With my witch magic unbound, I can do spells now."

Torrence glared at me, and I froze. "My mom taught

me this spell when I was a kid," she said. "I don't need help."

Her words were knives to my chest, and for a moment, I couldn't breathe. "Of course you don't," I said, relieved when her gaze softened. "Sorry."

I hated saying it the moment the word came out of my mouth. I had nothing to apologize for.

But the apology seemed to appease Torrence, and she refocused on the setup in front of her. She picked up the green candle, walked over to the hearth, and lowered the wick to one of the glowing embers. It caught flame, and a woodsy, earthy scent filled the room.

I could have easily lit the candle with my electricity. But after her reaction to my offering to help with the spell, I didn't suggest it.

She settled back into her spot in front of the book and used the green candle to light the others. They each smelled like the element they corresponded to.

Once they were all burning, a light breeze circled around Torrence.

She took a deep breath, unclasped her necklace, and held it up. A clear quartz set in diamonds and shaped like an upside-down pyramid dangled at the end of the thin gold chain. A pendulum. I'd given her the necklace for her thirteenth birthday, and she'd been wearing it ever since.

"Sage," she said. "Your slicer."

Sage pulled a plain, steel dagger from her weapons belt and handed it to Torrence. Apparently, that dagger matched the one her best friend Noah had used when she'd joined him in the first *ever* demon hunting mission appointed by my mom. She'd been using it to kill demons for nearly as long as I'd been alive, so it had seen its fair share of demon blood.

Its memory of that blood was a key part in locating whatever demon—or *demons*—had infiltrated the Otherworld.

Torrence gripped the dagger in one hand, and used the other to dangle the pendulum over the book. She started to speak the Latin words of the spell... but the pendulum began swinging after the first syllable.

That shouldn't happen.

Spells needed to be spoken before they activated.

But none of the others looked surprised.

Maybe the magic of the Otherworld was enhancing Torrence's power?

I didn't know, but whatever she'd managed to do, it was working. The pendulum directed her toward the west of the map. It stilled, she raised it, and the pages flipped themselves.

They settled on a zoomed-in version of the western part of the realm. The pendulum started swinging again, and Torrence repeated the process until we finally had a location.

The westernmost part of the Western Wild Lands, on the cliffs near the ocean.

The crystal glowed, and Torrence took another long breath, her eyes closed.

"There's only one demon," she said, and then the candles snuffed out, and her eyes snapped open.

We silently looked around at each other with shifty eyes, and Torrence handed Sage back her dagger.

"The demon must have been here for a while," Sorcha finally said. "Since the plague originated in the west."

Right. Before becoming known as simply "the plague," it had been called the Wild Plague, since it was said to have come from the Western Wild Lands.

"It must have," Thomas said. "And now that you know where the demon is, Avalon will be open to negotiations regarding how to help the Otherworld. In return, you'll remove the dome imprisoning Prince Jacen and Bella at the Crossroads, and let the four of us return to Avalon with Selena."

"And with Julian, his mom, and his sister," I chimed in, although Julian refused to meet my eyes.

The Empress paused, pursed her lips, and said, "We have no holy weapons. If you leave, the Otherworld won't be able to defend ourselves against the afflicted and kill this demon."

"We're carrying two holy weapons each," Sage said. "If you agree to the terms, we can leave them all with you."

I held my breath, waiting.

Can this actually work?

"No," Sorcha replied, and my heart dropped. "Given how widely the plague has spread, eight holy weapons won't be enough. We'll need far more."

"How many?" Sage asked.

"With my strongest living chosen champions on the job, we'll need one hundred, at the very least."

My eyes widened.

Thomas remained unfazed. "We don't have that many holy weapons to spare," he said simply. "The Earth Angel is the only one who can create them, and the process is neither easy nor quick."

"It sounds similar to the process of creating portal tokens." Sorcha sighed. "I suppose I can make do with fifty weapons. But only you and Reed may leave to retrieve them. I'll enchant the tokens so they can only be used by the two of you. If you try to break the enchantment, the tokens will self-destruct. Once I have all fifty weapons, and proof that they're true holy weapons and not imitations, I'll have the dome at the Crossroads removed."

"And our second request?" Thomas asked.

Time slowed as I waited for her answer.

"Selena can still do much good in the Otherworld," she said, and then she focused on me. "Unless you want to bequeath the Holy Wand to me?"

"No." I held the wand closer to my side. "Never."

"As I thought."

I tightened my grip on the wand and looked to Thomas. "Make the deal with the weapons," I said. "Free my dad and Bella from the Crossroads."

Uncertainty passed over his eyes. "Are you sure?"

"I'm not giving anyone the wand. The Empress and I will come to another agreement that will allow me to go back home." I glanced at her, and she nodded. "For now, I want my dad freed."

"This is crazy." Torrence stepped toward me, her expression wild. "Give her the wand. Come home."

"I'm not giving anyone the wand," I seethed, and she flinched back slightly. "This is the *Holy Wand*. And it's *mine*."

I narrowed my eyes, willing her to understand.

You know about the prophecy. About the Holy Objects, and the Four Queens.

Her mouth opened slightly. Then the meaning of my

words must have set in, because she shut it. "I'm not leaving here without you," she said.

"I'm not asking you to."

Neither of us moved.

Finally, she nodded, even though she still looked pissed.

Thomas remained focused on me, studying me. "I'll do this for Prince Jacen and Bella, but we're not leaving here without you," he said, and then he faced the Empress again. "To most easily get you the weapons, Reed and I will need tokens that can bring us straight to Avalon."

"No tokens can bring you straight to Avalon," she said. "If they existed, we would have used them by now."

"Fair point," Sage said.

"But I do have personal tokens that will bring you from my house to the Trevi Fountain in Rome," she continued. "From there, I expect Reed will have no issues teleporting the two of you to Avalon and back."

"None at all," Reed said.

"As I thought," she said, still focused on Thomas. "I accept your deal."

"It's done, then?" he asked.

"It's done." She nodded, and looked over at all of us. "Now, follow me to my side of the portal, and we'll see Thomas and Reed off to Earth."

11

SELENA

SORCHA'S QUARTERS were the size of a house, and she led us out to her private atrium.

Red lighting flashed in the night sky, thunder rumbled through the thick cover of clouds, and heavy raindrops splattered against the outside of the dome. Torches along the walls lit up the area, but the flashes of red reflected everywhere.

A woman stood next to the square fountain in the center of the atrium. She wore a sleeveless sky-blue dress, a red tattoo circled her bicep, and her wings glimmered gold.

The same color as Bridget's.

This woman was one of Minerva's chosen champions. A previous winner of the Faerie Games. Which meant that like Bridget, she had future sight.

The Empress walked forward, her glass shoes clacking against the tile floor, and joined the woman by the fountain.

The woman lowered her eyes, and the gold pointed cuffs at the tops of her ears stuck out through her hair. "Your Highness," she said.

"Aeliana," the Empress said, and the woman—Aeliana—raised her gaze. "I assume you already know why we're here?"

"I have news for you," she said. "But it's something you must see for yourself." She reached into a small satchel tied at her waist, removed two tokens, and looked to the group of us waiting by the entrance. "Thomas. Reed. These are for you."

They walked over to her and took the tokens. The rest of us followed, so we stood around them. Julian was at one of my sides, and Torrence was at the other.

Sorcha turned to Thomas and Reed. "Hold out your hands with the tokens so I can bind them to you," she said.

They did as she asked, and Sorcha turned her palms upward to create two orbs of diamond-colored magic. The orbs floated forward, surrounded their hands, shrank down, and disappeared into their skin.

They each opened their hands, took the token with

the other, and flexed their fingers like they were getting rid of pins and needles.

"Until I remove the enchantment, the tokens are bound to you," the Empress said.

"All fae can do that?" I asked.

"Only the fae who created the token. And few fae are both powerful and skilled enough to do so."

Thomas moved to Sage and pulled her in for a kiss. "I'll see you soon," he promised.

"I know," she said. "I'd wish you luck, but—"

"I make my own luck." He smirked, and she smiled in return.

I leaned closer to Julian. "How much longer until we start finishing each others' sentences like that?" I asked.

His expression hardened, and he looked away from me.

Torrence glared at him.

My best friend just saw my soulmate acting like a jerk to me. Great. I was never going to hear the end of this.

Although it would also be good to have someone to talk to about it.

"We'll be back with your weapons soon," Reed said to Sorcha, and then he turned to Torrence. "No more deals until we're back."

Torrence bristled. "I can't promise that," she said.

"I know you won't. But you should."

They stared each other down—again.

"Don't worry," I broke the silence, although they didn't look away from each other. "Julian's well-versed in the games of the fae. None of us will get roped into any more tricky deals."

Reed ripped his gaze away from Torrence's and stepped up onto the ledge of the fountain. Thomas joined him, and together, they tossed in their tokens.

We all stared at the water, waiting for the tokens to expand into a purple galaxy of stars.

Nothing happened.

Sorcha's brow knitted so much that her forehead creased. She placed her hand gently on the ledge and gazed down into the water, looking as confused as the rest of us.

Reed spun around and stared down at her. "You lied to us," he said, and he jumped off the ledge. Thomas did the same.

Sorcha remained focused on the water. She might as well have not heard him at all.

"Fae can't lie," Julian said. "If she didn't want to give us the tokens, she wouldn't have agreed to the deal." He turned to Aeliana—the only one of us who didn't look confused. "I'm guessing this is what you wanted us to see for ourselves?"

Sorcha straightened and looked to Aeliana as well.

"The Red Storm is blocking anyone from leaving or entering the Otherworld," she said. "Our realm will be blocked as long as the storm rages on."

Sorcha glanced up at the sky, and turned to me. "You have more than just lightning magic," she said. "I've seen you control the wind, too. You have *storm* magic. You can end this."

"I couldn't even create a portal back to Avalon," I said. "How am I supposed to stop a storm that's blocking the *entire realm*?"

"It's worth a try," Sage said. "Hop on one of those pegasi, create another hole in the top of the dome, and see what you can do."

"It's not worth a try," Aeliana cut in. "The Empress is right that Selena can end the storm. But she can't do it like that."

"Then how can I do it?"

"A demon and a witch have taken up residence in the western part of the realm," she said. "But you already know this."

"We knew about the demon," Torrence said. "Not the witch."

"Well, now you know."

"They must have worked together to create the plague," Torrence continued, her eyes brightening like a lightbulb had gone off in her head. "I should have realized it sooner. Because whatever magic created this plague is far too powerful for a demon to have managed alone. Of course they'd need the help of a witch. A powerful witch, at that."

"A Foster witch." Sage's eyes shifted into their wolfish yellow, then back to brown again.

"Their names aren't clear to me," Aeliana said. "But the clearest thing I see is this—to stop the storm, you need to kill the demon."

I glanced up at the angry, raging sky, and then refocused on Aeliana. "You mean a *demon* is causing this storm?"

"Yes."

"But the amount of magic they'd need to create and maintain the storm... it's not possible. Not even greater demons have that kind of power."

"This one does," Aeliana said simply.

I nodded and turned to Sorcha. "If I kill this demon, will you let me, Torrence, Reed, Sage, Thomas, Julian, and his mother and sister go to Avalon?" I asked.

"If you kill this demon, then your friends will be able to follow through on the deal we made regarding the holy weapons and releasing your father from the prison dome at the Crossroads," she said. "If you don't kill this demon, then we're all trapped here, and the Otherworld will perish because of it."

I looked to Julian for help.

"She's right," he said. "We promised to get her those weapons. We can't do that if your friends can't leave the Otherworld. And they can't leave until we turn this demon to ash."

Thunder boomed so loudly that it rattled my bones, and fear crashed through me.

Because I'd never seen a demon, let alone fought one.

But I'd been training for this for my entire life. Maybe not *me* in particular—since my parents had never intended for me to leave Avalon—but learning how to fight demons was part of the curriculum at the academy.

I could do this. Especially with my soulmate and my friends by my side.

"All right," I said, and the crystals on the wand glowed, as if the wand agreed with my decision. "I'll kill this demon."

"And I'll take the witch," Sage all but growled. "Especially if it's the witch I think it is."

"Absolutely not," Aeliana said. "You must keep the witch alive."

Sage's top lip curled upward. "Why?"

"Because you'll regret it if you don't. You also might

regret it if you do, but you'll most certainly regret it if you don't."

Sage didn't say okay.

She also didn't fight back. Which, for her, meant she was saying okay.

"So, it's decided, then," Sorcha said, back to her normal, composed self. "You'll leave for the Western Wildlands on the morrow. In the meantime, I'll walk you back to the guest wing so you can retire early and get a good night's sleep. It sounds like you're going to need it."

SELENA

I DID NOT, in any way, get a good night's sleep. We were locked back inside the rooms we'd been staying in before, which meant Julian and I were separated—again.

At least Sorcha let me keep the wand in my room. Probably because she knew I'd never use it, since I wouldn't put Julian's mom and sister at risk.

She woke me before dawn and brought me back to Bryan and Finn's house to have another go at curing Kyla.

It didn't work.

Apparently, I could relieve the symptoms and push back the infection's progress, but I couldn't cure it.

"Hopefully killing the demon will destroy the plague," she said on the carriage ride back to her house.

"Hopefully," I agreed.

We rode the rest of the way in silence.

At mid-morning, Sorcha gathered the group of us in the central courtyard. The temple at the end was collapsed inward, the roof blown apart from when I'd tried to create the portal back to Avalon.

Three pegasi waited for us. They were ready with saddles designed so two people could ride together, and satchels of supplies hung from the sides.

"Six spots." Aiden frowned. "Seven of us."

"As a full fae, you can't wield a holy weapon to defend yourself against the infected," Julian said simply. "You'll hold us back."

"So this was your doing?"

"It's for your own safety," he said. "And to make sure we have the best chance of succeeding on our mission."

"You're dead weight, fae-boy." Reed smirked. "Go back home to frolic and dine on fruit and honey wine, or whatever your kind does for fun."

Aiden created orange balls of magic in his hands and threw them at Reed.

Reed's eyes flashed black, and he shot dark smoke at Aiden's magic, consuming it like a black hole.

Aiden watched, shocked, as Reed's magic ate his up.

Torrence rolled her eyes and glared at Reed. "Was that necessary?" she asked.

"Yes." He brushed his hands off, and tendrils of black magic drifted up out of them like smoke. "He attacked me. I defended myself."

"You instigated him into doing it."

"*Enough*," Sorcha said, firmly but calmly. "Aiden, you'll remain a guest in my home. The rest of you, it's time to get going."

I glanced up at the sky. The Red Storm raged as strongly as it had yesterday. I couldn't imagine what it would be like when we left the dome and were fully exposed to its wrath.

"Traveling through the storm will be rough," Sage said. "But we can handle it."

"You've been out in it?"

"No." She shrugged. "But we *have* to be able to handle it. So that's what we're going to do."

Torrence looked to the pegasi, and then to Reed. "Why don't we join forces to create a defensive barrier around the pegasi?" she asked. "Like we did with the yacht. It'll protect us from the elements."

"Good idea," he said.

They jumped onto the closest pegasus, situated themselves on the saddle, faced each other, and joined hands. Their magic swirled around them in a magnificent, sparkly helix of yellow and purple.

The two of them hopped from pegasus to pegasus, casting the spell around each of the winged horses. They zeroed in on each other, like they weren't just connecting their magic, but their minds, too. They looked at each other like they were the only two people in the world.

It was the same way Julian looked at me.

From the amused way Sage watched them, she saw the connection between them, too.

After completing the spell around the final pegasus, they hopped off the saddle and walked back over to us. Torrence's face was flushed, and they both refused to look at each other.

She didn't look at me, either.

They were *totally* into each other. And she definitely knew that I knew.

But we needed to get going if we wanted to reach the Eastern Mountain Range before sunset. So I walked confidently toward the central pegasus and hopped onto the front saddle.

Julian sat behind me, Thomas and Sage claimed the pegasus on the left, and Reed and Torrence took the pegasus on the right.

"Time to see if this worked," I said, and then I pressed my heels into the sides of the pegasus, and we were off.

13

SELENA

THE BARRIER SPELLS around the pegasi protected us from the Red Storm, just like the dome around the city. The cracks of thunder were louder, since we were closer to the clouds, but the rain didn't touch us. And the barriers absorbed any lightning strikes that hit them.

Just like before, the number of zombies grew larger as we traveled farther west. They grunted as they ambled around aimlessly, and we flew as high as possible so we wouldn't be assaulted by the smell of rot and decay.

The thunder cracking overhead and the wind howling around the barrier domes made talking impossible. All we could do was observe the land below.

So much had changed in less than a week.

The grass was yellowed and brittle. The tree leaves

were brown. The flowers were dull, shriveled, and curled inward.

The Otherworld was dying.

Despite having every reason to hate this realm, seeing it like this broke my heart.

The pegasi pushed themselves to fly against the storm. We barely made it to the peak of the Eastern Mountains by the end of sunset, and by then, we were all more than ready to break for the night.

As expected, the peaks of the mountains were clear from zombies. They might have figured out how to get across the mountain range, but they couldn't climb *that* high. They needed to stick to the roads. Even then, only the strongest ones could get across the steepest parts. That was why there weren't full-blown hordes of them east of the mountain, like what Julian and I had seen on the other side.

We found a suitable location near a stream of fresh water, removed the packs from the pegasi, and set up camp. I used my fae magic to create a strong protective dome, and my lightning easily started a fire. Owls hooted in the distance, and squirrels scurried up and around the trees.

Other than the storm raging overhead, the camp was surprisingly cozy.

Julian studied our surroundings. "There are enough

small animals here to hunt that we don't need to eat our preserved rations yet," he said.

"I was thinking the same," said Thomas.

Julian nodded at him respectfully, and continued, "Three of us should stay back and guard the camp. Selena and I will go hunt, plus either Sage or Thomas. You choose."

Torrence's expression hardened. "Why one of them?" she asked.

"Their vampire and wolf senses make them natural hunters," he said.

"We won't have to go far," I added. "It won't take long."

She glared at me—the same way she had when I'd offered to help with the locating spell. "You're not the only ones who can kill," she said, and she spun to face the forest, raised her hands, and shot a stream of black magic out of her palms.

I watched, shocked, as she walked to the edge of the dome. Her magic expanded around multiple treetops in a plume of black smoke.

Objects fell out of the branches and thudded to the ground.

Birds and squirrels. Dozens of them. All dead.

It was far more than we could eat, and we already had enough smoked meat that we didn't have any space to take more with us. She was killing those poor animals for no reason.

"TORRENCE!" I yelled. "STOP!"

She held onto her magic and pushed it farther out into the trees. More small animals fell to the ground. In the distance, a flock of birds cried out and scattered up toward the red sky.

Reed rushed toward Torrence and wrapped his arms around her from behind. "You need to save your magic for bigger things," he said, so softly that I could barely hear him. "You need to stop. Please. Stop."

She breathed heavily, leaned back into him, and let go of her magic. The black smoke dissipated into nothing, revealing the horrifying extent of the damage she'd caused.

The brown leaves had dissolved, and their dust scattered in the wind. All that remained of the skeletal trees were gnarled and twisted canopies of branches. A tree cracked at the trunk and crashed down on the ones nearby, creating a domino effect of fallen trees until reaching the end of Torrence's deadly ring of magic.

"Torrence," I said her name slowly and carefully. "What did you do?"

She pushed herself out of Reed's arms and spun around, refusing to meet any of our eyes. "We needed food," she said. "So I got us food."

"But witch magic can't kill."

"Maybe not." She shrugged. "But my magic can."

She picked up an empty sack that had been holding our camping gear, marched out of the dome and into the dead forest, and started collecting the fallen animals. The five of us watched in stunned silence.

She shouldn't have magic like that.

But I knew my best friend well enough to know that she needed time to cool off. Trying to force answers out of her would just make the situation worse.

"Go with her," I said to Julian, since I trusted him the most. "Make sure she's safe."

He nodded and headed into the forest.

I made sure he was near her, and then I turned to Reed. "How did she do that?" I asked, putting magic around my words so she couldn't overhear. The barrier dome I'd created protected us from the elements, but it wasn't soundproof. We needed to be aware of the sounds around us so we could defend ourselves if necessary.

Reed's eyes flashed yellow, and he released matching colored magic from his hands to create a small sound barrier dome around me, him, Sage, and Thomas. It was a light magic barrier, so anyone outside of it wouldn't be able to hear us, but we'd be able to hear them.

"She'll be back soon, so we need to be quick," he said.

"Remember the story of how we used my magic to kill that cyclops together?"

"Yeah." I nodded and waited for him to continue.

"She kept using it after I let go of her. Ever since then, she's been using mage magic on her own."

"No—it was before that," Sage chimed in.

"When?" I asked.

"When we were fighting Scylla. She created the barrier spell and expanded it outward to make one of the heads explode, like she told you. But I was right there, fighting the head next to her. She didn't say a spell. She just... created the barrier on instinct."

"Mage magic," I said.

"I asked her about it, and that's what she said it was."

Reed's eyes raged nearly as intensely as the storm overhead. "She never told me."

"Can you blame her?" Sage asked. "You've been an ass to her every time she gets near you."

"No, I haven't."

"Yes, you have."

"You have," I agreed.

Thomas stepped closer to Sage. He agreed, too.

Reed didn't try to fight back.

"It happened after the two of you made the barrier spell around the yacht together," Sage continued. "She said it was a remnant of tethering your magic. Is that true?"

"Maybe," he said. "I've never done dark magic with a witch before. No mage has, as far as I know."

"So it could be too much for a witch to handle," I said. "Even one as strong as Torrence."

"I don't know." He shrugged.

I stared at him, waiting for him to say something more. Anything that might help us understand what was happening to her.

He didn't.

"Aren't you worried about this at all?" Electricity buzzed through me, lighting up my scars. "Your magic is changing her. You need to stop."

"Even if it means she has less magic to use to defend herself?"

I paused, since I hadn't thought of it that way.

"Guys?" Thomas said before I could reply. "They're back."

I spun around, and sure enough, there was Torrence. Her eyes were glassy, like she'd been crying.

Next to her, Julian held the lumpy sack. The dead animals inside weighted it down to the ground.

"I know you're talking about me," she said. "You can drop the sound barrier."

Reed's eyes flashed yellow, and the transparent dome around us shimmered out of existence.

I opened my mouth to speak, but Torrence got to it first.

"I shouldn't have done that," she said in a rush. "I don't know what came over me. All those animals… they didn't deserve to die."

"No," I agreed. "They didn't."

She glanced back at the devastation behind her, and then she refocused on me. Guilt was splattered across her face. "Once we're back home, I'm going to ask the three mages for help," she said. "Until then, I won't do it again."

I wanted to make her swear it in a blood oath.

But Reed's words echoed in my mind.

What if she needs the dark mage magic to defend herself?

If she made a blood oath not to use it until we spoke with the three mages, breaking the oath would kill her.

I couldn't ask that of her.

"Good," I said instead.

And then, like nothing had happened, we all gathered around the fire and worked together to prepare dinner.

Once the food was ready, we sat down to eat.

"So," Julian said. "Selena and I have a lot to fill you in on. Things we couldn't speak about in the citadel."

"Like what?" Sage sat forward on her log, intrigued.

He nodded for me to take it from there, and I jumped right in.

"We weren't honest with the Empress about how we got the Holy Wand," I started. "Well, we were, up until the part about the Fomorians. Because they weren't the ones hiding the wand. They were just a roadblock on our way to the place that *really* had the wand. An ancient, half-blood refuge called the Sanctuary."

14

SELENA

THE OTHERS AGREED that free half-bloods would make an excellent addition to Avalon's army. They also agreed that I was right to tell the citizens of the Sanctuary to remain there in safety until I returned with a plan, and to wait to free the rest of the half-bloods in the Other-world. We needed to focus on one battle at a time. Right now, that meant finding and killing this demon.

As we continued west, the Red Storm worsened. Because of the strong winds, our progress was far slower than it had been when Julian and I had traveled from Hypernia to the capital. It had been over a week since leaving the city, and we still hadn't reached the Western Mountain Range.

The rotting smell of the plague grew stronger by the day, even though we were flying the same distance above the hordes. Probably because there were more and more zombies the farther west we flew.

Every morning, Torrence did the spell to locate the demon.

The demon remained in the cliffs in the west. It was like she was waiting for us—like she wanted us to find her.

Bring it on.

If she wanted a fight, then we'd give her a fight.

Safe places to set up camp were hard to find in the Central Plainlands. But since the zombie hordes stuck together, we searched out areas where fewer of them congregated and managed to find nearly empty caves inside of hills. Once we killed off any zombies lingering in the vicinity, the caves were relatively safe for a night.

We created barrier domes around the caves. They were secure, but one person still stayed awake at all times to keep watch. We switched who that person was every two hours.

All things considered, we were holding up pretty well.

Except for Julian.

He started each day all right. But each afternoon, he kept nearly falling asleep while on the pegasus. His skin was clammy, and he was sweating through his clothes while he slept.

Something was wrong.

Very, very wrong.

And deep inside—in a place I'd avoided exploring—I had a guess about what that something was.

The sun started to set on the eighth night of traveling, and we located a viable cave to camp out in for the night. A handful of zombies wandered around it, and a few ambled about inside, but we easily took care of them with our holy weapons.

I created the barrier dome—with Torrence's and Reed's help—and we launched into our routine of laying down our sleeping rolls and setting up for dinner.

This far west, all the greenery was dead, or close to it. With no food sources, the animals that hadn't died or migrated away were skin and bone. We hunted what we could, but had to supplement each meal with the dried food we carried with us. As long as we rationed it reasonably, we had enough for another two weeks.

By then the demon would hopefully be long dead, and we'd be back in the citadel.

"Selena's turn for first watch," Sage said as we cleaned up after dinner. She had dark circles under her eyes, and other than Julian, she was struggling the most for sleep.

"Yep," I said, and my stomach swirled with anxiety.

Because after our long days of traveling, everyone

zonked out quickly each night and fell immediately into a deep sleep. Which made tonight the perfect time to pull Julian aside without any of them knowing. And even if one of them did wake up, they'd probably assume we wanted time alone as a couple.

I sat at the cave's entrance, listening and waiting for their breathing to slow. Julian fell asleep first. Then Sage. Torrence and Reed fell asleep at the same time, and Thomas was last.

It was now or never.

I kneeled down on my empty sleeping roll next to Julian, picked up the Holy Wand, and created a sound barrier around us. His skin was ashy, his brow damp with sweat, and every so often, a slight dimness flickered over his wings. The dimming could easily be explained by the dancing fire, but it was just one of the many things I'd been trying to explain away for the past few weeks.

He was sleeping so peacefully that I didn't want to wake him. But I had to.

So I placed my hand on his shoulder and gently shook him awake.

He forced his eyes open and stared up at me, confused. "Selena?" he asked, and he slowly pushed himself up to check on Torrence. She was supposed to keep watch after me, so he probably thought something had happened. But Torrence, of course, was fine. So he looked back to me. "What's wrong?"

"I need to talk to you," I said.

"About what?"

"Let's go up above the cave and talk there." I'd already thought this through. On the hill above the cave, we'd still be able to keep watch around camp. We'd also be able to talk without anyone waking up and seeing us.

"All right," he said, which surprised me. I'd expected him to put up a fight. Something about me not being responsible, because we all needed as much sleep as we could get. I was sure he'd think of something.

Instead, he tiptoed with me out of the cave without another question.

At the top of the hill, I surveyed our surroundings. A few lone zombies wandered out in the distance. But they couldn't hear us through the dome, and despite the red lightning flashing through the night sky, they were too far away to see us.

We were in the clear.

I released my violet and silver magic, and created a small soundproof dome around us so the others wouldn't overhear.

"Let me guess," Julian said lightly. "You're being driven just as crazy about the two of us not having any time alone together as I am?"

"No," I said, and disappointment flashed in his eyes. "I mean, yes, that's definitely been driving me crazy. But it's not why I brought you up here."

His expression hardened. "Then what's going on?"

Just be out with it.

I took a deep breath and said, "You have the plague."

He ran his hand through his hair and refused to meet my eyes.

No.

My heart shattered.

I'd wanted him to deny it. To tell me that was crazy. To assure me that if he'd been bitten, he would have told me.

Not answering was as good as admitting I was right.

"When we were journeying for the wand, there was a tear in your left sock," I said, remembering how the first time I'd seen it, I'd told myself the tear must had been from when I'd accidentally electrocuted him in the Night Forest. "Right above your ankle. Show it to me."

He lowered himself to sit on the dead grass.

In a daze, I sat beside him and placed the wand down next to me.

He unlaced his left boot, removed it, and pulled his breeches midway up his shin. I held my breath as he took off the sock.

There was no wound. His skin was ashy, but unmarred.

My heart leaped, and I could breathe again. But it felt too good to be true.

Especially because socks could fit on either foot.

I glanced at his other leg. "Your right sock," I said steadily.

I waited for a sarcastic remark. Something about this being an interesting new way of getting him to undress. But as calmly and emotionless as ever, he removed his right boot and sock.

The skin there was unmarred, too.

I stared at it in disbelief. I'd been so sure…

Then, the air around his ankle wavered. It could have been a trick of the light, caused by the Red Storm. But that would just be another excuse. Because it was the same way the air around his wings occasionally wavered.

The same way the air around the wand had wavered when the guard was disguising it as a sword.

Glamour.

I narrowed my eyes and focused on seeing through the magic.

Ghostlike outlines of a bandage appeared around his ankle, like a hologram.

He must have realized what I was doing, because the

glamour disappeared, and the reality beneath it sharpened into place.

A tan bandage—the same material as the clothes worn by half-blood servants—wrapped multiple times around his ankle. A few faded black splotches stained the outside of it, and the tips of small green leaves peeked out under the edges. And the worst part—the part that made the truth impossible to deny—was the thick black veins covering his foot like spiderwebs. They crawled up along his skin above the bandage as well, disappearing under the elastic cuffs at the bottom of his breeches.

My throat tightened, and I forced myself to swallow.

"Do you want to see it?" he asked.

I kept my eyes glued to the bandage, dug my fingers into the dirt, and nodded.

He untied the knot and carefully unwound the long strip of cloth. As he peeled off each layer, the black stains grew darker. The innermost layer was damp, shriveled, and completely stained black.

Small, green, oval-shaped leaves were pressed into the skin above the inside of his ankle.

"Boswellia," he explained as he peeled them away. "It numbs the pain."

Underneath the leaves, two crescent moon-shaped scratches faced each other on his skin. The marks weren't nearly as deep as Kyla's bite, but the skin was still slightly broken and covered in a layer of thick black goo. The dark, angry veins originated from the scratches, and again, I followed them up to the cuff of his breeches.

It's almost to her heart, I remembered Sorcha saying about Kyla's infection. *I fear she'll be lost to us once it gets to her heart.*

"How far up does it go?" The words didn't feel like mine. It was like someone else was in my place, and I was merely an observer.

"Up to my hip," he said. "It's been moving slowly. Probably because its teeth only grazed my skin."

My blood heated and crashed through my body like angry rapids. My head throbbed. Time slowed.

This can't be real.

"Does it hurt?" I asked.

"It did. But on the walk back from visiting Kyla, I stopped by the herb shop where I used to buy medicine for my sister. The boswellia numbs the affected area. I've also been chewing on willow bark, like Kyla recommended. It's not perfect, but it helps with the rest of the pain."

"Oh," I said. "That's good."

I couldn't move. I couldn't breathe. All I could do was stare at the wound.

The *bite.*

I'd been so upset since Julian had started pushing me away. So much that it hurt me physically.

But it clearly hadn't just been my own emotional pain I'd been feeling.

Because the soulmate bond connected Julian and me. The pain I'd been feeling must have also been his physical pain from the plague eating its way through his body.

"Selena," he said, and he sounded so vulnerable. "Look at me."

I did.

And I shattered.

He pulled me into his arms, and I cried until my tears soaked his shirt.

He was dying.

My soulmate was *dying.*

But not if I had anything to say about it.

I untangled myself from his arms, wiped the tears off my face, and grabbed the Holy Wand. Its crystals brightened at my touch. "I can fix this," I said, and I stood, backed up to put some space between us, and reached for my magic.

It swirled around me in a cyclone of blue, violet, and silver. Electricity crackled through the ridges of my scars and traveled farther up my arms. The crystal at the top of the wand lit up so brightly that it hummed with power.

Julian used his hand like a visor to block his eyes from the light and wind. "Don't sacrifice yourself for me, Selena," he said. "You're the Queen of Wands. The Otherworld needs you. Avalon needs you. Your parents need you. You can't desert them now."

"You're right—I *am* the Queen of Wands," I said, and lightning flashed through the sky. *Blue* lightning. "I'm going to get Avalon's help to save the Otherworld, and I'm going to free the half-bloods. And you're going to be with me when I do it."

I raised my arm, pointed the top of the wand toward Julian, and pushed as much magic as I could through it and out through the crystal. A beam of tri-colored light shot out from it and cocooned around him.

He braced himself, ready when the tendrils crawled forward and pierced his skin. This time, he didn't scream. He arched back, dug his fingers into the dirt, and focused on the sky raging with both red and blue lightning overhead.

Time to switch gears.

I stopped pushing out magic, and focused on sucking out the poison. I pulled as hard as I could.

But just like with Kyla, the poison wouldn't release

into my magic. It was a stubborn, thick, gooey thing that latched onto his bones and refused to budge.

No, I thought. *Let go. Come out of him.*

I grunted and pulled harder.

The wand's crystals burned brighter. Their humming intensified. Hot pain exploded in my palms and crawled up my arms.

"SELENA," Julian screamed. "STOP."

"NO." I dug deeper and pulled harder. This had to work. It *had* to.

I didn't want to live in a world without Julian in it.

My magic clawed under my skin, trying to rip its way out.

Selena, a warm, soothing voice echoed around me. The wand. It wasn't a voice, really, but a feeling. *You've done all you can. You can't cure him. At least, not like this.*

"Then how?" I asked.

There's always a way. But it won't do anyone any good if you die for nothing.

I wouldn't be dying for nothing. I'd be dying for Julian.

But if there were another way to cure him…

I released my hold on the magic, and the orb around Julian floated back toward me and into the crystal. It traveled down the wand, wrapped itself around my arms, and cooled the fire that had been trying to tear through my skin. The swirling magic absorbed into me and disappeared.

Rivulets of tar-like goo streamed out of Julian's wound and puddled on the ground. The black veiny lines on his skin had retreated, but just like with Kyla, the bite remained.

The poison was still inside of him.

Anger raced through me. Thunder cracked so loudly that the ground shook, and a bolt of blue lightning struck the ground between me and Julian. The brown, brittle grass disintegrated, leaving behind a mound of dirt with a small, black crater in the center.

I threw the wand like a javelin into the scorched ground. The top crystal embedded into the dirt. The other crystals dimmed and went dark.

Julian and I stared at each other, saying nothing.

Thoughts raced through my mind at a million miles per second. It was too much to process.

So I sank down to my knees next to the wand, and Julian started re-packing the herbs into the wound.

"When did it happen?" I asked one of my many questions.

"The only time it *could* have happened," he said. "When we fought the horde in the Central Plainlands, on our way to Sibyl's tree."

I nodded, since I'd already figured as much. It was

the only time we'd gotten close enough to the zombies for them to bite us.

"It was after you dismembered them, and they started growing their limbs back," I remembered. "Right before we jumped into the trees."

"Yes."

"Why didn't you tell me?" Tears blurred my vision again. "You pulled away. You all but ignored me. You treated me like crap. *Why?*"

Thick silence hung in the air between us.

He tied the bandage tight and made sure it was secure. "I didn't know what to say," he finally said. "I was about to tell you, in the Green Lake. But then you almost drowned. I thought I'd lost you, and the pain I felt in those minutes was unbearable. I didn't want you to feel even a fraction of that."

"You didn't think I could handle it."

"We needed to stay focused on finding the wand." He put his socks back on, and then his boots.

How was he being so nonchalant? Especially when…

"You were going to come with me to Avalon," I said. "You could have infected my parents. My friends. My entire *realm*."

"I was never going with you to Avalon," he said. "Not while I was infected, and not while my family was still here."

"So that was another lie."

If I couldn't trust my soulmate, who *could* I trust? I wished I could say Torrence, but now that she had dark magic, she wasn't herself, either.

"Knowing would have distracted you from what needed to be done," he said. "If we didn't bring the wand to the citadel, we both would have died. If we don't kill this demon, we'll *all* eventually die in this hellscape."

"You're not going to die." I stood and yanked the wand out of the ground. Its warm, comforting magic flooded through me, but it barely touched the depth of my anger. "You saw what I did for Kyla. If you'd told me you were infected, I could have pushed back the plague's progression earlier."

He stood as well, and he walked toward me, stopping when there was only a foot of space between us. "I saw you push your magic too far when you were trying to cure Kyla," he said. "If that's how far you went for someone you'd just met, then how far would you go for your soulmate? I didn't want you to risk killing yourself to cure me. Which is exactly what you just did."

"But I didn't kill myself. I helped you. And I'm going to *keep* helping you, every day until we find the cure."

"No," he said. "You have to be at full strength when we fight that demon. And the bite is only a scratch. The infection's moving slowly. This one time was enough."

"For now," I said, since the moment I noticed another flicker of weakness, I was going to help him no matter what.

He nodded, apparently realizing I wasn't going to budge. "You need rest after using all that magic," he said. "Let me take your shifts tonight."

"You're sick," I said. "You shouldn't be on guard duty, either. This entire trip, you've been in no condition to keep watch."

"I was still more than capable. But Sage kept guard with me, just in case."

Betrayal twisted at my heart. "Sage knew?"

"And Thomas. They smelled the infection the moment we met."

"And they didn't tell me."

"I asked them not to. I wanted to do it myself."

"That went well." My tone dripped with sarcasm, and he sucked in a sharp, pained breath.

Anger heated me down to my core. Anger at him for not telling me the moment he knew he was sick, anger at myself for not being able to cure him, anger that he'd gotten bitten in the first place, and anger at the plague for existing at all.

But snapping at him wouldn't do either of us any good. So I took a deep breath and got ahold of myself. "We need to tell Torrence and Reed," I said.

His expression hardened. "They don't need to know."

"We're working as a team, and one of our team members is compromised," I said. "So yeah, they do need to know."

He paused and looked out at the storm. A few seconds passed, and then he turned his attention back to me. "We haven't run into any trouble in the plains," he said. "I'll let them know before we cross into the Wildlands."

"You better," I said. "If you don't, I'll do it for you."

"You don't trust me," he said simply.

I wished I could say he was wrong. But I couldn't. So I shook my head instead.

He reached for me, but stopped. Because a shield of electricity hummed around my skin. It was protecting me from *him*.

Sadness—and regret—shined in his eyes. "Will you ever be able to forgive me?" he asked.

My heart melted, because I didn't need to think twice about the answer.

"It'll take time. But eventually, yes," I said. "Besides, I can't exactly be mad at you when you have the plague. So ask me again after you're cured."

"Deal. But if you won't let me take over this shift, then I'm sharing it with you."

"Fine." I sighed and sat in the dirt, unable to be angry at him anymore. It was exhausting.

He sat down next to me, and I stilled, not wanting to budge. But eventually, I caved and rested my head on his shoulder.

I could be as angry at him as I wanted after we found the cure.

Until then, I was going to treasure every moment we had together as if it were our last.

15

SELENA

BECAUSE OF THE growing intensity of the Red Storm, it took us a few more days to reach the Western Mountain Range—the mountains that separated the Western Wildlands from the rest of the Otherworld.

According to Julian, back when queens ruled the Otherworld, they sent all exiled fae to the Western Wildlands. Then the Empire took hold of the Other-world and deemed the exiled fae too much of a threat. So they hunted down all the exiled fae, threw them into a newly created prison realm—Ember—and have been sending them there since.

The Western Wildlands were said to be ruins now.

The Western Mountain Range was smaller than the Eastern Mountain Range, but the peaks were still high and steep enough that they were clear of zombies. There were far fewer trees, and the greenery was long dead. Any animal that hadn't been able to escape the storm was rotted to the bones. So, with no option to hunt or gather, we depended solely on our remaining rations for dinner.

The next day, we were supposed to cross into the Wildlands. Which meant that tonight, either Julian was telling Torrence and Reed about having the plague, or I'd do it for him.

We ate around the campfire, listening as Sage and Thomas told us about their journey years ago that had brought them, Noah, and Raven—the Queen of Swords —to Avalon. They'd been telling it to us in bits for the past few nights. Even though we learned about their adventure in school, it was far more exciting to hear it straight from them.

But I could barely focus on what they were saying. I was too distracted thinking about how I was going to break the news.

Julian's been keeping something from you.

Julian's been keeping something from all *of us.*

Julian was bitten by a zombie while we were searching for the wand.

Julian has the plague.

Julian's dying.

"Selena." Torrence snapped her fingers in front of my face to get my attention. "Where have you been all night?"

"Here." I shrugged, since it was true.

"You might physically be here, but your mind's not. And you've barely touched your food."

I glanced down at the hard bread and chewy strips of dried meat on my plate. I'd picked at them, but nothing more.

"You need to eat," Julian said from next to me. "To keep up your strength."

I wanted to pick up the roll and throw it at that ridiculously hard head of his. I *would* have, if we didn't need every bit of food we had.

I ripped the roll in half and settled for a glare instead.

He simply nodded, took my hand, and looked around at the others. "There's something you all need to know," he said. "I was going to tell you after we all finished eating, but it seems like it needs to be now."

Torrence's eyes widened, and she stared straight at me. "Are you pregnant?" she asked, and the piece of bread I was holding fell from my fingers back onto my plate.

"What? No." I stumbled over the words. "That's not even possible."

"You mean you haven't..." She looked at Julian, then back at me, *more* shocked than before.

Sage stifled a chuckle.

Thomas couldn't meet my eyes.

Reed kept eating.

"No. I mean, we have." I couldn't believe we were talking about this in front of Sage and Thomas. "But the reason it isn't possible is because the seeds from the pomegranate the gods gave us also act as birth control."

"Thank God." Torrence breathed out in relief. "I can go back to relishing the fact that Reed's the only virgin in the group."

Reed stopped chewing, and now *I* was the one who was shocked.

I'd learned on our journey that Reed was betrothed to a princess on Mystica because of some political arrangement. But he'd struck me as the type of guy who'd want to have his fun before tying the knot.

Judging from his silence, I'd been wrong.

"Julian was about to tell us something," Reed said stiffly, and all eyes turned back to my soulmate.

"Right." Julian fidgeted and cleared his throat. "There's no easy way to say this, so I'm just going to be out with it. When Selena and I ran into that horde of zombies while we were searching for the Holy Wand, one of them bit me. I'm infected with the plague."

Everyone stilled and silenced. Including Sage and Thomas, even though they already knew.

Julian explained what had happened, ending with how I'd pushed back the plague's progress a few days ago in the Plainlands.

"I can kind of understand why you waited to tell us," Torrence said once he was finished. "But not telling *Selena*?"

"Stop," I said, and she looked at me like I was nuts. "What's done is done. We need to focus on working together to kill that demon, and then on finding a cure."

She pressed her lips together and nodded, although she gave Julian another dirty look. The type of look that said, *If you lie to my best friend again, you're in trouble.*

I loved her for it.

"The witch," Sage said suddenly, and we all looked to her. "The one with the demon—the one Aeliana told us not to kill. Maybe she has the cure."

"She might," I said, since I'd wondered the same thing. "If she does, we're getting it from her. We need to be as ready for this battle as possible. Which means that tonight, I'm going to use my magic to push back the progression the plague has made on Julian these past few days."

"Then you'll be weakened when we cross into the Wildlands tomorrow," Torrence said. "Absolutely not.

We need you." Her voice was strained at the last part, like it hurt her to say.

"We're not leaving tomorrow," I said. "We'll stay here an extra night to give me time to regain my strength. Then, once we're all rested and ready, we'll head out, find the demon, and take her down."

16

SELENA

THE NEXT DAY, Torrence did another locating spell to make sure the demon was still in the same spot.

She was.

The general consensus was that the demon was clueless we were coming for her. But I thought she was waiting for us. I had no evidence—it was just a *feeling*.

"I've been thinking," Reed said once the spell was complete.

"Really?" Torrence chuckled and blew out the candles. "That's a first."

His eyes flashed black, then quickly returned to their normal color. "You know, you'd be less likely to get tangled up in your own messes if you stopped talking all the time and listened to other people every so often," he said.

"I *don't* get tangled up in my own messes."

"Says the girl who jumps into everything without thinking about the long-term consequences."

She glared at him in warning.

"Whoa." I reached for the Holy Wand—I'd rested it against a log while we were doing the locating spell— and also glared at Reed. "It's not Torrence's fault that I got stuck here."

"I never said it was."

"Not directly. But you implied it."

Torrence put her pendulum necklace back on, threw the maps and candles back into the sack, and stood up. "What's done is done," she said, which surprised me, since she'd never been one to back down from a fight. "No use getting worked up about it now."

"I wasn't worked up," he said. "I was just stating a fact."

Another silent staredown. Torrence's anger radiated off her so much that I could feel it.

After over a week of traveling together, I no longer secretly hoped that Reed and Torrence would get together. He was an arrogant, smug jerk. Torrence deserved way better. It was a good thing they hated each other, because once we got back to Avalon, they could happily go their separate ways.

Thomas got up from where he was sitting next to

Sage and marched over to us. "Enough," he said, and he focused on Reed. "Torrence is right. What's done is done. Now, care to share what you were thinking?"

Reed gave Torrence another death glare, and then refocused on Thomas. "I was *thinking* that pendulums can be used for more than just locating someone on a map," he said. "They can also be used for more precise tracking."

"That's dark blood magic." I glanced at Torrence— who looked more intrigued than she should have—and then back at Reed.

"It is," he said.

"But the locating spell has been telling us where the demon is hiding out. We don't need tracking magic."

The less Torrence was around dark magic, the better.

"What if the demon runs when she sees us approaching?" he asked. "We won't have time to get out a map and do a locating spell."

"She's not going to run," I said. "She's a demon. She'll want to fight."

"We can't know that."

Sage stood up and joined us. "*Most* demons want to fight," she said. "But not greater demons. They're smarter than that. They know when to teleport out of a situation. Well, run, in this case, since teleporting is blocked in the Otherworld."

"So annoying," Torrence said, and I nodded in agreement.

"It is annoying," Thomas agreed. "But Aeliana said we can kill this demon, and greater demons can only be killed by Nephilim. None of us are Nephilim. So this demon isn't a greater demon."

"If she's not a greater demon, then how does she have so much power?" I asked.

"No idea," he said. "It's unprecedented. So I agree with Reed. We need to do anything that gives us an advantage. Even if it means using dark magic."

"Julian?" I turned to my soulmate. "What do you think?"

"An advantage is an advantage," he said. "As long as using the advantage doesn't hurt anyone on our team, it's worth it."

I paused, since that was the question, wasn't it? What was the dark magic doing to Torrence?

But I also knew that their point was a good one.

"Fine," I said. "But Reed will be the one who does the spell."

"Obviously," he said. "I'm the most powerful one here."

"Are you so sure about that?" I sent my magic through the wand, and the top crystal glowed so brightly that it was like staring into a spotlight.

They all held their hands in front of their eyes and turned away.

Julian moved closer to me, his head turned away from the light. "Selena," he said. "Don't expend any more magic than necessary."

I sighed in annoyance. "I know." I pulled back on the magic, and the light dimmed. "I was just making a point."

"Point made," Reed said. "But you know what I meant. I'm the only one here with true *mage* magic."

I glanced at Torrence, since I wasn't so sure about that. But that was a whole other can of worms that we needed to wait to open until we were back on Avalon. Plus, Reed was right. Mage magic was his territory.

An image of Torrence killing all of those animals and trees in the forest flashed through my mind.

Another day, I reminded myself. *Worry about that another day.*

That was how I'd gotten through the Faerie Games— by tackling one big problem at a time. Right now, that problem was tracking this demon and her witch companion.

"There's only one issue with this plan," Torrence said. "If we want the pendulum to track a demon, we need demon blood. Not just an object with an intense memory of demon blood, like how we use the knife to do locating spells. We need *actual* blood."

"Which we have." Reed glanced at Julian. "At least, we have a trace of it."

Right. That was part of how we'd figured out that the demons had something to do with the plague. The trace of demon blood that Sage and Thomas had smelled in the zombie blood.

The same blood that was oozing out of Julian's wound.

Julian remained as calm and stoic as ever. "What do you need me to do?" he asked.

"Unwrap your bandage and let me dip the pendulum in the infected area," Reed said. "I don't need much. Just a drop will do it."

Julian sat down to remove the bandage, and Torrence handed her necklace to Reed.

"Don't get any blood on the diamonds," she said before letting him take it. "And be careful with it. It was a present from my best friend." She glanced at me, and I smiled.

"I'll do my best," he said, and then he knelt down next to Julian, dipped the tip of the pendulum into the black ooze coming out of his wound, and cast the spell.

SELENA

ON THE OTHER side of the Western Mountains, the storm raged like the eye wall of a hurricane. The wind flung the zombies into the sides of the mountains like rag dolls. Endless piles of them collected at the base, and they squirmed like dying worms. Their black blood stained the ground and the rocks, and the overwhelming smell of death and decay was inescapable, no matter how high we flew.

Luckily, the wind must have dumped all of the zombies along the mountains, because once we flew over the thick of them, they quickly disappeared. So did their smell.

But the wind intensified the farther west we flew. The roaring storm assaulted my eardrums. The rain pounded so densely on the boundary domes surrounding our pegasi that we could barely see in front of us. Debris kept smashing into the domes, too. And the clouds were so dark that if it hadn't been for the red lightning brightening the sky, we wouldn't have been able to see at all.

We were only a mile past the mountains, and the pegasi were straining their wings so much that we were making zero forward progress.

"We need to go on foot from here!" Julian screamed so I could hear him. "Land our pegasus. The others will follow."

I used the Holy Wand like a spotlight to double-check that there weren't any zombie stragglers beneath us. We were in the clear. So I squeezed my heels into the pegasus's sides and eased him to the ground.

Sure enough, the others followed.

We stood as closely together as we could, and then Julian, Reed, Torrence, and I used our magic to create a super dome around all of us and our pegasi. It was more powerful than the type of dome we used whenever we set up camp, or when we stopped for lunch, because it blocked the weather *and* the noise.

The wind must have been pummeling the area for a while, because it was a barren, dusty wasteland. Most of the trees were snapped at their trunks. The ones that remained were bare of leaves and tilted so much that their tips touched the ground. Besides the occasional zombie impaled through their thick branches, there was nothing green or alive in sight.

Although, I supposed the zombies weren't technically *alive*.

My pegasus lowered himself down onto his knees and rested his wings on the ground. Blood seeped through the edges of some of his feathers.

I ran my fingers through his silky mane, wishing I could help him. Unfortunately, healing magic was a rare gift among royal full fae that I didn't possess. When I'd "healed" the half-bloods, I was technically reversing the spell inked on them by the fae. And Torrence and her group hadn't brought any healing potion with them from Earth. Even if they had, healing potion only worked on humans and witches. We had no idea if it would work on pegasi.

"I've never been to Hell, but I always imagined it being nicer than *this*," Sage said as she looked around the stormy wasteland.

"Yeah," I agreed, since we'd learned enough about Hell to have a general idea of what it was like. This was most definitely worse. And despite common misconception, Hell wasn't the same place as the Underworld. Bad people didn't go to Hell after they died.

Hell was simply the name of the realm where the demons lived.

"We need to discuss our plan from here," Julian said, getting all of our attention. "We're not making any progress on the pegasi. Their wings are too fragile to fly in these conditions."

"What are you proposing we do?" Reed asked. "Go on foot?"

"Yes," Julian said, and Reed balked. "We can't travel nearly as quickly as the pegasi, but we're stronger and more durable than they are. According to the map, we only have a bit over ten more miles to go. It won't be easy, but if we all hold hands in a line to ground ourselves, we can push a boundary dome forward as we walk."

"So Reed and I will create another traveling dome," Torrence said. "One that surrounds the six of us. The pegasi might be too fragile to fly the domes against the wind, but like you said, we're physically stronger than they are. Not as fast, but we're more durable. It'll take us longer to travel on foot, but you're right. Together, we should be strong enough to push the dome against the wind."

Julian glanced at me and said nothing.

He wasn't going to approve of Torrence tethering her magic to Reed's again.

That was on me.

But before I could say anything, Torrence grabbed Reed's hands, and they did the spell. The purple and yellow of their magic lit up the barren landscape and created a shimmering dome around us, inside the super dome that also blocked noise.

The dome turned nearly transparent, and Torrence and Reed pulled away from each other in a daze.

She shook it off, turned her back to him, and tossed her hair over her shoulder. "There we go," she said with a bright smile. "Easy."

Reed's eyes were dilated, and he didn't say a word.

"We'll send the pegasi back to our camp at the mountains," Thomas said. "Once we're done with the demon, we'll meet up with them and fly them back to the city."

Sage kneeled down next to the pegasus she'd been sharing with Thomas and examined the spot where the creature's wing attached to its body. It was bright red, and the skin was so stretched that there were small tears along the edges. "Will they be able to make it back?" she asked.

None of us said anything.

Because none of us knew.

"Let me try something," she said, and then she bit the inside of her wrist. Blood flowed to the surface, and she held it up to the pegasus's mouth. "Here," she said. "Drink."

The pegasus snorted and turned its head away.

Thomas hurried to Sage's side and wrapped his hand around her wrist to stop the bleeding. "Let it heal," he said sternly. "We're getting ready to face a demon with strength we've never seen before. You need to be at your strongest. You can't lose any blood."

They held each others' gazes for a few seconds.

Then he pulled his hand away. Blood coated Sage's skin, but the surface was smooth.

Vampire and shifter healing abilities were incredible. Of course, they couldn't heal like that after being injured with holy weapons—or the Nemean lion's claws—but I supposed that was why she bit her wrist instead of slicing it with her dagger.

She looked helplessly at her pegasus. "I hoped my blood might be able to heal her," she said sadly.

"Vampire blood can only heal humans," Thomas said. "You know that."

"I know. But I had to try."

He slowly stood up, bringing her with him.

"The wind is blowing toward the mountains," I said. "The pegasi won't have to strain their wings, since they'll be flying with the wind and not against it. So they should be able to make it back to our campsite in the

Western Mountains. They'll need to heal first, but they have magic. I don't imagine the healing process will take long."

"Good idea," I said, and I looked back at my pegasus.

He bobbed his head up and down—a nod.

We set up camp and made ourselves comfortable.

The next morning, the pegasi were healed enough to fly with the wind behind them. And so we said sorrow-filled goodbyes to our winged horses, joined our hands together, and pushed forward.

18

SELENA

REED TOOK the left side of our "wall," and I took the right. Julian wasn't thrilled about having me on the end, but I needed a hand free to hold the wand. With the wand, I could send strength through our linked hands.

Torrence's pendulum pulsed steadily with light as we continued forward. It was like a game of hot and cold. If she stepped back, the pendulum dimmed. When she moved to the west—toward the demon—it started to pulse again.

Once we were within feet of the demon, it would flash like a strobe light.

We had to leave as much of our supplies as possible with the pegasi to lighten the load. So we carried only the essentials—weapons, food, and water. It was a good thing we'd cast the spell on the pendulum, because the atlas and the four candles had been left behind.

The wind was so strong that each step felt like my shoes were bricks. After hours of walking, the sun set, and we stopped for the night.

Sleeping without bedrolls on the dead, muddy grass wasn't the most comfortable thing in the world, but we made do.

Sage and Thomas snuggled together, and Julian, Torrence, and I snugged together—with me in the middle facing Julian. Reed slept alone. He glanced at Torrence a few times when we were getting situated, but she ignored him.

We did the same thing the next day, and the next. Pushing against what had to have been category five strength winds was no easy task, even for supernaturals.

Finally, on the third day, we stepped out of the wind. One moment the storm roared, and the next, the air was still. Unnaturally so. Clouds darkened the sky, and red lightning flashed between them, but the wind was gone. The calmness extended for as far as I could see.

I spun around and looked out to where the storm raged on only a few feet away. An invisible line separated the wind from the calm. The protective bubble climbed all the way up to the sky. It was incredible and beautiful, in an exceptionally creepy way.

"It curves toward the horizon," Thomas said. "We're in the eye of the storm."

"What would you bet that the demon and her witch are right in the center?" Sage asked.

"I don't need to bet," Julian said. "I was counting each footstep, and I memorized the map. We just walked ten miles. Ten miles more, and we'll reach the cliffs where the demon made her lair. Now that we're not walking against the wind, it shouldn't take long to get there."

"I should heal you first," I said. Even though I wasn't actually healing Julian, it was easier to refer to the process of pushing back the plague that way. "We'll make camp again to rest tonight, and launch our attack in the morning."

From Julian's steely gaze, he didn't like that plan. He didn't like *anyone* being held back because of him. But he didn't say no.

Sage spun slowly around and sniffed the air. "You guys?" she said. "We're gonna have to hold that thought."

"Zombies?" I asked, and she nodded.

"About half a mile out. They're heading in this direction."

"From which way?" Julian asked.

"From *all* ways. They're trapping us in a semicircle, with our backs toward the storm. It has to be a planned attack."

"How many?" he asked.

"A lot. We're gonna need all hands on deck."

Thomas's hand went to the handle of the sword strapped to his weapons belt.

Julian looked around at all of us. "You all know the plan?"

We snapped to attention and said yes, since we'd been through this many times.

"Good," he said. "Let's take them down."

We located the nearest hill and hurried to the top of it, ready with our weapons—and with our magic. Working together, we created another super dome around us. We'd be able to move in and out as we pleased, but it would keep the zombies out. It technically should have been able to hold against endless amounts of them, but we'd yet to put it to the test.

No time like the present.

Rot and decay grew thick in the air, followed by the first of the zombies stumbling into the valley. They were clumped so thickly together that I couldn't see the grass beneath their feet.

They closed in, and their groans chorused around us. There had to be four times as many as the horde

Julian and I had fought on our way to Sibyl's tree—or more.

But back then, we didn't have holy weapons. We didn't know what we were facing. We didn't have a plan.

Now, we were ready.

The others formed a circle around me, faced the zombies, and held out their holy weapons.

Sage had both the slicer and the longsword she'd been loaning me. I'd have no use of the longsword while I was safe inside the dome, so it was more useful with her. The wand was all I'd need.

Reed and Julian had one holy weapon each, since Reed had loaned Julian his extra. They'd insisted it made the most sense for them to be the only ones without two holy weapons, since Julian could pull a regular weapon from the ether if needed, and Reed had his dark mage magic.

I double checked that everyone was ready, raised the Holy Wand above my head, and shot my electricity through it. Just like when I'd freed the half-bloods, the crystals conducted the magic, heightening it and giving me extra strength.

Hundreds of blue lightning bolts shot down from the clouds and struck the zombies below. I rotated around in a circle, making sure to hit them all.

The zombies collapsed to the ground. Smoke drifted

off of them, the scent slightly covering the smell of rot. Their sprawled bodies looked like the aftermath of a massacre.

But they still weren't *dead* dead.

Julian, Reed, Thomas, Torrence, and Sage bolted toward the approaching zombies.

One, two, three, four, five, I counted the seconds in my mind.

They wielded their holy weapons, and they swung them in a blur, stabbing the zombies through their hearts and turning them to ash. They watched each other's backs, and ashed the entire inside ring of zombies.

Twenty-one, twenty-two, twenty-three, twenty-four.

"COME BACK!" I yelled, and they all spun around, quickly rejoining me inside the dome.

Thirty seconds.

That was the shortest length of time it took for a knocked down zombie to start pushing itself back up. Which, sure enough, a few of them did.

We waited another minute, until all of the remaining zombies were back on their feet.

Then we did the same thing again. And again. And again.

I itched to go out there and join them. But the wand thrummed in my hand, as if it was warning me away from my thoughts. Because even though I wasn't in the midst of the action, my role was important. This entire strategy wouldn't be possible without me.

By the fifth round, nearly three-fourths of the zombies were gone. Ash covered the majority of the ground in the valley.

The five of them had moved on to slaying the zombies in the outermost ring, nearly half a mile away.

Seven, eight, nine...

A thick bolt of red lightning struck a hill in the distance.

Crap.

So far, the red lightning had stayed up near the clouds. This was the first ground strike I'd seen.

The others were powerful.

But powerful enough to withstand a direct lightning strike?

I wasn't about to find out.

"COME BACK!" I screamed, but an exploding boom of thunder drowned out my call.

A thick bolt of red lightning struck the top of the dome. I spun around just as it pierced the barrier.

Impossible.

But even more impossibly, it didn't strike the ground.

It spread out into the shapes of two people made of

pure, red electricity. I shot a blast of electricity toward them, but it passed right through.

The electricity around them sizzled out, and two women solidified into place.

One had skin so pale it nearly matched her white dress. Her hair was as black as zombie blood.

The other was as tall as a model, and her dark, wavy hair flowed down to her waist. She smiled at me, and her eyes flashed red.

A demon.

My heart leaped in terror. Because I didn't have a holy weapon.

So I pointed the wand at her and sent electricity through the top crystal.

But she was a second ahead of me. And that second was all she needed to move out of the way, come at me from the side, grab my wrist, and send a searing pain through my body that boiled my blood and ripped me to shreds.

19

SELENA

I SCREAMED.

At least, I *tried* to scream.

But I couldn't. Because I wasn't anything. I was split into nano-sized bits down to the cellular level, zooming through the air as energy stronger than any voltage I'd ever conjured rushed through me.

No, not *through* me.

The energy *was* me.

I was light. Pure electricity zooming through the clouds. I was free.

Am I dead?

Then, piercing pain. The bits of me snapped into place, and the cells rearranged themselves like a jigsaw puzzle piecing itself together at super speed.

Please, stop, I pleaded to whoever might be listening.

It didn't stop. Instead, thousands of needles stabbed through me, stitching me back together.

Finally, the pieces settled into place.

Bright red light surrounded me.

I tried screaming again.

Again, nothing.

Just when I thought I couldn't take it anymore, the pain vanished. Ground solidified beneath my feet. The red light dimmed, and went out.

A hand was wrapped around my arm.

The demon.

I slammed my knee into her groin, and she released me. Then I pushed her down with my other foot for good measure, hurried away to put space between us, and spun back around.

I shot a beam of blue, violet, and silver magic through the wand's crystal and out at her.

Red magic shot from her hands and crashed into mine. It was like hitting a wall.

"How'd you like the ride?" She grinned.

I grunted and pushed harder. But her magic didn't budge. She didn't even look like she was trying.

"It hurt, didn't it?" she continued. "I wish I could say you'd get used to it, but I can't. Not that it matters, since there won't be anything left of you to get used to once we're done here."

Still holding onto my magic, I glanced up at the dark red sky. We were at the bottom of a huge crater that must have been fifty feet deep. Zombies crowded around the perimeter of the circular cliff, pulling at an invisible fence as they stared down at me like angry fans watching a wrestling match.

The landscape behind them was flatter than where we'd been fighting a minute ago.

Whatever the demon had done to me had transported us somewhere else.

How?

It wasn't teleporting—teleporting didn't hurt like that. Plus, teleporting was blocked in the Otherworld.

It was some other method of travel.

But I'd worry about that later. Right now, my focus needed to be on defeating the demon.

I opened the hand that wasn't holding the wand.

Blue lightning struck down from the sky toward the demon.

She dropped her hold on her magic and rolled out of the way. My magic slammed into the rock wall behind where she'd been standing. Then, she stood up and opened her hand.

Move.

I jumped out of the way a split second before red lightning struck where I'd been standing.

I raised the wand and brought down ten bolts at once—all aimed at the demon.

A dome of red electricity surrounded her and absorbed the blast.

I slammed it with another bolt, and then another. But the dome was an impenetrable cage. No matter how much lightning I struck it with, I couldn't get through.

"I'm Fallon, by the way." Her long hair blew behind her as she maintained her hold on the electricity surrounding her. "In case you were wondering."

"I wasn't."

"That's too bad. Because I'm a fan of yours, Selena. I loved watching you in the Faerie Games."

I sent another lightning strike at her, although of course, it did nothing.

"This is a Faraday cage." She laughed and motioned around at the electrical cage-like dome around her. "There's a whole scientific reason behind how it works, but basically, it blocks electromagnetic fields to protect whatever and whoever's inside."

"So you're just gonna stand in that thing and taunt me?" It seemed like it, since if she was going to attack from in there, she would have done it by now.

Apparently, the cage blocked magic from both the outside *and* the inside.

"You're easy to rile up." She smirked. "I learned that

while watching the Games. It's fun watching you waste your energy trying to get through."

I raised the wand, its crystals glowing, but I didn't attack. Because as much as I hated it, she had a point about wasting energy.

Plus, the more she talked, the more time the others had to use the pendulum to track her here and bring me a holy weapon.

I couldn't kill her without one. Not even blowing up everything around me like a bomb—like how I'd killed Octavia—would do it. That would just drain me so much that I wouldn't be able to defend myself.

I *needed* a holy weapon.

The longer she stayed in that cage, unable to attack me, the better. Although since she found it "fun" to watch me try to get through, I'd have to keep her entertained by throwing a bit of electricity at her every so often.

"I also figured I'd give Lavinia some time to take care of your friends back there," she continued. "She gets real pissy if she doesn't feel like she's being useful."

Lavinia, I thought, and it clicked into place.

Lavinia *Foster*. A notorious traitor witch who'd been working with the demons since they'd escaped from Hell. Before I was born, she'd bound Sage and the rest of the Montgomery pack to the greater demon Azazel, which forced them to serve him. They were finally released after the Queen of Swords killed Azazel.

After being freed, Sage had tried to kill Lavinia. But Lavinia ran away before she could.

Sage better keep herself from killing Lavinia now. We need the witch alive so she can give us the cure.

But I kept my expression as calm as Sorcha's, not wanting Fallon to see a hint of my worry.

"My friends can handle themselves against your witch," I said.

"Maybe." She shrugged. "Maybe not. I don't care. She's already had her use."

"And what *use* is that?" I slammed her stupid Faraday cage with another bolt of lightning, and she chuckled, amused.

"All of this." She looked around at the zombies crowding the ledges, her red eyes wide in wonder. "The plague. Lavinia created it—at least, the spell for it. My mother will be annoyed if she dies, but oh well. Casualties happen in war. Like your sweet friend Cassia."

I sucked in a sharp breath at my friend's name.

Then I pointed the wand at Fallon and shot multiple bolts of lightning at her cage. They surrounded it, hissing and buzzing around her red electricity.

I can put my fae and witch magic behind it and push harder, I thought. *I can break through.*

But I pulled back and let my magic fizzle out. Because as satisfying as it would be to destroy her cage, I still didn't have a holy weapon.

I needed to keep stalling.

She pulled her hair over her shoulder, brushed her fingers through it, and smiled. "How did it feel watching Cassia die?" she asked.

I raised my hand and aimed a bolt of lightning at her face. The cage stopped it, of course, but the release was satisfying.

"You saw me afterward," I said. "You should know."

"Actually, I didn't see you afterward. Lavinia banished the orbs from our castle. She said they were distracting me from mastering my magic." She toyed with electricity in her hands, thunder rumbled overhead, and the sky flashed red.

I raised my wand, shot electricity out in all directions from the top crystal, and created a massive blue electrical cage around the crater.

Red bolts of lightning struck the top, but they didn't break through.

"A cage around a cage." Fallon looked up at it approvingly. "Smart."

I lowered the wand, and the blue cage around us held.

She snarled at me, and her eyes flashed red. Hurricanes of rage swirled within them.

She was going to snap.

Keep her talking.

"The Nephilim army has been hunting demons since before I was born," I said. "None of them have ever had lightning magic. So how do you?"

"That was the beauty of Lavinia's spell. Because the plague eats away at fae magic. Then, when it reaches the heart, it transfers the remnants of that magic to me." The sky boomed and lit up with red streaks again. "The plague killed hundreds of thousands of fae." Her long hair blew around her, and her skin glowed red with electricity. "All of their magic is stored inside me."

The weight of that settled on my shoulders, and fear coated my tongue.

But I swallowed it down. Because I was the Queen of Wands.

I could fight her.

I *had* to be able to fight her.

The entire realm—and maybe more—depended on it.

I glanced up and around the crater's edge, trying to see through my blue cage to the zombies surrounding it.

Come on, guys, I thought, searching for my friends. *Where are you?*

There were no signs of them.

I needed to keep stalling.

"I guess that kind of makes sense." I toyed with my electricity, mimicking her. "But lightning magic isn't fae magic. It's *Jupiter's* magic. So how do you have it?"

Did Jupiter gift Fallon with his magic, too?

"Your magic is impressive, and I wanted it for myself," she said simply. "And remember, I've absorbed magic from *hundreds of thousands* of fae. Their magic exists in tiny orbs inside of me. Rub enough of those orbs together, and BOOM. Electric charge." The sky cracked with thunder and flashed red again, as if accentuating her point.

"So you saw my magic and copied it."

"Not copied." She frowned. "I was *inspired* by it."

"Same thing."

She snarled, the cage around her vanished. She raised both hands and shot a thick beam of red electricity toward me.

I clutched the wand with both hands and shot out a beam of my own. Just like earlier, my blue magic crashed into her red magic. Together, it formed one long beam—her side red, and my side blue. White sparks ignited and flared out in the center where they touched.

We both held on, braced ourselves, and pushed harder.

I screamed and threw as much power as possible into my magic. Silver and violet helixes swirled within the blue beam of electricity.

But it wasn't enough. My hands shook around the wand. It was taking all of my strength to hold out against her.

If I could force past her magic and reach her, maybe I could trap her in a Faraday cage of my own. Then I'd have to either hope my friends got here in time with a holy weapon, or leave her to seek them out, hoping she'd still be there when I returned.

I didn't like either option. But they were both better than her winning and finishing me off.

While I'd been thinking, her magic had climbed forward, making its way closer to me.

We circled around each other, both keeping hold on our magic.

Sweat beaded on my brow and dripped down the side of my face, narrowly missing my eye.

The cage surrounding us, I realized. *It's taking too much magic to hold onto it* and *defend myself against her.*

I let it fizzle out, and a surge of magic rushed through me. I pushed it toward her, and she stumbled back.

But her hold on her magic didn't weaken.

She steadied herself, screamed, and sent a surge straight back at me.

I pushed harder, but her magic inched closer. One foot, two feet, three feet. She was gaining on me too quickly. And with each bit of progress, the weight of her magic grew heavier and harder to hold back.

It wasn't supposed to end this way.

Distract her, I thought. *Get her lost in her thoughts, like how I just got lost in mine.*

"What do you want?" I screamed to be heard over our crashing magic and the blowing wind.

"The wand." Her eyes glowed brighter red. "Kill you, and the wand's mine."

She forced her magic further forward. Most of the beam between us was red now. One more foot, and she'd reach me.

Part of me wanted to let go and roll to the side, like she had earlier. Then I could lock myself in a Faraday cage of my own to buy myself some time while I figured out what to do.

But her magic was much closer to me now than mine had been to her then. If I let go, I wouldn't have enough time to move before her electricity reached me.

I needed to stand strong.

So I bent my knees, every muscle in my body shaking as I tried to stop her progress.

Sweat coated my body. My palms were slick with it, the wand slippery in my grasp. I held my breath and tried as hard as possible to hold on.

But her magic inched closer. Only a sliver of blue protected the top crystal of the wand from her magic, and then, nothing.

Red exploded around the crystal, and the force of it threw me backward in a burst of light. My back smacked against the ground. Dots floated in my vision, and I gasped for air, but it sliced my lungs like knives. The wand lay beside me, its crystals dead of light.

But they weren't broken.

Just like I wasn't broken. And I wasn't going to lie there and give up. I had too much to fight for. My parents, my friends, Julian, and my *home*. I was going to get back to Avalon, and I was going to make sure the demons couldn't do to Earth what they'd done to the Otherworld.

I was the Queen of Wands. Fallon might have knocked the wind out of me, but the wand gave me strength. With it, I could still fight.

I sucked in my first good breath since being slammed to the ground and reached for the wand.

But I was too late.

Because Fallon got it first.

SELENA

"Yᴇs," she said, and she tilted her head back, raising the wand to the sky.

Red electricity danced along her skin. But it didn't travel up the wand.

Instead, the wand's invisible magic traveled down to me. Tendrils of it brushed against my skin, like it was begging me for help.

Of course it was. Because the Holy Wand was *mine*.

The *Holy* Wand.

If the wand's holy, then maybe...

The wand and I were connected. We'd been connected since I'd hovered my hands over it in the Sanctuary and held it for the first time. So I pulled the tendrils of the wand's magic into me.

The crystals pulsed with blue light, in sync with the beats of my heart.

Fallon smiled. She must have thought the glowing crystals were *her* doing.

Now, I thought, and blue electricity ignited around the entire wand in a bright burst of light.

Fallon screamed as the electricity spread over her body, covering her completely. It cracked and buzzed around her, and she seized, like Felix had when I'd fried him.

But she kept her hand wrapped around the bottom of the wand. It was like her palms were covered in superglue. And the longer she held on, the longer the electricity continued to fry her.

I pushed myself up and backed away, putting a few feet between us.

Her strangled screams echoed through the crater, so loud that they drowned out the thunder overhead. Her veins popped out so much that they looked like they were about to burst. Her eyes widened, bloodshot and about to pop out of their sockets. The ends of her hair fried and burned upward, like ropes on fire. The sickening smell of cooked flesh filled my nose.

I reached out my hand and focused on the wand.

Come to me.

It yanked itself out of her grasp, flew toward me, and smacked into my palm.

The electricity around Fallon fizzled out. She collapsed to the ground in a burnt heap, and rolled over to look up at the red sky.

She blinked a few times and moaned like the zombies surrounding us.

Not dead.

At least, not yet.

Please work, I thought, and then I raised the wand with both hands, pointed the top crystal down at her chest, and plunged it into her heart.

The crystals glowed blue—as did her eyes. She opened her mouth to scream, and blue light flooded out of it. Her skin cracked open, and blue light flooded out of the growing crevices, too.

The wand was burning her up from the inside. The light clawed through more and more of her skin, ripping it to shreds and consuming her in a Fallon-shaped blue orb.

The light exploded in a burst. Then the wand slid past her body like there was nothing there, and it wedged into the ground.

The thunder overhead silenced. The eerie red light faded away to nothing, and the sun shined down, basking me in its warmth.

The light around Fallon dimmed and disappeared.

All that remained was a big pile of ash. The tip of the wand was buried in the spot where Fallon's heart would be. About half a foot away—on top of the ash that had been her head—was a pile of pointy yellow teeth.

I pulled the wand out of the ashes and stared down at Fallon's remains.

It worked.

The Holy Wand *was* a holy weapon. It could kill demons.

I reached down, picked up one of the teeth, and pocketed it. Most members of Avalon's army had a "tooth bank" where they kept a tooth from each demon they killed.

Hopefully Fallon's would be the first in my own very large collection.

I stood there, staring at the pile of ash, smiling at the fact that I'd truly killed her.

Thump, thump, thump.

The sound echoed around me, like falling rocks.

I whipped my head up to see what was making the noise, and froze.

Zombies were tumbling over the edge of the crater like lemmings. They rolled down, hit the ground, and pushed themselves up to stand. Their eyes were on me, and they groaned, opening and closing their jaws as they shuffled toward me. More kept falling over the edge—a never-ending stream of them.

I spun around to find a way out.

But they surrounded me from all directions.

So I raised my wand, and clouds rolled in overhead, blocking the warm sun. Then I called bolts down from the sky and struck the zombies down. They collapsed to the ground—stunned, but not dead.

Time to get out of there.

I ran forward, rammed the top of the wand into the ground, and pushed off of it, flying up and through the air like a pole-vaulter. I landed at the rim of the crater, on the back of a fallen zombie, and bent my knees to absorb the impact. Then I held my arm out and called to the wand. It unwedged itself from the ground in the center of the crater, soared through the air, and landed in my palm.

The crystals glowed brightly, and adrenaline rushed through my veins.

I hopped off the back of the zombie and looked around to figure out a way back to the hill where Julian and the others were fighting.

The adrenaline evaporated away in an instant.

Because apart from the ruins on the brown, barren land, zombies stretched out for as far as I could see.

Tons more than I'd been fighting with the others back on the hill. There must have been *thousands* of them.

They started getting up, and I called down lightning again, frying the ones closest to me.

I needed to clear a path and get out of there.

My heart pounded, and I spun around to figure out where to go. The ruins meant this place was in the Western Wildlands. The crater had been in the "eye" of the hurricane—because of the lack of wind and rain—so the others had to be nearby. And we'd just entered the eye from the east when the zombies had attacked.

I needed to go east.

But nearly identical hills rolled in every direction. The trees were dead, so I couldn't use their moss to figure out which way was north. Using the stars to navigate was out, since it was the middle of the day. And even though Fallon's storm had stopped, I needed to maintain the cloud cover overhead so I could keep zapping the zombies. So using the position of the sun wasn't an option, either.

I rammed the wand into the heart of the zombie in front of me and turned it into ash. Then I ashed another, and another, until I stood in the center of a circle of it.

A few of the zombies nearby started to get up. So I called down another round of lightning and knocked them back down. Then I ashed a few more of them for good measure.

Breathing hard, I stopped and looked around at the piles of ash surrounding me. Because as good as it felt, taking my anger out on the living dead wasn't helping anything. Plus, there might be a way to cure them. That was why we were planning on keeping Lavinia alive—in case she knew a cure. So I needed to stop killing them. At least, I needed to kill as few of them as possible.

There has to be a way to quickly find the others. There's always *a way. I just have to figure out what it is.*

I looked down into the center of the crater, at the pile of ash that had been Fallon. I should have gotten her to tell me where we were before killing her. But thanks to the strange way she'd brought us here, I was clueless.

How exactly *had* she brought us here?

Wind gusted around me, thunder cracked overhead, and a thick bolt of lightning struck the ground in front of me.

The storm.

That had to be it.

Fallon had somehow *turned us into electricity* and transported us through the Red Storm. I'd never heard of such a thing, but then again, I was still discovering the limits of my new magic.

I straightened, tightened my grip around the wand, and took a deep breath.

Time to create a storm of my own.

I brought another round of lightning down on the zombies to make sure none of them started to get up while I was attempting lightning travel. Then I raised the wand and pictured the valley where Julian, Torrence, Sage, Thomas, Reed, and I had fought the zombies after entering the eye of Fallon's hurricane.

Thunder rumbled loudly overhead, and the wind blew stronger. The gusts picked up the zombies and blew them away, clearing the area where I was standing.

The clouds overhead darkened. Blue lightning flashed between them, casting its light down upon me. A Blue Storm. The storm was a part of me. I could feel the area where the storm clouds spread, like I was running my fingers over a raised map.

I could go anywhere in its reach.

But the further the storm spread, the more magic I expended. And I wasn't trying to create a storm across the entire Otherworld. It needed to be just large enough to get me to the others.

I closed my eyes, hoping I could see down from the clouds. No such luck. Feeling the topography of the land would have to be enough.

The storm touched the start of the Western Mountain Range, and I pulled at it to stop it from expanding.

While locating Fallon, I'd studied the map enough times to know the layout of the Western Wildlands. So I reached my magic down from the clouds and touched as much of the land as I could. My storm covered nearly the entirety of the Wildlands, and finally, a map of the land beneath the storm formed in my mind.

Where do I need to land?

I had an idea of where we'd camped out in the mountains, and an idea of the path we'd taken through the eye wall to reach the valley where we'd fought the zombies. Pinpointing the exact valley was impossible, but to teleport, witches didn't need to pinpoint locations exactly. They just needed to be able to picture it clearly in their mind—what it looked like, and where it was on a map.

I wasn't sure how similar lightning travel was to teleporting, but at least it was *something* to work with.

Take me to them, I thought, and I pushed my lightning magic up into the clouds. *Now.*

A blue bolt struck down from the sky and surrounded me.

My cells ripped apart in an explosion of pain, and I *became* lightning, zooming through the clouds like electricity through a wire.

SELENA

EVEN THOUGH I was prepared for the pain, it didn't make the feeling of my cells being ripped apart and stitched back together again any better. And while I knew light-speed travel was basically instantaneous, the pain made it feel like an eternity.

Finally, the ground solidified under my feet.

"Where's Selena?" Julian's voice was the first thing I heard before the light around me disappeared.

I was back on the hill, inside the super dome.

Julian had forced Lavinia onto the ground, and he was holding a knife to her throat. Thomas and Sage prowled around them in their wolf forms, their eyes locked on Lavinia. Torrence and Reed stood opposite each other at the edges of the dome.

Bits of black swirled along the dome's walls. The remaining zombies stumbled around outside the dome, but luckily, everyone seemed to have gotten back to safety unharmed.

Julian's knife disappeared into the ether, and he ran to me, pulling me into a hug so tight I could barely breathe.

Over his shoulder, I saw Lavinia get up and run. But she smacked into the dome's wall. The black magic kept her locked inside. She cursed, and Torrence ran for her, holding her knife to her neck just like Julian had been doing before. Lavinia clawed at Torrence's arms hard enough that she drew blood with her long, pointy nails, but Torrence didn't loosen her hold.

Julian pulled away and took my face in his hands, as if making sure I was real. "What happened?" he asked.

"Fallon—the demon—took me somewhere to fight me. But she lost. I killed her."

"I figured as much when the Red Storm ended," he said, still looking down at me like he was worried I might disappear at any second. "But *how* did you kill her? You didn't have a holy weapon."

"Turns out the Holy Wand *is* a holy weapon." I smiled, and the wand's crystals glowed slightly, like they were showing themselves off. Then I reached into my pocket, opened my hand, and revealed the tooth. "She's gone."

The storm I'd created overhead disappeared, and sunlight shined down upon the tooth. It was an ugly, pointed, yellowed thing, which was why demons used their version of glamour to make them look normal. But right then it felt like the most precious thing in the universe.

Well, not *the* most precious thing.

Because there was one thing I wanted more.

I looked at where Torrence was still holding down Lavinia. Sage and Thomas prowled around them, and while Sage's wolf was smaller than his, the murder in her eyes made her look far more deadly. Blood dripped to the ground from the scratches along Torrence's arms, and she dug the edge of the blade into Lavinia's throat, drawing blood herself.

Lavinia's lips quivered, and she whimpered.

Weak.

"She's not skilled in combat," Julian said. "It wasn't difficult to corner her."

I nodded, remembering how Fallon had said that she didn't care if Lavinia lived or died. "Have you tried getting her to tell you the cure yet?"

"Not yet. Our priority was finding out where the demon took you."

"Well, I'm back," I said. "Now, we need the cure."

Lavinia pressed her lips together, saying nothing.

Reed stepped forward so he was near us, and his eyes flashed black. "Want me to torture it out of her with dark magic?" he asked.

"No." I faced Lavinia straight on, and electricity raced from my palms up along my scars. "I'll do it."

"You sure about that?" He looked me up and down, like he didn't think I had it in me.

"Yes."

My anger grew hotter as I walked toward Lavinia, and dark clouds rolled back in overhead. Thunder cracked with each of my steps. I stopped when there was only a foot between us.

Julian and Reed walked behind me, but I kept my gaze locked on the Foster witch. Her ragged white dress was filthy with dirt, and her ink-black hair was a tangled mess. She was barely fighting back.

Whatever had happened before I'd returned must have been good.

But I'd hear about that later. Because the cowering witch before me was responsible for the plague that was slowly killing my soulmate, and that had already killed an unimaginable number of fae and half-bloods.

I was ready to break her.

I raised the hand that I wasn't using to hold the wand

so it was right in front of her face. Mini bolts of electricity hummed and crackled between my fingertips, and I smiled, hoping I looked as deadly as Octavia in the arena.

Lavinia flinched backward, and Torrence tightened her hold around her waist.

"Tell us how to make the cure," I said.

"There is no cure."

"Lies." I shot a mini-bolt of electricity at her chest—enough to hurt her, but not kill her. I held onto her with the electricity to keep her from thrashing forward into the edge of Torrence's knife.

She seized and dropped her hands from Torrence's arms. Red shot through the whites of her eyes, and I released my hold on her.

She fell back into Torrence, her breaths shallow. Tears streamed down her cheeks.

Torrence propped her up and smirked. Her eyes flashed black, and black smoke drifted up from her hand around Lavinia's waist.

Lavinia gasped and jerked forward. Just in time, Torrence moved the knife away and held Lavinia's neck in a strangle instead, keeping her upright.

"Torrence," I warned. "Stop."

"Why?" More smoke rose from her palm. "You're not the only one who can play this game."

"Because we need to keep her alive."

She didn't let go of her magic.

I gathered more electricity in my hands. "Don't make me hurt you," I said, even though I knew I'd never be able to bring myself to use my magic against my best friend.

Torrence must have known that, too, because she didn't stop.

Lavinia groaned, flopped into Torrence's arms, and went limp.

Thomas pounced at Torrence, shifting back into human form midair. Moving in a blur, he pushed Torrence toward Reed and propped Lavinia up. "Control her," he said to Reed, and Reed created a yellow and black mini dome around himself and Torrence. Satisfied, Thomas turned back to me. "Use your magic to shock her back into consciousness."

I pressed my hand flat against Lavinia's chest and jolted her with electricity.

Her eyes snapped open, and she sucked in a sharp breath.

"The cure," I said before she could speak.

She glanced over at where Reed had trapped Torrence and wiped her bloodied fingers on her dress. Her eyes traveled to Julian, to Sage, and then back to me, defeat splattered across her face.

"Fine," she said. "You're right. There is a cure."

"Of course there is." I stepped back and gathered a ball of electricity in my hand. "Tell us what it is."

"And then what?" She smirked. "You'll let me go?"

"We'll test it to make sure it works. Then we'll let you go."

She chuckled, apparently not believing my lie. "Are you ready to make a blood oath on it?"

"I'm fae," I said, and my wings sparkled brighter. "I can't lie. A blood oath isn't necessary."

"You're half-fae," she said. "And you absolutely *can* lie. Like you did just now."

I sighed, since she was right.

"It's a solid offer," Julian spoke up from beside me, and he sized up Lavinia. "What, specifically, are you requesting from us?"

"First, I want you to stop holding a knife to my neck. Your point has been made, and I'm willing to work with you."

"Do you promise not to try anything against us?" I asked.

"I'm not stupid like Fallon," she said. "I know I can't win a fight against the six of you, and I plan on getting out of this alive. So let's figure out how to make that happen in a civilized manner."

I held my wand at the ready. Then I nodded to Thomas, and he let Lavinia go.

Her legs wobbled. She took a few seconds to steady herself, then she adjusted her dirty, bloodied dress.

Thomas moved to stand next to Sage, who'd also shifted back to human form.

"Much better," Lavinia said with a satisfied smile. "Now, as I was saying. I'll tell you how to create the cure. In exchange, you'll let me live, and you'll let me use my token —or any token I can get my hands on—to return to Earth."

"We'll have to verify that the cure works," I said. "But fine. If you give us a true cure, we won't stop you from returning to Earth."

I didn't like it, but I'd do anything for that cure.

"Hold on," she said, and I stilled. "I wasn't finished."

"Go on."

"Until I portal out of the Otherworld, none of you will portal back to Earth without my consent," she said. "So if I die while still here, the blood oath will keep you from ever portaling back. I can't risk you leaving me here at the mercy of the fae, and it'll give you incentive to help me return home. And along with letting me live, you won't make *any* moves against me, ever. So none of you will be able to purposefully harm me, and you won't be able to help anyone harm me, either."

"I don't like it," Sage said.

"I didn't think you would." Lavinia smiled at Sage. "What would you propose, instead?"

"Safety until we all return to Earth. Then, once we're back, all deals are off."

"And then, if we end up taking the same portal, you'll kill me the moment we land on the other side." She chuckled. "No can do."

Sage narrowed her eyes, not denying it.

"How about this," I said. "We'll give you the safety you asked for. If we take the same portal to Earth, we'll let you teleport away from the landing site unharmed. But that's it. Once you teleport away, the blood oath is complete."

"And what will you do if I say no?" Lavinia asked. "Kill me?"

I pressed my lips together, because no, of course I wasn't going to kill her. We needed that cure too badly.

"I didn't think so." She squared her shoulders, looking extremely pleased with herself. "My deal is reasonable, and it benefits us all. I recommend taking it."

"It's reasonable, except for one part," Julian said. "If we can't harm you, we won't be able to defend ourselves if you attack us. So it's only fair if it goes both ways. We can't hurt or kill you, and you can't hurt or kill any of us."

I nearly smacked myself. Because I should have thought of that loophole, too. But like fae deals, blood oaths were tricky things. I was grateful that Julian was skilled at making them.

"Hm." She looked at him approvingly. "I can agree to that."

"Selena's offer was good, too." Sage stepped forward, but Thomas took her hand, stopping her from getting any closer to Lavinia. "Unless you're afraid we'll be able to easily hunt you down and kill you once we're all back on Earth, even with the protection of the witches in your circle and the demons you work for?"

"You're not going to trick me by trying to wound my pride," she said calmly. "Perhaps that works on shifters, given how *reactive* you all can be, but it won't work on me. It's Julian's deal or nothing."

I looked to Sage, who was staring at Lavinia like she wanted to murder her on the spot. "Sage," I pleaded, but she didn't budge. "This is Julian's life we're talking about. My *soulmate*. If the situation were reversed, and it was Thomas who needed the cure, wouldn't you want us to do whatever was necessary to get it for him?"

Sage looked to Thomas, and her eyes softened.

"You would," he said. "Just like I'd do anything to get the cure for you, if you were the one who needed it."

Silence. We all just stood there, staring at Sage, waiting for her to change her mind.

Instead, she ran to Lavinia, grabbed her by the neck, and pushed her up against the wall of the dome. She shifted her fingernails into claws and slashed them across Lavinia's pale white cheek. Blood seeped out of the three slices and dripped down the witch's face.

Lavinia struggled, but after my electrical jolts and Torrence's dark magic, she barely had any strength left in her.

"The others can take whatever deal they want," Sage said, her face right up to Lavinia's. "I'll agree that we don't harm each other until we're back on Earth and you teleport away. After that, all bets are off. Unless you want scars on your other cheek, too?"

Lavinia looked to me, as if I'd help her.

I said nothing.

Sage tightened her grip around Lavinia's neck.

Lavinia gagged and scratched futilely at Sage's hand. "Fine," she choked out, and Sage released her. She fell to the ground, and Sage rushed back to Thomas's side.

Lavinia's fingers went to her cheek, and she pulled them away, staring at the blood.

Since the marks were made with shifter claws, they'd leave permanent scars.

She blinked a few times. Then she stood up, wiped the blood on her dress, and held out her palm. "Who wants to go first?" she asked, and then, one by one, we stepped up, sliced our palms, and entered into the blood oath.

SELENA

I was the last to make the oath. The oath's magic sealed the slice on my palm, and the skin was good as new.

Once finished, I rejoined Julian and the others. We all faced Lavinia.

"It's done," Torrence said to the witch. She'd gotten control over herself in the dome with Reed's help, so her eyes were back to normal. "Now, tell us how to make the cure."

"Firstly, you should know that the antidote will only cure those who have been bitten, but have yet to fully succumb to the plague," Lavinia said. "Those mindless, black-winged creatures are beyond saving."

"You lied," I said, and lightning flashed above us. "You said you'd give us the true cure."

"That *is* the true cure. I thought you'd be happy about

it, since it means your soulmate will live?" She glanced to Julian, and then back at me.

"But all those others will die."

"They already *are* dead," she said. "They died the moment the poison entered their hearts and transferred their last remaining magic to Fallon."

"What are you talking about?" Julian asked.

"The plague is one of a kind. I created it with Fallon's blood," Lavinia said, and she continued on to explain everything Fallon had told me in the crater.

"So Fallon absorbed fae magic," Julian said once she was finished. "What about half-bloods?"

"The spell can't break through bound magic. I'm sure you saw the remnants of what happened to the half-bloods on your way here."

"The puddles of goo," he said.

"Yep. The poison ate right through them. It's unfortunate, really. If their magic hadn't been bound, it would have been more magic for Fallon to absorb."

I shuddered, because even though I'd suspected that the black tar was the remnants of the half-bloods, it was different to have it confirmed. If I'd freed them beforehand...

They'd be as lost to us as the black-winged fae, and Fallon would have had more magic when we fought at the crater.

In a way, the half-bloods' having bound magic might

have saved me, and therefore, saved the Otherworld from total destruction.

"I can't say I'm sad that Fallon's dead," Lavinia continued. "I was the reason she had so much magic. She was supposed to use it to protect me."

"That's what you get for trusting demons." Sage laughed with dark satisfaction. Her eyes flashed yellow, and her nails shifted into claws.

"We need to stay focused," I said before Sage could do or say anything she regretted. "You promised you'd tell us how to make the cure. So now, tell us."

"Fine," she said, and she listed off a bunch of ingredients—a combination of flowers, leaves, and tree sap. Many were similar to the ingredients used to make healing potion. There were just a few changes here and there, and one major one.

"Do you have all of these in the Otherworld?" I asked Julian.

"I'm not a botanist, but I've heard of some of them," he said. "But given the state of the Otherworld, I'm not sure how easy they'll be to come by."

We looked sadly around at the barren, dead land around us. Judging from what we'd seen on our journey, the rest of the Otherworld was in a similar condition.

"We have all of those ingredients—except the obvious one—in Avalon's apothecary," Torrence said, and she narrowed her eyes at Lavinia. "If you give me *permission* to portal back to Earth, I can easily get my hands on them, create a test vial of the cure, and bring it back here."

I waited for Lavinia to say no, or to propose another deal.

"Go ahead," she said instead, and I stood on edge, ready for her to continue on with some sort of catch.

She didn't.

"Just like that?" I asked.

"Just like that. Although, I don't imagine you can portal back from here, can you?"

"I have a portal token," Torrence said. "The one that brought us to Ryanne's villa. We need to get back there, and then I can use it."

"That token will bring you back to the foyer of King Devin's penthouse," Thomas said. "Like all vampire kingdoms, there's a boundary dome around the Tower to keep you from teleporting in or out of there. You'll be trapped inside. And who knows what he'll do to you if you show up alone."

"I can handle him." Torrence's eyes flashed black—but only for a second.

Still, it was one second too long.

"Why don't we go straight to Sorcha?" Sage said. "She needs the cure for Kyla. I'm sure she'll be open to a deal in return for loaning you one of her portal tokens."

"We need to think more long term than that," Julian said in that confident way of his that got everyone's attention. "We can't show the Empress our cards this early. The less time she has to figure out how to use our knowledge against us, the better."

"What are you proposing?" I asked.

"We need to go to a fae who likely has a token of their own. Someone in our corner who won't use this as an opportunity to take advantage of us. Someone we can trust."

"Fae can't be trusted." Lavinia chuckled. "They're tricksters—all of them. Including you half-bloods."

"Many are," I agreed. "But I can think of one or two who I'd trust with my life. Ones I technically already *have* trusted with my life."

I looked to Julian, and he gave me that knowing smile of his—the one that meant we were on the same page.

From there, we filled in the others, and figured out a plan.

SELENA

"ARE you *sure* I can lightning-travel all seven of us at once?" I asked Lavinia.

"I'm sure," she said. "Fallon did a lot of testing."

"With zombies. Not with real people."

"And she said that bringing a zombie along was the same as bringing me along. As long as there's skin-to-skin contact, you can bring as many people as you want."

"It seems risky..." I looked over at the others, worry swirling in the pit of my stomach.

"Even if the pegasi reached our campsite in the mountains and healed, they can only hold two people each," Julian said. "One of us would have to be left behind."

"But we can't just leave the pegasi there," Sage said.

"There was fresh water at the campsite, and they can

go for a long time without food," I said. It was one of the many tidbits Bridget had shared with me during our long days in Vesta's Villa. "Pegasi are good at surviving. Once they heal, they should be able to easily return to the city on their own, especially since they won't have the storm pushing against their wings."

"They'll be fine," Julian said confidently. "But like I was saying, we can't ride them back to the city. And it's too risky to travel on foot. Not only because of the hordes of zombies we'd encounter, but because we barely have any food remaining. We can't count on there still being animals out there to hunt. Lightning-travel is our best bet."

"But I've only ever used it on myself. Maybe I should test it out with someone else first." Remembering how painful the lightning-travel had been, I turned to Lavinia. "Since you're so certain this will work, do you want to volunteer?"

"No," she said, and I frowned, since I was looking forward to putting her through lightning-travel twice in such a short period of time. "But I'm sure one of your heroic friends will gladly step up."

"Me," Torrence said, just as Julian started to say that he'd do it. "As much as he tries to hide it, Julian's weakened from the plague. So you're taking me with you."

I walked toward her and held out my hand.

She took it and smiled—the mischievous, excited smile that I'd missed since we'd reunited in the Otherworld. She nodded, and I called down a thick bolt of lightning from the dark clouds overhead.

It surrounded us, one long, painful second passed, and then it dropped us off on top of the closest hill, about a hundred yards away.

"Damn." Torrence stretched out and gazed down at the zombies lumbering around the bottom of the hill. "That hurt."

"Told you it would," I said. "You ready to go back?"

"Might as well get it over with."

Another bolt of lightning, and we were back inside the super dome with the others.

"The ability to pass through barrier domes makes lightning-travel far superior to teleporting," Thomas observed.

"It does. But I can only travel as far as the storm reaches," I reminded him. "It would look pretty suspicious if once we're back on Earth, a storm spans from—for example—the Vale to Utopia."

Sage cracked a smile. "A storm that spanned from the Canadian Rockies to New Zealand would *definitely* look suspicious," she agreed. "But you could always just teleport to wherever you wanted, and then lightning-travel through the domes protecting the vampire kingdoms from there."

"Which means once we're on Earth, Selena will hide this ability from everyone who doesn't need to know," Julian said. "From what I've heard of your vampire kings and queens, they won't take kindly to someone who can easily break into their kingdoms."

I nodded in agreement. Because while Avalon currently had an alliance with all the kingdoms so we could fight together against the demons, there was no saying what would happen once the war was over. The more volatile kingdoms—like the Tower, the Ward, and the Carpathians—were too unpredictable to mess with.

"Don't worry." Lavinia smirked, her voice dripping with sarcasm. "I won't say a word."

"Do you *want* to give us another reason to send our army after you once we're back home?" I asked her, and her smirk vanished. "That's what I thought. If you have as much self-preservation as you claim, you'll keep this to yourself."

"Noted," she said, and I had a feeling she might actually keep my secret.

At least, until it benefited her to share it.

"Let's not delay this any longer," Reed said, and he fidgeted, like he might actually be *nervous*.

Torrence smirked, amused by his discomfort. "It hurts as much as they said it would," she said.

He glared at her. Then he walked toward me and put his hand on my arm.

The others followed suit, and I raised the wand to create my biggest storm yet. The crystals answered my call, and I felt the clouds as they spread over the Western Mountain Range, crossed the Central Plainlands, traveled over the Eastern Mountain Range, and settled above the citadel.

"You all ready?" I asked, and they all said a variation of yes.

I pictured our destination in my mind, called down a giant bolt from the sky, and then, we transformed into electricity and zoomed through the clouds.

SELENA

WE LANDED in an alley on the outskirts of the fae section of the city.

Reed and Sage cursed right after our bodies reformed. Torrence whooped with glee, and Thomas and Lavinia looked shaken. Julian's hard expression revealed nothing.

If Julian was able to hide his pain after that, I didn't want to know how agonizing his infected wound must be.

Apparently, withstanding pain was one of the many abilities of being a chosen champion of Mars.

Once we got ourselves together, I lightning-traveled to a bunch of other random places inside the dome, leaving before my body fully re-formed so no one could see me. The goal was to create a bunch of lightning strikes that went through the dome. They had no idea that the lightning was my unique way of teleporting, so hopefully they'd think the lightning was connected to the Blue Storm overhead, and they wouldn't come investigating.

I ended a few alleys away from where we'd first landed, and released my hold on the storm. The clouds rolled away, and the first rays of sunlight peeked through. Hopefully people would assume that those final bolts of lightning were a result of the storm ending.

Next, I glamoured myself invisible and hurried to find the others. It had been less than thirty seconds since we'd arrived, so they were still there, waiting.

I removed the glamour, and they smiled in relief when they saw me.

Julian and I glamoured our wings back to only being one color. His steel gray, and mine light blue.

With our wings back to their expected colors, we led the way out of the alley, turned the corner, and stopped in front of our destination.

Sage looked over the plain, marble, one-story house, less than impressed. "This is it?" she asked.

"This is it."

"You're right," she said. "After everything you told us about them, it *is* more modest than I expected."

I smiled, since given that the Montgomery pack lived

in a compound of mansions in the Hollywood Hills, I wasn't surprised that her definition of "modest" was different from most. Then again, I grew up in a castle, so who was I to talk.

But the longer we stood there, the more likely the rare person passing by might take notice of us. So I hurried up to the front door and knocked.

The door opened slowly—cautiously. But the moment the man behind it saw me, he beamed.

"Selena!" Bryan bounced in excitement and looked over my shoulder at the others. "Come in, all of you, and quickly so you're not seen. I can tell from the looks in your eyes that you've got a story to share—and I can't wait to hear all about it."

Finn joined us in the kitchen, where he and Bryan set out sandwiches and fruit for us to enjoy while we filled them in on everything that had happened since Julian and I had last seen them. Finn was quiet as he listened, unlike Bryan, who peppered us with question after question.

"You've come a long way from being that scared little girl about to enter the Games," Finn said to me once we finished. "Now, I'd like to give you something."

He stood up, spun around, and left the kitchen before I could ask what that "something" was.

"Any idea what he's getting?" Torrence asked Bryan.

"Yes." Bryan smiled and raised his eyebrows. "But I'm not saying a word. It should be a surprise."

Finn returned quickly, holding a small, black velvet pouch. He sat down and handed it to Torrence. "I'm loaning this to you," he said. "So you can bring back the cure."

She opened it and pulled out a golden token with Finn's likeness etched into the back. Her eyes lit up, but then they filled with suspicion. "What do you want in return?" she asked.

"I want you to bring back two test vials of the cure. One for Julian, and one for Kyla."

Dread filled my stomach, and I couldn't look at Finn.

Julian reached for my hand under the table and said, "We can't bring a vial back for Kyla. At least, not yet."

"She's nearly succumbed to the plague," Finn said. "She's down there, locked up and suffering. She needs that cure."

I looked back up at him and swallowed down the lump of guilt in my throat. "I'll push back the poison and keep her alive until she gets the cure," I said. "I promise."

"Why wait?" Finn clenched his fist, the muscles in his

arms growing more defined, and I feared he was about to snatch the token out of Torrence's hand.

"Because Sorcha will do anything in exchange for getting Kyla that cure," I said. "And I want exactly what I've wanted since I was brought here. I want to return to Avalon."

"You're going to use Kyla as leverage."

"As much as I hate it—yes. But you know me." I looked over at Bryan, and then back to Finn. "I won't let her die. Too many people have already died here because of me. I refuse to add her to that list. All I can do now is ask for you to trust me."

"I trust you," Bryan said, and then he looked to Finn, his eyes begging for his soulmate to agree.

Finn stared down at the table, not looking at any of us as he thought it over.

I barely moved as I waited for his decision. Neither did the others.

Finally, he refocused on me. "I'm a strategist," he said. "And I can't deny that your strategy is a good one. I also know that you have a good heart, and I trust you'll try your hardest to save Kyla."

"I will," I said. "I promise."

"Good. So I'll loan Torrence the token in exchange for her bringing back one vial of the cure, to test on

Julian." He gave me a single nod, stood up, and looked to Torrence. "The token will bring you to the Fonte Gaia in Sienna, Italy. The fountain to get there is in our court-yard. Follow me, and we'll send you off."

25

SELENA

As PROMISED, I pushed back the plague for Kyla. But I didn't tell her about the cure. I didn't want to get her hopes up until we were sure it worked.

Bryan stayed in the basement with her afterward and told her the story of how we'd killed Fallon.

I went up to the courtyard to wait with the others for Torrence to return.

Finn brought a wide variety of ancient Roman board games to the courtyard and taught us how to play, but I couldn't focus. Not that I would have been able to beat Julian or Thomas, anyway. They were both *really* serious about winning.

With every hour that passed, I worried that Torrence had run into trouble. I couldn't even bring myself to eat when Bryan brought out a huge roast for dinner.

"She has a lot to explain to your mother, and it takes time to brew potions," Sage assured me at nightfall.

"This one shouldn't take any longer than an hour," I said.

"But you're forgetting about the time dilation. A day on Earth is equal to a week here. I'm no math genius, but that means an hour on Earth is…"

"About seven hours here," Thomas finished. "There's no getting around it—we'll be waiting for a while."

Still, we were *all* worried—including Lavinia. Although her pacing was probably due to annoyance, too, since Reed had used his dark magic to lock her inside a small boundary dome. The dome didn't hurt her, so it technically didn't go against the blood oath.

Eventually, Bryan brought out sleeping rolls so we could get some rest.

I didn't think I'd be able to sleep. But it had been a long day, and eventually, exhaustion kicked in and sleep took over.

———

I woke to a light nudge on my shoulder.

"Selena," Julian said softly, and I opened my eyes to the sight of his face framed by the beautiful pinks and yellows of sunrise. "She's back."

I pushed myself up and smiled at the sight of Torrence standing next to the fountain. She had a large, full, brown sack strapped to her back, and my heart leaped in excitement.

It fell a second later. Because Torrence's green eyes lacked the sparkle they *always* had when she'd succeeded in something. And her face looked drawn and aged, like years had passed in the time she'd been gone—even though because of the time dilation, it should have only been about an hour for her.

"What happened?" I held my breath, preparing for the worst.

She dropped the sack to the ground, and the items inside clanked loudly against each other. Then she smiled, and said, "I have the cure."

"I was worried there for a second." I relaxed, able to breathe again. "You look..." *Exhausted? Defeated?* "Stressed."

"I'm fine." She pulled a vial of white, milky potion from her weapons belt, and looked to Finn and Bryan. "Which one of you wants to do the honors?"

Bryan stepped forward and squared his shoulders. "Finn loaned you his token," he said. "I'd like to give my blood."

I smiled to express my gratitude.

But despite Bryan being a friend, he was also a fae. I needed to be aware of that, always.

"In exchange for what?" I asked.

"In exchange for promising that if the cure works, you'll do everything in your power to get a vial to Kyla as soon as you can."

I quickly analyzed his precise words. He could have given me an exact deadline of when I needed to get Kyla the cure, and he could have made sure that I'd *definitely* get it to her instead of doing "everything in my power." There was a lot of wiggle room with his phrasing.

"I'd already planned on it," I said. "So yes, I accept the offer."

Torrence pulled out her dagger and held it out to Bryan. "I only need a drop," she said. "A prick on the pad of your finger should do it."

Bryan shuddered and stepped back. "That blade has iron."

"Here," Julian said, and he pulled a gold dagger out of the ether. "No iron."

Bryan took the dagger, and Torrence uncapped the vial. With a swift jab, he pricked the tip of his middle finger. A drop of blood bubbled on top of his skin, he held his finger over the vial, and squeezed it so his blood dripped inside. It diluted in the milky potion and turned pink.

"That's enough." Torrence popped the cap back on the vial and slowly turned it upside down. The blood spread evenly throughout the potion, until the opaque white liquid was only slightly tinted pink. Then she turned it right-side up, walked to Julian, and held it out to him. "It's ready. In twenty-four hours, you should be cured."

"Not *should* be," Lavinia said. "He *will* be cured. Assuming you brewed the potion correctly."

"Of course I brewed it correctly," Torrence snapped, and she turned back to Julian. "It'll work. It might make you a bit woozy, but I know it'll work."

He took the vial, and my heart beat so hard that it felt like it was trying to punch its way out of my chest. Then, without hesitation, he uncapped the vial, brought it to his lips, and downed the potion.

He made sure to get every last drop, and then I took the vial from him.

"How do you feel?" I asked.

He blinked a few times, and his eyes glazed over, like he was trying to focus but couldn't. "Tired," he said, although the word was slurred. He swayed slightly, and I reached out to steady him.

He sounded—and looked—drunk. No, that was an understatement. He looked *wasted*. Even more so than when he'd had to drink all of that wine for the discus competition in the Faerie Games.

"Milk of the poppy will do that," Lavinia said casually.

I moved closer to Julian and propped him up to keep him from falling over. "Milk of the poppy makes people woozy," I said. "It doesn't do *this*."

"It's a strong potion." She shrugged. "His body will be working hard to reverse the effects of the poison, so he'll be out until he's recovered."

"You could have warned us *before* he drank it."

"I could have. But there's no harm done, and it's more entertaining this way."

I glared at her and helped Julian down onto the nearest sleeping roll.

He fell down onto it and conked out in a second.

I placed a pillow under his head, made sure he was comfortable, and then brushed a finger over his cheek, studying him. His face was pale, but he didn't appear to be in pain. In fact, he looked more at peace than ever.

But sitting there staring at him wasn't doing any good. So I moved to his feet to take off his boots and socks.

The fresh cloth we'd wrapped around the wound that morning was already soaked with tar-like blood. The skin around it was black as well, and dark, thick veins covered his foot. I pushed his breeches up to his knee to see where they stopped, but they kept going. A quick lift of the bottom of his tunic revealed that the infection had traveled to his hip.

I winced at the thought of how much pain he must have been in. Each time I pushed back the poison, it came back faster and faster.

It was a good thing we had the cure.

It better work.

Bryan retrieved a bowl of warm water and a cloth from the kitchen, and got to work cleaning Julian's wound. He was gentle, despite Julian being so knocked out that he wouldn't have felt a thing.

Once the wound was clean, no more black blood spilled back over the surface. That had to be a good sign.

"What should we expect next?" I asked Lavinia.

She stopped pacing and smiled sweetly. "Get the mage to release me from this dome, and I'll tell you."

"You realize that with the Holy Wand, I'm strong enough to remove the dome myself, right?" I asked.

"Really?" She faked disbelief. "Then show me."

"Nice try. But no."

"Figured." She shrugged. "Anyway, this is the first time anyone's ever taken the antidote. I have no idea what to expect. So, we'll just have to wait and see."

I glared at her again.

Thomas walked to Torrence's side, opened the sack she'd brought back with her, and inspected the contents. "They're all here?" he asked.

"Yep," she said. "All fifty of them."

"Good."

She left the sack with Thomas, and picked up her sleeping roll. "Can I bring this inside?" she asked Bryan. "It's too light to sleep out here."

"Of course," he said. "Follow me, and I'll show you to the guest room."

"Wait," I said, and Torrence turned to face me.

"What?" She yawned, as if telling me to hurry up. And she wouldn't meet my eyes.

Something was bothering her. But she was so exhausted that she clearly wasn't up to talking about it yet.

In the meantime, there was one thing that couldn't wait.

"You saw my mom, right?" I asked. "Back on Avalon?"

"I did."

"And..."

She glanced down at the ground, and then finally met my eyes. "She was relieved to hear that you're still alive," she said, and I nodded, since obviously I'd expected that. "She sat with me in the apothecary while I made the potion, and I told her everything. Afterward, she called Skylar in to look into the cards."

Anxiety pooled in my chest, and I prayed the prophetess's reading was a good one. "What'd she see?"

"She can't see into the Otherworld. But she saw us returning to Earth."

My heart leaped—that was one of the best answers I could have hoped for. "When?" I asked.

"She said I looked similar to how I look now. So… soon."

"Good," I said, and I shook my head, hardly able to believe it. The future could always change, but Skylar's vision meant we needed to stay on our current course. Which meant our plan was a good one. "That's fantastic."

"It is." She smiled, although her eyes still looked sad. "Your mom's proud of you. She told me to tell you how much she loves you, how much she believes in you, and that she can't wait to see you again soon."

Tears pooled in my eyes, and I wiped them away. "How's she holding up?" I asked. "With both me and my dad gone, I can't imagine…" I trailed off, since it hurt to think how alone she must feel. Even though it had only been a few days for her, I bet it felt like a lifetime.

"As expected," she said. "But hearing from me—and from Skylar—gave her hope."

"I'm glad," I said, and then I tried to put some humor into my tone. "I can't believe you were about to go to sleep without telling me all that."

"I'm tired." She yawned again and rubbed at her eyes. "Sorry."

"It's okay," I said, even though I still couldn't get rid of that nagging feeling that something was off. "Go get some sleep."

She nodded, pulled her sleeping roll closer, and followed Bryan inside.

26

SELENA

"Is it just me, or was Torrence acting strange?" I asked Sage once Torrence was gone.

"She always acts strange," Reed said from the table off to the corner, where he was setting up a solo game of backgammon.

"Shut up." I narrowed my eyes at him, and then refocused on Sage.

She looked at where Torrence had left the courtyard, and then back to me. "It wasn't just you," she said.

"Do you have any idea what's going on with her?"

"It could be anything," she said. "I'm sorry. I wish I had a better answer."

"It's okay," I said, even though it wasn't.

There was nothing more to say, so I pulled my sleeping roll up next to Julian's and made myself comfortable. Thomas and Finn brought some of the board games over, and they set them up on the sleeping rolls. Sage joined us, as did Bryan when he returned.

It was like one strange sleepover—especially with Lavinia sulking in her prison dome.

I couldn't take my eyes off of Julian. With each passing hour, the black veins retreated closer to his wound. It was similar to when I'd used my magic to push back the progression of the infection, but slower. By nightfall, the veins only spread from his ankle up to right below his knee.

Torrence still hadn't returned. I quickly left to check on her, but she was sound asleep, so I went straight back to the courtyard.

"She's still sleeping," I told the others, and then I settled back next to Julian's side.

He hadn't moved since falling asleep. If I hadn't been constantly checking his pulse to make sure he was alive, I would have thought he was dead.

But he's not dead, I reminded myself. *Once he wakes up, the poison will be gone, and he'll be cured.*

I held onto that belief with everything I had, and did the only thing I could do—I stayed by his side and waited.

I fell asleep before Torrence woke up.

The next thing I knew, someone stirred by my side.

Julian.

I was awake in a second, and I sat up, my eyes instantly going to the wound.

Except there *was* no wound.

My breath caught in my chest. But just to make sure I wasn't getting excited too soon, I brushed my fingers over the smooth skin above his ankle.

I couldn't believe it.

Yesterday, it had been a mess of black pus.

Now… he was cured.

"Told you." Lavinia smirked from where she was sitting inside the dome.

Julian stirred again and slowly opened his eyes. He smiled when he saw me.

"It worked," I said, and he sat up to see for himself.

He touched the spot where the wound had been, and he stared at it, his eyes wide as he soaked it in.

He'd spent all that time thinking the plague was going to kill him. Now, his entire life was ahead of him again.

I wasn't going to lose my soulmate before we had time to relax and enjoy our lives together. Of course, we still had a long way to go until truly being able to relax, but the peaceful, happy future I imagined for us felt closer than ever.

"You're okay." I scooted closer to him, wrapped my arms around his waist, and rested my head on his shoulder. "You're going to be okay."

He draped one arm around me and leaned into me. "I love you," he said softly, for only me to hear.

The others woke up, too—including Torrence. Apparently, she'd moved back into the courtyard after I'd fallen asleep.

They all took turns looking at Julian's ankle. Sage gasped, Bryan spun around in excitement, and Thomas told Julian congratulations. Even Reed nodded at Torrence in respect.

"Good job," he told her.

"Potions are one of my specialties," she said, although she shrugged, her normal confidence gone from her tone. "I'm glad it worked."

"Of course it worked." I smiled, trying to lift her spirits. "I never doubted you for a second."

"Thanks." She managed a small smile back. But then she looked away and gazed at the fountain, her eyes far off.

Something's wrong.

Maybe she was just impatient to get home. If there

was one thing Torrence didn't have much of, it was patience.

Julian stood up, and I did, too. His steel-colored wings sparkled with brightness I hadn't seen since we fought that first horde of zombies, and his cheeks were flushed and *alive*.

"How do you feel?" I asked.

"Great." He bounced on his toes, like he was testing out how his leg worked. "Incredible."

I was so relieved about his recovery that I couldn't stop smiling at him. I must have looked like a total airhead, but I didn't care.

Julian was better. He was alive.

And he was going to *stay* that way.

"Now, for the next part of the show." Finn strode into the courtyard, and all eyes were on him. "Getting the witch home."

Lavinia stood up in her prison dome and smiled wickedly. "I'm assuming you have a plan," she said, and he nodded. "Tell me what it is."

Finn walked up to her prison dome and stood right in front of her. Then he reached into his pocket and pulled out a small black velvet pouch—the same one he'd given to Torrence yesterday. "I'm giving you my token," he said.

She crossed her arms and studied him. "In exchange for what?"

"In exchange for you promising that you'll leave the Otherworld immediately after I hand it over, and that once you leave the Otherworld, you'll never return again."

"Deal," she said, and she pressed her palm to the inside of the prison dome. "Now, free me from this thing and hand over the token."

But Finn made no effort to move. "Once you leave, I'll be draining this fountain," he continued. "Without an anchor point, the portal will be closed off, and the token will no longer be functional."

Smart. Not only would Lavinia be unable to enter the Otherworld again, but she also wouldn't be able to give the token to someone else to use.

"Understood," she said, and she looked to Reed. "Time to let me out." Then she paused, focused on me, and smiled. "Unless you want to do it, given how you boasted about your abilities earlier?"

"As a matter of fact, yes," I said, and I picked up the Holy Wand. "I'd love to do it."

I reached for my electricity, raised my hand, and shot a bolt of lightning out of my palm. It hit the dome, and the electricity spread out along it in dancing, humming webs.

It ate away the dome, and then both the electricity and the dome disappeared in a flash. Tendrils of smoke drifted up out of the courtyard. I inhaled, loving the burnt smell left behind.

Lavinia stepped over the line where the dome had been and smiled. "Very good," she said, and she held out her hand to Finn. "Now, the token."

He removed it from the pouch and pressed it into her palm. "You'll give the people in Sienna quite the fright when you arrive."

I looked over her dirtied, blood-stained dress and smirked.

"Let them stare." She snatched her hand away from his and clenched the token in her fist. "That is, if they can. I'll be gone before they can blink."

"I'm sure you will." Sage stepped in front of the fountain, blocking Lavinia's path. "But I promise you that someday—hopefully in the near future—I'm going to find you. And once I do, I *will* kill you in the most drawn-out, painful way possible."

Lavinia smirked, not breaking Sage's gaze. "Move out of my way," she said. "I told the fae that I'd leave immediately after he gave me the token, and I intend on following through on that promise."

Sage stayed there for a moment, staring down the

witch like she was challenging her to a duel. Then she snarled and moved to Thomas's side.

Lavinia stepped up to the fountain and smoothed her hands over her dirtied dress. "It was nice working with you all for the past few days," she said. "I assure you, it won't happen again."

"Good riddance for that," I said.

Finn held out his hand and shot a beam of sparkling orange magic toward Lavinia.

Against her will, one of her feet moved to climb onto the flat ledge of the fountain. The other one followed. She wobbled, then steadied herself.

"Like you said, you promised to leave immediately after I gave you the token," Finn said. "Now, leave."

"My pleasure."

She tossed the token into the fountain, jumped in, and finally, she was gone.

SELENA

NOT WANTING to go into the next part of the plan hungry, we scarfed down a breakfast of fruit, bread, and cheese. Then we returned to the courtyard, said bye to Finn and Bryan, and I lightning-traveled us to the Empress's house.

We landed in her public courtyard, in front of the temple where I'd presented the Holy Wand to Juno. The tall, marble building looked just like it had the first time I'd seen it, before I'd destroyed it with my magic.

Four fae stood at the bottom of the steps.

The Empress, Aeliana, Ryanne, and Prince Devyn.

None of them appeared fazed by our flashy arrival.

"Welcome back," Prince Devyn said, and he bowed his head in what looked like *respect*.

Butterflies fluttered in my stomach, and I tried unsuccessfully to swallow them down. Because with his omniscient sight, Prince Devyn could ruin everything. He was the biggest wild card in any possible plan.

But the future wasn't set in stone. Even his omniscient sight couldn't change that. And at the end of the day, we were the only ones who could brew the antidote.

Which meant we were the ones in control.

Sorcha eyed the sack that Torrence carried on her back. "Is that what I think it is?" she asked.

Torrence marched forward and dropped the sack to the ground in front of Sorcha's feet. A shiny, metal blade stuck out from the top of it. "Holy weapons," she said. "Fifty of them, as promised."

Sorcha glanced down at the sack, but made no effort to move closer to it. "Once we're done here, Aeliana will bring the weapons inside the temple," she said. "After they're verified as true holy weapons, I'll tell Nessa to release Prince Jacen and Bella from the Crossroads."

"How will you be verifying them?" Julian asked.

"I'll gather fifty half-bloods, arm them, and send them outside the dome. If the weapons slay the infected, then they're verified."

I nodded, since she wasn't going to be disappointed.

But she wasn't looking at me.

Her eyes were locked on Julian, like a cat ready to pounce. "You look healthy," she said. "I trust Selena has been pushing back the progress of the plague?"

I stiffened in place.

She knew he'd been bitten?

Had I been the last to find out?

"She did, for a bit," he said. "But she doesn't need to anymore. Because yesterday morning, I was cured."

Sorcha's lips parted, and hunger danced in her eyes. "Show me," she said.

Julian removed his boot and sock, and showed her the spot where the wound had been.

She lowered herself down to her knees and ran her fingers across his clear, smooth skin. "Incredible," she murmured, and a single tear rolled down her cheek. She wiped it away, composed herself, and stood back up. "Tell me the cure," she said. "Tell me, and I'll let you all return to Earth."

My mouth dropped open. I knew she'd want the cure... but I'd expected her to drive a harder bargain.

Apparently, even the serene Empress would do anything to save her daughter. And I certainly wasn't going to refuse.

"We'll need to clarify the details of that offer," I said,

and she nodded. "Plus, there's one more thing I want, too."

"I'm listening."

This is it.

I tightened my grip around the wand, needing all the support I could get, and said, "I want you to permanently end the Faerie Games."

28

SELENA

Sorcha looked to Prince Devyn. "I assume you want to take over from here?"

"I do." He cleared his throat, focused on me, and said, "The main purpose of the Games has always been so you could eventually play in them and rise to save the Otherworld."

The world felt like it stilled around me. Because the magnanimity of that was... overwhelming, to say the least.

"So you've been behind the Games this entire time," I said. "They were your idea."

"They were Bacchus's idea," he said. "He came to the Empress. She didn't have to accept his proposition."

"I actually didn't want to accept it," Sorcha continued. "Sending so many half-bloods to their deaths in such a brutal way was unnecessarily cruel, even for us. But then your father told me that the Otherworld would most likely be destroyed if we didn't agree to host the Games. So I sought out a compromise."

Julian stiffened and clenched his fists. "Thousands of half-bloods have died in the Games since their inception," he said. "I see no evidence of a compromise."

"Look closer," Sorcha said. "Because despite the many horrors that those thousands of half-bloods inflicted upon others before or during the Games, they all skipped judgment in the Underworld and were sent straight to Elysium. Why do you think that is?"

"That's thanks to the gods," I said. "Not you."

"Wrong." She smiled. "You're not the only one who's used the Golden Bough to journey to the Underworld. Centuries ago, I did the same."

"You met Sibyl?"

"I did," she said. "I needed to speak with the Queen of the Underworld, Proserpina. Sibyl helped me get to her. You see, as the patron goddess of plebs—common people, like the half-bloods—I suspected Proserpina would hear me out. I was correct. After I explained the situation, Proserpina argued to Pluto on my behalf. Pluto's biggest weakness is his love for his wife. She pushed the right buttons, and he agreed to give all chosen champions a free pass to Elysium."

"But that doesn't make their deaths irrelevant," I said. "Elysium or not, their lives were cut short."

"And the chosen champions weren't the only ones who suffered," Julian added. "What about our families?"

"I provided your immediate family members with a generous lifetime stipend," she said. "They're all well taken care of."

Hot rage shot through my veins, and I shook my head, unable to believe what I was hearing. "How would you feel if Kyla died?" I asked. "Would a lifetime stipend, no matter how generous, ever replace the loss of your daughter?"

She lowered her gaze, took a deep breath, and then looked back up at me. "No," she said sadly. "But I'm not only a mother to Kyla. As the Empress of the Otherworld, I'm a mother to the entire realm. I need to do everything I can to keep this realm from falling. That meant agreeing to the Faerie Games, so that was what I did. And my decision seems to have been the right one. If it weren't, then we wouldn't be standing here today."

"You don't know that," I said.

"She might not," Prince Devyn said. "But thanks to my gift, I do. Without the magic Jupiter gifted to you, you couldn't have beaten Fallon. And it goes beyond that. Our iron allergy makes it so fae can't wield holy weapons. But half-bloods can. And chosen champions are the strongest half-bloods, thanks to their gifts from the gods. The chosen champions who won the previous Games and who now reside in the citadel are the key to bringing down the afflicted fae in the realm. You see, the Faerie Games didn't exist solely so you could rise. They also existed to slowly create our army over time. That army is the only chance we have in slaying the afflicted."

Chills prickled along my arms.

Because as twisted as it was, it made sense.

"What's done is done," I finally said, since I couldn't change the past, no matter how awful it was. "And I'm happy to tell you the cure, as long as you promise to end the Faerie Games forever."

"Done," Sorcha said. "Now, regarding your return to Earth—"

"Immediately after we tell you the cure, you'll give all eight of us—me, Julian, Torrence, Reed, Thomas, Sage, plus Julian's mother and sister—portal tokens that will bring us from your private courtyard in this house to the Trevi Fountain," I interrupted. "We'll be able to leave when we want, and you'll do nothing to stop us. The tokens will remain ours for as long as we're alive, or until we choose to give them to someone else."

She tilted her head and smiled in that calm, knowing way of hers. "And if I don't have eight portal tokens that go from my private courtyard to the Trevi Fountain?"

I nearly rolled my eyes. Because she didn't actually think I was going to fall for that, did she?

"Do you have eight portal tokens that go from your private courtyard to the Trevi Fountain?" I asked.

"I do."

"As I thought." I nodded. It made sense, because if there was some sort of emergency in the Otherworld that would require her to quickly leave for Earth—for example, if the citadel became overrun with zombies— she'd need enough tokens for herself, her daughter, her advisor, and enough guards to keep them safe.

"So it's a deal, then?" she asked.

"Yes. It's a deal."

29

SELENA

TORRENCE LISTED off the ingredients for the cure, and gave instructions about how to make it.

The Empress's eyes narrowed as Torrence spoke.

"And that's it," Torrence finished. Despite all the sleep she'd gotten last night, she still had bags under her eyes, but she was pushing through. "The potion will be milky white, tinted pink from the blood."

Sorcha pressed her lips together and stared Torrence down like she was seconds away from strangling her neck. Then she turned her angry gaze to me.

I stood steady, refusing to be intimidated.

"You didn't tell me the cure was a potion," she finally said.

"You didn't ask."

She scowled, reminding me of Sage before she

burst into wolf form. "You know perfectly well that fae can't brew potions," she said. "This cure is useless to us."

"It's not useless. It works." I motioned to Julian as an example. He'd put his sock and boot back on, but his bright steel wings were a perfect picture of health.

"It may work," she said. "But that doesn't matter when we can't *create* it."

I wanted to shrug and say it wasn't my problem.

But there was still more I needed to get done on the Otherworld. I hadn't forgotten about the half-bloods—both the ones who were still alive and slaves to the fae, and the ones hiding out in the Sanctuary. As soon as I could, I was going to follow through on my promise of freeing them.

Making an enemy of the Empress wouldn't benefit my cause.

"Strong witches and mages can create potions," I said simply. "We have many on Avalon who are more than capable of brewing the cure."

"And we have all the necessary ingredients," Torrence chimed in. "Except for fae blood. But you've got that covered."

Sorcha glared at her, then returned her gaze to mine. "What are you proposing?"

"Nothing yet," I said. "I need to consult with the

leaders of Avalon first. But when I'm ready, I'll call for you at the Crossroads."

Silence.

Then Sorcha straightened, and the anger melted off her face. "We'll meet there on the next full moon," she said.

"We'll meet there when I call for you." My gaze didn't waver from hers. "Which will be whenever I'm ready."

"Why should I believe you'll ever be ready? You have no reason to have any love for the Otherworld."

"On Earth, we need all of the help fighting the demons that we can get," I said. "So we might be able to come to an arrangement that will benefit us both."

"We can spare some of our chosen champions," she said quickly. "They're stronger than most species' on Earth, *and* they can wield holy weapons. They'll be extremely useful to you against the demons. In return, you'll speak with anyone necessary on Avalon and devise a way to get us as many vials of the cure as we need."

The desperation in her tone caught me off-guard, especially because I didn't want any more fae or half-bloods to die, either.

But I needed to do what would be best in the long term.

In this case, that meant seeking guidance from those

with more experience than me, and not impulsively agreeing to something that hadn't been fully thought out. Especially because I suspected the Empress was preying on the fact that I'd acted impulsively in the past.

"I can't agree to any proposition until I speak with the leaders of Avalon," I repeated. "So it's in your best interest to get us there as quickly as possible. But first, a parting gift."

I glanced to Torrence, and Torrence reached into her pocket.

"No gifts," Sorcha said, and Torrence paused, the gift still hidden from view.

"Are you sure?" I asked, unable to keep a teasing lilt from my tone. "Because once you see it, you may change your mind."

The Empress narrowed her eyes, clenched her fists, and I braced myself for an attack.

Did I push her too far?

"Fine," she said, and I relaxed slightly. "Show me, and I'll decide if I want to accept it or not."

Torrence removed it from her pocket and held the vial of milky potion out to the Empress. "It's the cure," she said. "All it needs is a drop of fae blood and a witch's touch, and then you can give it to Kyla."

Sorcha gasped, her lips parted, and she reached forward to grab the vial. But she stopped herself and lowered her arm back down to her side. "What do you want in return?" she asked, although she spoke to me and not to Torrence.

I smiled, since I'd already prepared for this. "A future favor," I said.

"That's a big request."

"And this potion will save your daughter's life. Do you want it or not?"

She held my gaze, like she was trying to will me to offer something else.

I didn't.

"Fine," she said. "Hand it over."

"I will," Torrence said, and then she looked to Julian. "But first, we need the final ingredient."

Julian pulled a golden dagger out of the ether—it looked the same as the one he'd loaned to Bryan—and held it out to Sorcha.

"Prick the pad of your middle finger and squeeze it into the vial," I told her.

Torrence uncapped the vial, and Sorcha did as asked. The drop of her blood landed in the potion, and then Torrence popped the cap back on and slowly rotated it so it was upside-down. The Empress's blood spread out, tinting the milky potion pink. Once the color evened out, Torrence turned the vial right-side up and handed it to Sorcha.

Sorcha took the vial and held onto it as tightly as I held onto the Holy Wand. "It was kind of you to bring an extra vial for Kyla," she said.

"Kyla's a sweet girl," I said. "I couldn't leave the Otherworld in good conscience without providing her with the cure."

Sorcha simply nodded, and we watched each other for a few seconds, in what felt like a moment of understanding.

"Selena." Prince Devyn broke the silence, and I looked to where he stood next to the sack of holy weapons.

"Yes?"

"What do you intend on doing immediately after you return to Earth?"

"Shouldn't you already know?" I asked, and I pointed to my temple. "Omniscient sight, and all."

"I see every possible scenario," he said. "Some good… many bad."

I shivered, not liking the haunted look in his eyes. "Julian and his family won't be allowed onto Avalon until they pass the island's trials," I said. I'd already explained all of this to Julian, so he had an idea what to expect. "We're going to bring them to the starting place of the trials at the Vale. After seeing them off, we're teleporting back to Avalon."

He eyed me, as if he doubted me. "A good plan," he finally said. "But no matter what you learn from here, you need to remember that you're one of the Four Queens. To win the war against the demons, you must act like a queen and put the greater good above your own desires." He glanced to Torrence, and then returned his focus to me. "Can you do that?"

"Of course I can."

He nodded slowly, looking doubtful.

He knows something.

"What do you see?" I asked.

"Something that's not for me to tell. All I can do is encourage you to do what you've set out to do. Don't let anything—or any*one*—divert you from your plan. Do you understand?"

"I don't see what would stop me."

"You will soon," he said. "But I've done all I can to guide you toward the correct path. My job here is finished. And now, finally, I can move on."

"Move on to where?" I tensed, not liking how resigned he sounded.

He sounded like Bridget, at the end of the second week of the Faerie Games, when we were inside the chariot heading toward the Coliseum.

"A place where I can finally find peace." He smiled. "Throughout the years, many have been jealous of my gift. They imagine that if they knew every possible future, their lives would be perfect. But there's always so much more at stake than my own future. In fact, I most always end up sacrificing my own happiness for the greater good."

"Which is what you said I need to do as the Queen of Wands," I said.

"Exactly. You see, what most fail to understand is that my gift is a burden—one I've had to carry with me for over a millennium. But now the future is in your hands, along with the other three queens. I've lived my entire life to ensure that you rise as the Queen of Wands and return to Earth, ready to rule. And now, the time has come when I can finally release myself of my burden, and pass on to the Underworld."

My head spun, and the ground tilted beneath me. I held the wand tighter to steady myself.

There had been so many times when I'd wanted to strangle Prince Devyn. Even though he was my biological father, I hated him for what he'd done to me. I'd never forgive him for kidnapping me to the Otherworld and nominating me for the Faerie Games.

But I'd never wanted him dead.

"You can't mean…" I trailed off, unable to say the words out loud.

You can't mean you want to die?

Julian stepped up beside me and took my hand. "What if you don't end up in Elysium?" he asked Prince Devyn.

"I have omniscient sight." He smiled. "I know where I'll end up."

Before any of us could move to stop him, he pulled a holy weapon out of the brown sack, plunged it into his heart, and exploded into a sparkling ball of green light.

I watched, stunned, as the light that had been my biological father floated up and dimmed out like a firework. My feet were heavy as rocks, strapped to the ground below. I opened my mouth, and then closed it again, at a complete loss for words.

Sorcha also stared at the spot where Prince Devyn had been standing, looking as shocked as I felt.

The silence was so heavy that I could barely breathe.

Aeliana faced all of us, her expression solemn, and said, "May his crossing to the Underworld be a peaceful one."

"May his crossing to the Underworld be a peaceful one," I said with Julian and Sorcha, my voice hollow. It felt like I was watching all of this from above instead of experiencing it with my own eyes. My only anchor was Julian's hand in mine.

The others bowed their heads in respect and repeated the words as well.

Sorcha straightened and cleared her throat. "Aeliana," she said, sharply and swiftly. "Take the sack of holy weapons and make preparations to begin testing them to ensure they're not forgeries. I'll bring these six to my private courtyard and see them off to Earth."

"And my mother and sister?" Julian asked.

"They're already there, waiting for our arrival," she said, and she spun on her heel, leading the way.

30

SELENA

WE ENTERED THE COURTYARD, and Julian's mother and sister rushed at him to give him huge hugs.

I stood back and watched, tears in my eyes. Even though they'd already reunited while I'd been recovering from trying to create the portal to Avalon, this was different.

Because this time, they knew they were going to a place where they could finally be a family again.

They pulled apart, and Julian's sister—Vita—looked to me. She had Julian's ice-blue eyes and dark blond hair, but she was so fragile and pale that it was hard to believe they were twins. "Thank you for everything you've done for us," she said. "I can't wait to get to Avalon."

I startled at her outward expression of thanks, but

quickly recovered. Because even though half-bloods weren't bound to favors by thanking one another, they tended to avoid the words, since they didn't want to slip up while talking to a fae.

The fact that Vita had said them was a true, heartfelt expression of gratitude.

"You're welcome," I said warmly. "I can't wait for you to see Avalon. You're going to love it."

"I'm sure I will." She smiled, and in that moment, I knew I was truly gaining a sister.

"You can bond with each other later," Sorcha said, and she pulled a small golden pouch from one of the pockets in her skirts. "Here are eight tokens that will take you to the Trevi Fountain, as promised."

I stared at the pouch in her hand. "You had the tokens this entire time," I realized. "And you had Julian's family waiting here. You already knew you were going to agree to the deal."

"Your father was determined to have all of this play out in a particular way, and I trusted his guidance in these matters," she said. "But he only told me to have Julian's family wait here, and to carry the tokens with me. I knew nothing more."

She opened the pouch, and handed a token to each of us.

I took mine last.

It was gold, and about the size of a quarter—just like the one Julian had handed to me when we'd thrown them into the fountain in LA. But instead of Prince Devyn's likeness on the back, this one had Sorcha's. Her crown towered so high that it bled off the top of the coin.

"All right." I turned to face the fountain. "I guess this is it."

Julian nodded at me, and I prepared to toss the coin into the water.

"Wait," Torrence said, and I looked to her. She was shaking, and her big green eyes were full of fear.

"What's wrong?" I asked.

"There's something I haven't told you yet. Something I just found out when I went to Avalon. Something you need to know before we leave."

My heart leaped into my throat, since whatever this "something" was, it didn't sound like it was going to be good. "What is it?"

She held my gaze for a few more seconds. "Since you were brought here, the timelines in the Otherworld and on Earth have been different. For each day that passed on Earth, an entire week passed in the Otherworld," she said, and I nodded, since I already knew all this. "But at some point while the four of us have been here, the timelines merged back together."

"Oh, right." Sorcha smiled, and her eyes glinted with amusement. "The Red Storm made it impossible for anyone to leave or enter the Otherworld, so there was no need to have my fae use their magic to uphold the time dilation. You see, the larger the time difference becomes, the harder it is to hold on to. So I had them stop using their magic to alter time, and instead had them focus on upholding the dome around the citadel."

"And you weren't going to tell us?" I asked.

"I didn't see why it mattered."

I pressed my lips together, my head spinning. "When you say the timelines 'merged,' what exactly do you mean?" I asked Torrence.

She bit her lower lip and toyed with her token. "I mean that time on Earth caught up to the time here."

My stomach sank at the confirmation of exactly what I'd feared. "So on Earth, the four of you have been gone for weeks," I said, and Torrence nodded. "My mom must have been so worried. And my dad and Bella have been stuck in that dome this entire time..."

I didn't get a chance to finish, because Reed stepped in front of Torrence and grabbed her shoulders like he was getting ready to shake her. "Exactly how much time passed?" he asked, and he stared down at her like his life depended on her answer.

Her eyes welled with tears, and she lowered her gaze. "Almost three months."

He dropped his hands and cursed. "How much time is left?"

I looked back and forth between them, confused. "What are you guys talking about?" I asked, and I looked to Sage and Thomas to see if they had any idea what was going on. They both couldn't look at me, which I guessed meant they did. "What happened?"

The three of them looked to Torrence.

I did, too.

My best friend took a deep breath, and finally forced herself to meet my eyes. She looked so guilty that my stomach filled with more dread than I'd thought possible. "We ran into a bit of trouble when we were getting the four objects for King Devin," she started. "Specifically, on Aeaea."

"Circe's island," I recalled.

"Yes. When we told you what happened there, we weren't exactly being honest with you. Well, *I* wasn't being honest with you. I asked the others to go along with it, because we needed to focus on getting you back home. I didn't want you worrying about me when we had so many bigger problems to deal with here. I figured that once we were all back on Avalon, I'd tell you then, and we'd figure out what to do from there."

"Tell me what?"

"We weren't able to steal the staff from under Circe's nose," she said. "Circe was too powerful for us to pull that off. So, to get her staff, I made a deal with her."

"An impulsive deal," Reed said. "A *stupid* deal."

"Stop." I held up a hand, blocking his face from my view. "I want to hear it from Torrence."

"All right," she said, and then, she started from the beginning, and told me the truth about what had happened after they'd landed on that island.

31

SELENA

"CIRCE SAID she'd loan us the staff for three months." Torrence swallowed, barely able to say the next part. "If we failed to bring it back to her, she wanted me to go live with her, on Aeaea."

"Okay." I steadied myself, since maybe it wasn't as bad as it sounded. "For how long?"

"For forever."

Time froze, and I blinked as I processed her words.

I couldn't be hearing right.

This was too crazy, even for Torrence.

"Tell me you didn't take it," I said. "That you came up with something else she wanted." I looked to Sage, hoping she'd jump in and say she came up with a brilliant idea at the last moment to stop Torrence from going through with it.

She didn't.

I took a deep breath and ran my fingers through the roots of my hair. Because there was a solution to every problem. We just needed to figure out what that solution was.

In this case, that meant getting that staff back from King Devin and returning it to Circe before the time was up.

"You said almost three months have passed." I paced around, working everything through in my mind. "Exactly how much time do we have? A week? Two?"

"A day," she said, and I stopped in my tracks. "Well, it was two days when I got back to Avalon, and more than a day has passed since I got back here. So, less than a day."

"What?" I stood there and stared at her. "You can't be serious."

"I wish I wasn't."

"You shouldn't have done it," I said. "You should have left without the staff. Figured out some other way to get to the Otherworld."

"There *was* no other way," she said. "At least, not that we knew of. And we knew that for each day that passed for us, a week passed for you. We had no idea what was happening to you here. All we knew was that the sooner we got here, the more likely it was that you'd be alive.

And then, with the time dilation, not much time on Earth should have passed before we all got back home. I thought we had weeks to figure out how to get Circe's staff back to her."

"We still have time to get the staff back to her," I said, since we didn't have any other option. "We just need to do it quickly. How many hours do we have?"

"I made the deal with Circe in the morning, Bahamas time," she said. "I'm not exactly sure how time zones in the Otherworld correlate to the ones on Earth..."

"They can be sporadic," Sorcha said. "Usually a few hours earlier or later than Ireland's time zone."

I frowned, since that complicated matters. Then I looked to the Holy Wand in my hand, and suddenly, felt like the biggest idiot in the world. "Wait," I said. "I have all this new magic. We can just go straight to Circe's island, and I can... take care of her. If she's not alive, then there's no deal. Problem solved."

"I wouldn't test your luck," Sorcha said.

"Why not?" I asked. "You've seen what I can do."

"Because Circe isn't just an immortal sorceress. She's a goddess. The four of them were lucky to get off of Aeaea alive. Trying to fight Circe will get you turned into swine at best, and ash at worst."

I bit my lower lip and nodded, since I did see her point. Especially since there was a better option. "So we're back to plan A," I said, and I realized I was starting to sound like Julian. "Getting the staff back from King Devin and returning it to Circe. We're stronger than King Devin. It shouldn't be a problem."

"You can't just kill King Devin," Sage said. "He's allied with Avalon."

"Then it's a good thing I'm not planning on killing him off."

"So what's your plan?"

"He offered to trade his portal tokens for the items he sent you to retrieve," I said. "So why wouldn't he be open to another trade?"

"There has to be something he wants more than the staff," Julian said.

"Exactly." I smiled, glad that my soulmate seemed to be on board with the idea so far. "We'll offer him another trade. The four of you were powerful enough to get the original items he requested. Now, with Julian and me helping, we can get him something even more powerful than Circe's staff."

They were all silent as they thought about it.

"Do you have anything in mind?" Sage finally asked.

"Not yet. We need to go to him first. Propose the deal, and get him to work with us." I looked around at all of them, hoping I sounded strong and in control.

Like a true queen.

"Hold on," Thomas said. "We're forgetting one important detail here."

"What's that?"

"Prince Devyn said that Selena needed to go straight to Avalon after dropping Julian and his family off at the Vale. He was extremely clear that she shouldn't get side-tracked. And this mission—as honorable as it is—is a deviation from the original plan."

I glared at him, and electricity buzzed through my veins at the idea of doing anything *but* helping Torrence. "I'm not just going to do nothing and let Torrence get trapped on that witch's island," I said. "It won't take us longer than twenty-four hours. I'll be back on Avalon soon enough."

"But isn't this exactly what Prince Devyn warned you about?" he asked. "Putting aside your own desires—like helping your best friend—and doing what's best for the greater good?"

"The greater good *is* helping Torrence," I said. "My magic is the strongest of all of ours. With me helping, we have the greatest chance of success."

"Getting real full of yourself, aren't you now?" Torrence smirked.

"Just stating a fact." I couldn't joke about the situation—it was far too serious for that.

"If we're stating facts, then we should also remember

that Prince Devyn had omniscient sight," Thomas said. "He would have known this was coming. And he made it clear that you were to go straight to Avalon after bringing Julian and his family to the Vale."

"Prince Devyn could see every possible future," I reminded him. "Just because there may be one future where everything apparently ends up better if I don't help Torrence, I refuse to believe there isn't a future where I help her and everything turns out well."

I held his gaze, unwilling to back down. I was going to do this, whether I had his approval or not.

"It's your future," Thomas muttered. "And you're just as headstrong as your mother. I can't force you not to do this. I was simply reminding you of the facts."

"Noted," I said.

"What about what Torrence thinks?" Sage looked to my best friend. Torrence still looked stressed, but not *as* stressed as when she'd returned to the Otherworld. "Do you want Selena to come on this mission? Or do you want her to go straight to Avalon?"

"No matter what any of us say, Selena's not backing down. She's coming with us," Torrence said. "So how about we stop wasting time, and get started on getting that staff back to Circe."

32

SELENA

WITH THE DECISION MADE, we devised a plan.

We needed to get to the Tower so we could approach King Devin with our offer. Given that we had four portal tokens that would drop us off in his penthouse, and we needed to save as much time as possible, it made the most sense to use those. And it needed to be the four of us with the most powerful magic.

Torrence, Reed, Julian, and me.

After a heartfelt farewell, Thomas and Sage accompanied Julian's mother and sister through Sorcha's portal. They'd arrive in Rome, and then Thomas would use his gift over technology to contact a witch to bring them to the peaceful kingdom of the Haven.

Once Julian, Torrence, Reed, and I returned the staff to Circe, Julian and I would go to the Haven and bring his mother and sister to the Vale, so the three of them could start Avalon's trials together. The trials wouldn't take long—two days, maybe three at the most—and I was confident they'd pass. I'd be waiting for them on Avalon when they arrived.

I used my lightning-travel to bring Julian, Torrence, Reed, and myself to Ryanne's villa.

As expected, she was spending time in the courtyard with her husband, Prince Redmond. They were quietly reading on a bench, and they both startled when we arrived.

"Selena." Ryanne placed her book facedown on the table next to her and stood up, worry etched across her face. "Do you have news of my son?"

"Aiden is a guest of the Empress's, in her house in the citadel," I said. "He's being kept safe there, and he sends his love."

"So he's still alive?"

"Very much so." I smiled. "He looks forward to returning home once the roads are safe for travel again. But that's not why we're here." I held up the token that Sage had given me—the one with her initials engraved on the back. "Sorcha has lifted the law that prohibits Julian and I from portaling to Earth. The four of us need to go to King Devin's penthouse immediately. Which means—"

"You need the letter," Ryanne said.

"Yes." I nodded in confirmation of the deal we'd made during the meal Julian and I had shared with her before setting off to find the Holy Wand.

"Wait here," she said. "I'll be right back."

She hurried out of the courtyard. While she was gone, Redmond asked me some generic questions about lightning-travel. I told him what I knew, which wasn't much.

He visibly relaxed when Ryanne returned. Apparently, he wasn't one for socializing.

Ryanne kissed the seal of the letter. It shimmered, and transformed into a glittering, turquoise crystal that matched the color of her wings. The crystal was small, and fit perfectly in her palm. "Give this to King Devin," she said. "The crystal will only return to letter-form when he holds it."

I took the crystal and placed it in my pocket. "I'll deliver it safely to the king."

"I trust you will." She glanced up at the clouds clearing from the sky. "And I suppose I have you to thank for stopping the Red Storm?"

"Yes, but we're in an extreme time crunch, and it's a bit of a long story," I said. "We need to go to the lake so we can portal out now."

"I understand," she said. "There are afflicted outside

the villa, so I can take you as far as the front doors. You'll be on your own from there."

"Not a problem." I glanced at the Holy Wand in my hand, ready to use it to ash some zombies.

"On Earth, your wings won't be visible to anyone who's not fae," Ryanne said, and then she looked to the wand. "But I doubt the same rule will apply to the wand. You might not want to carry it so openly in the Tower. Or on Earth, in general."

"Hm." I pressed my lips together, since she was right. The Holy Wand was large, and I couldn't sheath it like a sword. Plus, King Devin couldn't know I had it.

Because if he asked to trade Circe's staff for the Holy Wand... as much as I wanted to help Torrence, I'd never hand the wand over to him.

I also wasn't going to leave it somewhere while we went on our mission. I needed it with me, in case I needed to use it.

But what else could I do with it? I wasn't Julian. I couldn't store it away in the ether and pull it out when I needed it.

Or could I...?

I glanced to Julian, and then back to Ryanne. "I have an idea," I said, although it involved Julian using his fae magic—which Ryanne and Redmond didn't know about yet. "But I need to speak with Julian alone."

"The dining room is empty." She motioned to the room off the hall of the courtyard, where we'd shared that meal together all those weeks ago. "You can speak there."

Julian and I made our way to the dining room, and he closed the door behind us. "So, what's this secret idea of yours?" he asked, watching me curiously.

"The magic gifted to you from Mars allows you to pull weapons out of the ether," I started. "Now that your fae magic is unlocked, I was wondering if you could use it to give me an 'ether cubby' where I can keep the wand."

That was how he'd described his ability to me before —like a cubby he could reach into, and find any weapon he desired.

"Maybe," he said, and he sized up the wand. "It's worth a try."

"Cool. What do you need me to do?"

He closed his eyes, his brow creased in thought, like he was internally communicating with his magic. Then he opened them again. "I'm just going on gut instinct here," he said. "But I'm thinking we should both hold onto the wand at the same time. I'll focus on doing what you asked, and we'll hope it works."

"Sounds like as good of a plan as any," I said. "Just don't break the wand."

"The Holy Wand has more magic than any other object in the world," he said. "Well, except for the other three Holy Objects. I don't think there's anything I could do to break it."

"Still," I said. "Be careful."

"Always."

He wrapped his hand above the wand, right above where I was holding it, and I nodded for him to continue. Then, with his eyes locked on mine, his steel gray and ice blue magic floated out of his palm and around the wand like a helix. It swirled out around my wrist, up my arm, and to my elbow. My skin tingled where it touched. The magic sank into me, and disappeared around both my arm and the wand.

All was still.

"Did it work?" I asked.

"There's only one way to find out," he said. "Picture the open space next to you as an invisible cubby. Imagine it opening, move the wand inside of it, and then let it go."

"All right." I shuffled my feet and tightened my grip around the wand. "What if it works and I can't get it back?"

"I can access the ether," he said. "If that happens, I'll get it back for you."

I nodded and took a deep breath.

Here goes nothing.

I imagined a cubby in the open space next to me, and the air brushed against my skin, like it was expanding outward. It pressed against me, slightly larger than the wand.

I moved my hand toward the space, and it sucked the wand inside. The wand disappeared in a flash.

But the wand's warm magic still brushed against my skin. It was there next to me, even if I couldn't see it.

"Nice," Julian said. "Now, imagine the cubby opening again. But this time, reach inside and pull the wand out."

I did as instructed.

The Holy Wand was back in my hand.

I stared at it in awe.

"It worked," Julian said. "Now, let's head out to the lake. We have a vampire king to bargain with."

33

SELENA

RYANNE WALKED us to the front doors of the villa and opened them. Black-winged zombies ambled around the lake at the bottom of the hill. They reeked of decay, and I breathed as shallowly as possible to block out the smell.

A breeze blew around us, they sniffed the air, and slowly turned to face us.

"This is as far as I can go," Ryanne said. "Good luck."

I nodded, since I didn't need luck.

I had my magic.

I called on it, and with the Holy Wand in my hand, electricity hummed across my skin. Clouds rolled in, thunder cracked overhead, and bolts struck down from the sky, knocking down the zombies.

"Come on," I said. "Let's go."

We hurried down the hill—jumping over fallen zombies in our way—and stopped at the edge of the lake. Even though the lake was natural, it had a fountain in its center, which was why we could use it as a portal. And it was big enough that we could all jump in at the same time.

"Now!" I said, and we tossed our tokens into the lake. Purple leaked out of them, spread through the water, and swirled like a galaxy of stars.

The glow brightened, and together, we jumped.

I anticipated a splash, but there was none. Instead, I floated into nothingness. I was weightless, like an astronaut in space.

Like the first time I'd portaled, I opened my eyes. The purple mist and sparkling stars fully surrounded me. There was no up or down. There was just open *space*.

But I didn't have time to fully take in its beauty, because mist covered my vision and blocked out everything.

My feet hit solid ground, the mist cleared, and I gazed around the foyer of King Devin's sleek, modern apartment.

I was back on Earth. I couldn't believe it.

Next stop: Avalon.

But first, it was time to find the king and do whatever was necessary to acquire that staff. And with Julian, Torrence, and Reed by my side, I had no doubt we'd succeed.

34

TORRENCE

I GLANCED at my Apple Watch for the time. But of course, its battery had died soon after I'd arrived in the Otherworld.

Luckily, there was a massive clock on the wall.

4:30 AM, Caracas time.

Caracas was an hour ahead of the Bahamas, which meant it was 3:30 AM in the Bahamas.

Four hours to go.

I took a deep breath, and the unmistakable iron scent of blood filled my nose. My sense of smell had gotten stronger since starting on this quest, and I wasn't complaining. Anything that benefited me was welcome.

I spun to face the dining room, which was where the scent was coming from. "This way," I said, and the others followed.

I stopped in front of the double doors and pushed them open.

A voluptuous, naked woman lay sprawled out on the table. King Devin hovered on top of her. He wore only Aphrodite's girdle, and he faced away from us, so we got a full moon view. He straddled her, his knees on the table beside her hips, and he caressed her breasts as he drank blood from her neck.

She writhed and moaned as he drank.

He licked the remaining blood from her skin, and moved to lower himself inside her.

Julian cleared his throat.

The king jumped off the table and spun to face us. The golden girdle covered practically nothing, providing a full frontal that I'd *never* wanted to see.

He smiled at me and tilted his head. "Torrence," he said, his voice silky smooth. "Might you want to join us? Your friends can stay and watch."

His dark, liquid eyes swirled with longing, and he beckoned me closer. Desire warmed my core.

How did I not notice how attractive he is the last time we were here?

I started to walk toward him, but Reed flashed to my side and wrapped his hand around my wrist, stopping me from going any farther.

"Let go." I tried to pull away from Reed, but he was too strong.

He tightened his grip around my wrist. "He's wearing the girdle," he said, as if I couldn't see for myself. "Do what you did in the Otherworld to block the compulsion."

Aphrodite's girdle. Right.

It made the person wearing it irresistible to anyone nearby.

I need to fight it.

I called on my dark magic, and a shadow flashed across my vision. The smoky magic swirled inside of me, raced to my head, and cleared my thoughts.

I swallowed down disgust at the way King Devin was leering at me.

The woman on the table pushed herself up to sit, but she must have been weak from the blood loss, because she fell back onto her elbows. "My king," she begged. "Come back."

King Devin's focus remained on me. "Come on, Torrence," he said. "Why settle for the boy when you can have a real man?"

"No chance in hell." I clenched my hands into fist, seething, and the dark magic continued to gather inside me. It would be so easy to throw it at his heart and end him…

Then Circe's staff would no longer be his. We could find it, take it, and return it to her. I'd be free to return home.

But killing King Devin would be the equivalent of Avalon declaring war on the Tower. We couldn't afford a war against another kingdom when we were already at war with the demons.

If I killed him, so many people would die because of my actions.

I wouldn't be able to live with myself if I did that. So I relaxed my hold on the dark magic, although I kept enough of it as a shield around my mind to protect me from the girdle's compulsion.

He looked around at the others, and his eyes narrowed. "None of you are affected by the girdle," he said, and then he zeroed back in on me. "How?"

"Just a little Jedi mind trick I learned in the Otherworld." I smirked. "Reed can do it, too."

"And the two others?"

"They're mates," I said, not yet wanting to give away Selena's identity. "Soulmates—like Sage and Thomas— are immune to the girdle's effects."

"Interesting," he said, and he studied me, fascinated. "No witch in the Tower is strong enough to resist the girdle's magic."

Revulsion curled in my stomach at the thought of

what he must be doing to them. Dark magic rose within me, but I reminded myself of the task at hand and quelled it.

"Get dressed and meet us in the living room," I said. "We need to talk."

"And why should I listen to you?"

Selena raised her hand, and a ball of electricity hummed in her palm. The sparks reflected in her violet eyes, making her look downright terrifying. "Because I've brought you a letter," she said. "From Princess Ryanne. I assume you want to read it?"

King Devin looked at her and licked his lips. "And who, exactly, are you?" he asked.

"Selena Pearce." She held her head high, her gaze not leaving his. "Chosen champion of Jupiter, and daughter of the Earth Angel of Avalon."

"Well," he said. "Aren't you fancy with all those titles."

"Do you want the letter or not?"

"Wait in the living room," he said. "I'll be down in five minutes."

"What about her?" I glanced at the woman on the table. She was lying on her side, making goo-goo eyes at the king.

"She'll stay here," he said. "I'll finish with her later."

He marched past us, left the room, and headed to the steps.

The woman frowned as she watched him leave.

Once he was gone, I rushed toward her and helped her sit up.

She blinked, and the vapid look in her eyes disappeared, quickly replaced by horror. She looked down at her naked body and wrapped her arms around herself. Tears rolled down her cheeks.

Reed joined us and covered her with his cloak.

"Can you get out of here?" I asked her, even though I knew the answer.

She was a human blood slave in the most brutal vampire kingdom in the world. Of course she couldn't get out of there. Or at least, not easily.

"Kill me," she begged, desperation plastered across her tear-streaked face. "Please."

"No." I yanked my hand away from her, appalled by her request. "But I promise you that after the demons are gone, we're coming back here." I leaned closer to her ear, not wanting King Devin to overhear the next part. "And I'm going to kill him myself."

35

TORRENCE

"I KNOW you said King Devin was a disgusting pig," Selena said as we stood in his living room, waiting for him to return. "But that…" She trailed off, stared out into the hall, and electricity raced along her scars.

Before she could continue, King Devin strolled inside. His hair was slick with water, and he wore a fluffy white bathrobe. Luckily, it was tied around his waist, so it covered the regions of him I never wanted to see again.

Aphrodite's girdle was nowhere in sight.

"You took a shower?" I asked.

"A cold one." His eyes hardened. "You didn't expect me to focus on our conversation in the state I was in, did you?" He laughed and looked over his shoulders.

"Lucinda!" he called. "Bring some of those pastries in here. I need to break bread with our guests."

The woman from the dining room—Lucinda—rushed in with a tray of pastries.

King Devin watched her place it on the coffee table, and he frowned. "I was wondering where the mage's cloak went," he said. "Take it off and give it back to him."

She shifted uncomfortably.

"Did you hear me?" he said. "Take. It. Off."

She looked to me, and I nodded, as if reminding her of my promise. Then she took the cloak off and handed it back to Reed.

He took it and put it back on, although he kept his eyes lowered in respect for Lucinda as he did.

"Much better." King Devin's gaze roamed approvingly over the woman's body. "Go back to the dining room. When I return, you better be just how I left you."

Dark magic coiled inside me.

He can't treat people like that.

He needs to pay for it.

A shadow shrouded the room. I was seconds away from letting my magic loose on him when she nodded, bowed her head, and hurried away. The dining room doors slammed shut behind her.

The penthouse was eerily quiet, and my magic retreated.

King Devin picked up one of the pastries, ripped a piece off, and popped it into his mouth. "I'd ask what happened to the vampire-shifters who accompanied you before, but I don't particularly care," he said. "Eat. Then, we'll talk."

We each picked a pastry up off the tray and took a bite. Mine was filled with blueberry jam. Yuck. I hated blueberry.

"The letter?" he asked once we were all finished.

Selena removed the turquoise gem from her pocket and held it out to him. "It should return to letter form after you touch it," she said.

"I know how fae letters work." He grabbed it and stepped back.

The gem shimmered, and then transformed back into a sealed envelope.

He ripped it open and unfolded the parchment. His eyes scanned the words, and his brow creased, as if deep in thought. Then he wiped all emotion off his face, folded the letter back up, and placed it into his pocket.

He crumpled up the envelope and tossed it into the nearest trash bin.

"Good news?" Reed asked.

"None of your business. Now, I'll personally escort you out of the Tower so you can teleport back to Avalon. And since Her Highness, the Earth Angel's daughter, has returned from the Otherworld, I'll be draining my fountain and demolishing it. The portal will be destroyed."

"We didn't just come here to give you letter," I said, and he stilled. "I have a proposition to make."

He raised an eyebrow. "I have a feeling this isn't the type of proposition I enjoy receiving from women."

"No, it's not," I said. "But I do believe it's the type of proposition that you'd want to hear from *anyone*, regardless of their gender."

"I'm listening."

He sat in the closest armchair, spread his legs, and leaned back.

The four of us remained standing as I told him about the deal I'd made with Circe. He grinned wickedly when I told him that Circe had sealed the deal with a kiss.

"I must say," he said once I was finished. "Circe will be one lucky woman to have you around as her pet for all eternity."

Dark, hot anger filled my chest and expanded through my veins. "I'm no one's pet. And I'm here because I want to make another deal with you." I paused to rein in my emotions, and he gestured with his hand for me to continue. "Julian and Selena are more powerful than Sage and Thomas," I said. "The four of us together are capable of retrieving an object far greater than any of the four you already have."

"Let me guess." He brought his legs together and straightened. "You think there's another, more powerful object I want, and you want to trade that object for Circe's staff."

"Yes." I didn't let my gaze leave his. This was too important to show anything that might be taken as weakness.

He said nothing for a few seconds.

Dread filled my stomach, and my throat went dry.

He's going to say no. I'm going to be stuck on Aeaea forever with Circe. And she's going to...

Shame flooded through me, and my cheeks heated. I couldn't bring myself to look at my friends.

"It's an interesting proposition." He stood up, and I breathed slightly easier. "But I have to consult with my witches to learn if there's an object that will satisfy my needs."

"And what, exactly, are your 'needs?'" Reed asked.

"They're none of your business." He headed out of the room, but then he turned to face us again. "You'll wait here. And don't go into the dining room to check on my little human. I have cameras installed every-where. If you speak with her—if you so much as *look* at her—then we don't have a deal."

I nodded, although I hated myself for it. Because I couldn't risk messing this up. And there was nothing we could do for Lucinda—at least, not yet.

"We understand," Julian said, and I was grateful for it, because I couldn't bring myself to say it. "But it's in your best interest to hurry, to give us most likely chance of success at retrieving the object."

"*If* there's an object I want," he reminded us.

Electricity danced between Selena's fingertips. A light breeze blew through the penthouse, and I had a feeling it was taking every last strength of will for her to not reach for the Holy Wand and use it against King Devin.

But when she'd introduced herself to the king, she'd left out the fact that she was the Queen of Wands.

Because there was one item we wouldn't trade for the staff—the Holy Wand.

"I'll return as soon as I can," he said, and then, he left to decide my fate.

36

TORRENCE

JULIAN WALKED over to the floor-to-ceiling windows that lined the wall of the living room, pressed his hand to the glass, and gazed out at the skyscrapers. They gleamed blue, and their windows glowed with light. The buildings were packed together so tightly that it was impossible to see out to the shantytowns beyond.

Reed walked to Julian's side and also stared out the window. "I'm not used to it, either," he said. "Not sure I ever will be."

Julian simply nodded in acknowledgment, and continued staring.

I supposed that compared to the Otherworld and Reed's home realm of Mystica, Earth's technology was like stepping into the future.

At the reminder of technology, I glanced at my watch again, annoyed by its dead, black face. "You don't think King Devin has an Apple Watch charger around here anywhere, do you?" I looked around, but of course, there wasn't one. If he had one, it would probably be in his bedroom. And there was no way I was going up there.

"Hand it to me," Selena said. "Maybe I can charge it up."

"You can do that?"

"No idea." She shrugged. "The Otherworld wasn't exactly a high tech place, and this is my first time back on Earth since getting my magic. But it's worth a try."

I unstrapped the watch and handed it to Selena. "Give it all you've got."

She held it in her palm, her fingers outstretched, and a soft, blue glow emanated from her hand.

The watch's face turned on.

"There you go." She smiled and held it out to me. "Fully charged."

I grabbed it and snapped it around my wrist. Sure enough, the battery gauge read one hundred percent. I dug into the settings and made it so the face displayed both Eastern Standard Time and the local time wher-ever we were, so we wouldn't have to worry about calculating time zones.

Since hidden cameras were watching us, we gazed out the windows as we waited for King Devin to return.

Ten minutes later, the elevator dinged. King Devin stepped out of it and into the foyer, and re-joined us in the living room. His dark eyes glinted in excitement, and he stopped, looked around at us, and smiled.

There's something he wants.

"I explained your proposal to an important advisor of mine," he started, and then he paused for dramatic effect. "It turns out that there *is* something I'd trade for Circe's staff."

"What?" I bounced on my toes, ready for anything.

"The heart of a dragon."

I stilled, and my mouth nearly dropped open. Dark magic slithered under my skin as I stared him down. "That's not possible," I said.

"Why not?"

"Because dragon's don't exist."

"Before we met, you didn't think any of the objects I asked for existed."

"That's different," I said. "Those were objects related to mythology. Dragons are supernaturals, like you and me. We'd know if they existed."

He raised an eyebrow, amused. "I'm surprised to hear such doubt from you," he said. "Especially given that you've seen evidence of their existence with your own eyes."

"No, I ha—"

I stopped mid-sentence.

Because King Devin was right.

And I knew exactly where we needed to go next.

37

TORRENCE

I SENT a fire message to our destination so our contacts there knew we were coming. Then, as promised, King Devin personally escorted us outside of the Tower's gates.

One by one, I teleported Reed, Selena, and Julian to our location. I was the only one of the four of us who'd been there before, which meant my teleporting would be far more precise than theirs.

The last thing we could afford to lose was time.

Once we were standing outside of the kingdom's boundary dome, I checked my watch.

8:23 PM, New Zealand Time.

4:23 AM, Eastern Standard Time.

A bit more than three hours to go.

Anxiety fluttered like butterflies inside my chest.

We can do this, I reminded myself, just as six witches appeared on the other side of the dome. *One step at a time.*

Alice and Harper, the witches who'd helped us last time we were in Utopia, stepped forward.

"Welcome back," Harper—the more talkative of the two—said to me. Then she looked to Selena and bowed her head slightly. "You must be the Earth Angel's daughter."

"I am." Selena reached into the ether and pulled out the Holy Wand. "I'm also the Queen of Wands."

Harper's eyes widened, and two of the other witches stepped back. Alice was as calm as ever.

"Your Highness," she said swiftly. "How can we assist you?"

Annoyance flared within me, but I took a long, deep breath and put a cap on it. "It's actually me you'll be assisting," I said. "I'm on a time sensitive mission, and we need an audience with Queen Elizabeth immediately."

Harper glanced warily at the guys, and then refocused on me. "Alice and I can take you and the Queen of Wands," she said. "Your male companions will wait here, outside of the dome."

"Understood," Julian said, since I'd already warned him of the high chance that he and Reed wouldn't be allowed inside Mount Starlight.

"Great," Harper said, and then she and Alice flashed out of the dome. Alice stood next to me, Harper next to Selena, and they both held out their hands. "Let's go."

We teleported to just outside the crater's rim, and Harper led us onto the elevator-pulley contraption that would bring us down the volcano and into the hollow magma chamber that housed the kingdom of Utopia.

Before we got on, Selena stored the Holy Wand back in the ether.

"Impressive." Harper smiled. "I need to learn how to use that spell."

"It's fae magic," Selena said simply, not bothering to go into detail about how it was also magic specific to the chosen champions of Mars.

"Oh." Harper frowned, but then her hand went to the handle of a sword on her weapons belt, and she brightened. "No matter. We have no reasons to hide our weapons in Utopia."

Alice walked over to the elevator's lever and pulled at it. The platform jerked forward, and Selena and I reached for the railing to brace ourselves. I looked down, and my chest tightened at the sight of the hole that seemed to go down forever.

It'll be fine, I told myself, and luckily, the elevator didn't jerk again as it moved down. *Small spaces can't hurt you. It's just in your mind. And it gets bigger at the bottom.*

Just like before, beautiful speckles of light dangling from the inside walls distracted me from my aversion toward small spaces. Selena stared wide-eyed at them, too.

"They're glowworms," I told her what I'd learned the first time I'd come here. "They're bioluminescent. Natural creatures from Earth that glow."

"I know what bioluminescent means," she said quickly, her eyes still glued on the worms.

I bristled at her tone. I knew Selena had been obsessed with learning everything she could about Earth, but that didn't mean she had to be a snippety know-it-all about it.

Finally, the tube opened up, and the elevator lowered into the magma chamber.

The vertical city of earthy, stone buildings connected by layers of rope bridges was just as impressive as it had been the first time I'd seen it. Warm, orange orbs of magic that glowed like miniature suns lit up the ceiling, mimicking the timing of the real sun. Except unlike the real sun, the light from the orbs didn't harm vampires.

"How do you have fae light?" Selena asked Harper.

"That's not fae light," Harper said. "One of our oldest ancestors cast her Final Spell here, to give us a home inside Mount Starlight. These orbs were the result of the spell."

"Hm." Selena didn't look convinced. "Interesting."

The elevator reached the bottom of the shaft, and the witches led us down a series of stairs and rope bridges. Vampires and witches wearing animal skins—all of them women—watched us out of the corners of their eyes. But they made room for us to pass and said nothing.

We followed the witches down to the lowest point of the vertical city, and then through a tunnel that brought us to the deepest part of the chamber.

Queen Elizabeth sat on a throne inside the open-jawed skull of a dragon.

"My Queen." Alice looked at Elizabeth straight on. "I present the Queen of Wands, the chosen champion of Jupiter, and the daughter of the Earth Angel of Avalon, Selena Pearce. And Torrence Devereux, of the Devereux witch circle."

I was an afterthought that followed Selena and all her new fancy titles.

I curled my fists as dark magic swirled inside of me. But I took a deep breath to control it, and kept my gaze focused on the queen. Just like before, she wore layered animal hides, shrunken heads that hung from a leather belt, and a crown of bones.

I'd warned Selena about the shrunken heads ahead of time.

"Come forth," the queen commanded, and Selena and I crossed the bridge to stand in front of her.

Harper and Alice handed each of us a bite-sized piece of multigrain bread. The bread was fresh and warm, and we popped the pieces into our mouths and quickly swallowed them down.

"Congratulations on successfully bringing the Queen of Wands back home," the queen said to me. "Now, what brings you here from Avalon?"

"I actually haven't been to Avalon yet," I said, and confusion passed over her face.

"Why not?"

As quickly as possible, I summarized the story of the predicament I'd gotten into with Circe.

"King Devin said he'll trade the staff, but only for the heart of a dragon," I finished. "At first, I thought he was crazy. Because dragons don't exist. But then I remembered the dragon skull that you're sitting inside of right now."

"And you thought I might be able to lead you to where dragon shifters live today."

Shifters.

Interesting.

"Can you?" I studied the massive skull surrounding her. The dragon's head must have been three or four times the size of me, and its teeth were long and sharp.

Monstrous teeth designed to kill.

"If dragons are still alive, I know nothing about them," she said, and I deflated, all of the air sucked from my lungs at once. "But all is not lost." I perked up, and she continued, "The bones that make up this dragon skull were gifted to me by the ancestors of a present-day witch circle."

"What circle?" I asked. My family knew all the big ones.

"The Gemini Circle."

"Hm." I frowned. "I've never heard of them."

"You wouldn't have," she said. "The Gemini Circle has lost a lot of their magic from generation to generation. There aren't many of them left, and they stopped communicating with me ages ago. But I still know where they live."

"And where's that?"

"Close by, in Australia, south of Melbourne. They own a beachfront café on John Astor Road and live in the space above it. I'll write down the address. I can also dig out a map for you. Once you get there, ask to speak with the leader of their circle. A witch named Rachael Brown."

"Rachael will know where the dragons are?" I asked.

"She might." She shrugged. "Or she might not. The only way to know is to go there and find out for yourself."

38

TORRENCE

SELENA USED her glamour to make it look like we were wearing modern clothes, so we wouldn't make a spectacle of ourselves in our breeches, dresses, and cloaks. Then Alice and Harper brought us back up the elevator, dropped us off with the guys, and blinked out. The four witches who'd been standing guard blinked out, too.

"Well?" Reed asked. "Do they know where to find the dragons?"

"Not exactly," I said, and I summarized everything Elizabeth had told us. "Teleporting with such little information isn't easy, but given how powerful we all are, we should be able to get decently close."

We took a few seconds to study the map. John Astor Road was a long road that wound around Australia's southern coastline. The café—Twin Pines—was at the start of it.

"Everyone good?" Julian asked.

"Yep," I said, and Selena and Reed said the same.

We stood in a circle, held hands, and blinked out to what would *hopefully* be the parking lot of Twin Pines Café.

We landed on sand.

The air smelled like salt, and waves crashed ahead of me. I opened my eyes, and sure enough, we were standing in the middle of a beach. The beach was nestled in a cove of tall cliffs. Narrow wooden stairs along the side of the cliff wound up to the top. It was empty, and judging from the branches, rocks, and leaves flung out on the sand, it was normally that way.

The sun hung low in the sky, and it was that perfect temperature where you couldn't feel the weather. I glanced at my watch, where the two clocks ticked next to each other. 7:33 PM, Sydney Time, and 5:33 AM, Eastern Time.

Two hours to go.

"Let's teleport up to the top of those steps and try to

get an idea about where we are." I blinked out and landed at the top of the steps less than a second later.

The others appeared next to me.

Trees lined the opposite side of the winding, two-lane road ahead. A car zoomed by, but other than that, it was empty.

I held my watch up near my mouth. "Hey, Siri," I said. "Take us to Twin Pines Café."

She replied that we were half a mile away. Not bad for going in basically blind.

"This way." I faced east, and ran.

The others followed behind in a straight line, and we all stayed to the side of the road. We probably looked like a high school cross-country team during practice, except that thanks to our supernatural strength, we ran way faster than any human could possibly dream of.

Not many cars drove by. Each time they did, we slowed down to normal human speed. Then, once they were out of sight, we picked up the pace again.

A few minutes later, my watch told me to turn right onto a small side street.

I did, and there it was, looking out toward the ocean. Twin Pines Café. A cute, two-story freestanding house with worn gray siding and a light teal roof. Flowers surrounded the entrance, a sign with the café's name hung above the door, and a chalkboard displayed the daily specials.

Dragon fruit tea was right at the bottom.

It has to be a sign.

We walked to the door, I pulled it open, and the warm smell of coffee flooded my senses.

Shelves of books lined every empty wall space possible. All the comfy sofas and armchairs were full, and people sat at pretty much every table, happily chatting away.

After so much time in the Otherworld, it was strange to be somewhere so *normal.*

A girl around my age with blonde, highlighted hair worked at the register. She was tan, and she wore light blue jean shorts and a white crop top. Her wrists were stacked with shell bracelets, and she gave off the vibe that she'd rather be at the beach than cooped up inside working.

As I approached her, I caught a floral scent buried beneath the overpowering smell of coffee.

Witch.

The smell was so slight that it could have easily been mistaken for perfume.

"Hi," she said in an Australian accent, and smiled brightly. "What can I get for you?"

"I'm actually looking for someone," I said. "Rachael Brown."

The girl glanced over my pendulum necklace and gemstone rings, and her ocean blue eyes filled with suspicion. "She didn't say she was expecting anyone," she said slowly.

"She's not expecting us. But we need to see her." I scanned the area, even though I had no idea what Rachael looked like. "Is she here?"

"Why?"

Selena leaned against the counter, held up her hand, and created a violet fae orb in her palm. "Witch business," she said, and then she closed her hand into a fist, and the orb disappeared.

Since Elizabeth had told us that the Gemini Circle had basically no magic left in their bloodline, hopefully the girl wouldn't realize that was fae magic and not witch magic.

The girl's eyes widened, and she looked to her right, where another girl was finishing up making a cup of coffee. The other girl smelled slightly of witch, too. "Gemma," she said, and the girl looked at her over her shoulder. She had long brown hair, green eyes, and wasn't as tan, but other than that, the girls were identical.

Twins.

"Yeah?" Gemma asked.

"Take these four up to see Mom. *Now*."

Gemma placed the cup of coffee down on the counter for a customer to pick up, and then walked over to stand next to her sister. "What's going on?"

"They asked to see mom, and they said they're..." The blonde twin surveyed the room to make sure no one was listening, then turned back at her sister and lowered her voice. "*Witches*."

"No way." Gemma's eyes lit up, and she smiled at us with sudden interest.

"Way," her sister said, and she looked at Selena. "Show her."

Selena held out her hand and created a fae light again. She only held it for a second—just long enough for Gemma to see—and then snuffed it out again.

Gemma scooted around the counter so she was standing next to us. The floral scent was stronger now.

Was Elizabeth *sure* they didn't have much magic left?

"This way," Gemma said, and she walked to a door that led to the back, and we hurried behind her.

39

TORRENCE

REALIZING we hadn't told Gemma our names, we introduced ourselves as she led the way up the stairs.

"Mom hates being interrupted while she's doing bookkeeping," she said when we reached the top. "But I think this'll be an exception."

"I'd think so," I agreed.

She walked us down a narrow hall and stopped at the door at the end. "Wait here," she said, and then she let herself into the room and closed the door behind her.

I glanced at the others, but stayed quiet. They didn't say anything, either. It was like if we spoke a word, we risked Rachael turning us away.

Finally, the door creaked open, and a woman who looked like an older version of Gemma faced us. The biggest difference between her and her daughter was that her eyes were brown instead of green, and they had slight wrinkles around them.

She sized us up, conveying absolutely no emotion. "Come in," she said, and she opened the door wider, revealing what looked to be a master bedroom. "I'm afraid I don't normally have visitors, so you'll either have to stand or sit on the floor."

"No worries." I strolled inside, the others right behind me. "Thanks for seeing us."

The hardwood floors were covered with a worn blue Turkish rug, the furniture had a shabby chic beach cottage feel, and a large window looked out to the ocean. One side of the room had a bed and dresser, and the other had a desk and bookshelves. The shelves held items I knew well—candles, crystals, and jars of flowers and herbs.

It was like a mini-apothecary.

"Gemma," Rachael said once we were all standing inside. "Go downstairs and get back to work."

Gemma gave her mom a longing look—she clearly wanted to stay. But Rachael stood firm, as strict as ever, and Gemma sighed in defeat. "Bye," she said to us. "I hope you get whatever you're looking for."

"Thanks," I said, and then Gemma left the room—but not without a final longing glance over her shoulder.

Once the door was closed again, Rachael sat down in

her office chair and swiveled around to face us. "So," she said. "Who are you, and why are you here?"

I shuffled awkwardly as we launched into introductions, unsure whether to sit or stand. But the others remained standing, so I did, too.

We told her we were all witches, since we didn't have time to explain about fae and mages. Plus, Rachael's floral witch scent was nearly undetectable. She likely didn't have supernatural senses, so she wouldn't be able to smell the differences between the four of us.

"We're not here to hurt you," I finished. "We're here because we need your help."

"Gemma said that you conjured up some sort of magical ball of light," she said, and I nodded. "Show me."

Selena created another fae orb, and Rachael's eyes widened.

"Incredible," she said in a daze. "My daughters and I are witches ourselves. But magic like that..." She paused and stared up at Selena like Selena was a goddess. "I didn't realize it was possible." She faced her palm to the ceiling and stared at it, like she was trying to create an orb of her own. She was, of course, unsuccessful. So she closed her fist and dropped it to her side. "How did you do it?"

"You don't have nearly as much magic as we do," I

said simply, and her eyes narrowed in suspicion. "Not enough to do anything like that."

"So why do you need my help?"

"We're looking for something, and a very powerful supernatural told us you might know where it is."

No need to tell her that the "powerful supernatural" was an immortal vampire queen. Judging by her shock at seeing visible magic, that would involve an explanation we didn't have time to give.

She tilted her head and looked over each of us. "What sort of 'something' are you looking for?" she asked.

This is it.

I took a deep breath, and said, "We're looking for a dragon."

She flinched slightly, and her expression hardened.

She knows something.

"Why are you seeking a dragon?" she finally asked.

"It's kind of a long story," I said, and I glanced at my watch. "And we're running out of time. But basically, I made a deal with someone to save my best friend's life." I glanced at Selena, she gave me an encouraging nod, and I turned my attention back to Rachael. "Now, in order to make sure I don't end up trapped alone with an evil witch for all eternity, I need to find a dragon. And I have

—" I paused to glance at my watch again. "Less than two hours to do so."

Rachael pressed her lips together and nodded slowly. "Interesting." She crossed her arms and leaned back in her chair. "And why do you think I can lead you to one?"

"Because the powerful supernatural who sent us here has a dragon skull in her kingdom," I said. "I asked her where she got it, and she said the bones were presents from *your* ancestors."

A few beats of silence passed.

She knew something.

She *had* to know something.

"I'm afraid I can't help you." She stood up and glanced at the door. "I need to get back to work, but I'll see you out."

"Wait," Selena said, and Rachael looked to her. "Tell us everything you know about your circle's connection to dragons. Now." Her voice was fuller and richer—she was using compulsion.

We hadn't wanted to force Rachael to tell us anything. If she'd been honest with us, we could have made a new ally.

But it was past the time to do this the nice way.

Rachael's expression slackened, her eyes unfocused. "The Gemini Circle has dragon magic in our blood," she said, her voice devoid of emotion. "Every other generation, twins are born. Legend says that when the fated twins come of age, the dragon magic will ignite and bless them with great power."

"And has that happened to Gemma and—" I paused, realizing I hadn't caught Gemma's sister's name.

"Mira," Rachael said. "And no. They've yet to come of age. The ceremony will happen at their next birthday, and the magic is strong in them. They're the fated twins of the prophecy. I can feel it."

"How so?" Julian asked.

"I don't know." She shrugged. "I just can. Let's call it motherly instinct."

I nodded, since given the war with the demons, it wouldn't surprise me if they *were* the fated twins. But that was something to worry about another day—after I returned the staff to Circe and was back home on Avalon.

"So, the twins are dragons," Selena said, and she looked at me with worry.

"No," Rachael said quickly. "Dragons are monsters."

I relaxed, since if I had to cut out Gemma or Mira's heart, there was no way I'd go through with it. I'd take a thousand lifetimes on Circe's island before killing an innocent in cold blood. Just the thought of it sent chills up my spine.

"Are you saying that dragons exist?" I asked.

"No." Rachael smiled. "And if they did, why should I tell you?"

Black magic gathered at my fingertips, and I stepped forward, ready to *force* her to tell me. After all, Selena wasn't the only one with powerful magic. And this was my problem to solve. I should be able to handle it myself. I didn't need anyone's help.

Then, Reed moved closer to me and wrapped his pinky around mine. Warmth shot through me, and I froze.

Why does his touch affect me so much?

I glanced over at him, and he nodded at me, as if telling me to calm down. His eyes were so soft that I might have even believed he *cared* about me.

The surge of anger disappeared, and realization weighed heavy on my shoulders.

Had I really just wanted to *torture* the answer out of Rachael?

I was better than that. And if I let this anger and jealousy toward Selena consume me, I feared what I'd become.

I pulled my pinky out of Reed's and moved closer to Selena. She visibly relaxed, as if she was worried that I'd been about to do something I'd regret, too. Then, she returned her focus to Rachael.

"Do dragons exist?" she repeated, her voice dripping with compulsion.

"Not anymore," Rachael said. "As far as I'm aware, they died out long ago."

"But you don't know that for sure?"

"No," she said. "I suppose I don't."

Relief coursed through my veins, and I toyed with my necklace.

My *pendulum* necklace.

That was the answer. Why hadn't I thought of it immediately?

"You're going to have to get the twins back up here," I said to Rachael. "Because if the legend about the Gemini Circle is true, then I know how we can track a dragon."

40

TORRENCE

GEMMA RUSHED INTO THE ROOM, and Mira followed behind. It was a miracle that Mira was walking straight, because her eyes were glued to her phone as she typed away.

"What's going on?" Gemma asked, her green eyes bright and excited.

"I'm going to do a locating spell to find a dragon," I said. "And I need both of your help to do it."

That tore Mira's gaze away from her phone *real* quick.

"Say what?" she asked.

"It's a long story, but I need to find a dragon in the next few hours. And I need your help to locate one."

She held her phone to her side and looked at me like

I belonged in a mental ward. "Dragons don't exist," she said simply.

"That's funny, because we just learned that you and Gemma have dragon magic," I said, and I looked to Gemma. "Is it true?"

She paused, as if unsure how to answer. "Maybe," she said slowly.

"We don't," Mira said. "We don't have *any* magic, let alone dragon magic."

"I wouldn't be so sure about that," Selena said. "The two of you—the *three* of you—have the scent of witch. It's slight, but it's there."

"What about dragon?" Gemma asked. "Do we have their scent, too?"

"I don't know," I said. "I don't know what dragons smell like."

"Because you've never seen one." Mira rolled her eyes. "Because they don't exist."

"We won't know for sure until our birthday," Gemma said.

"Right. The *ceremony*." Mira's voice dripped with sarcasm.

"I told them that you won't know if you're blessed with dragon magic until then," Rachael said. "But they insisted this spell might work anyway. So I'm leaving the decision up to you."

"Yes," Gemma said, at the same time as Mira said, "This is crazy."

The twins glared at each other. But Mira didn't walk away, which I took as a good sign.

Gemma turned her attention back to me. "What do you need us to do?"

"If the legend is correct, then your blood could be the key we need to find a dragon," I said. "All I need to do is a locating spell."

"How much blood are we talking about here?" Mira asked. "Not like I think it'll work. I'm just curious."

"Just a few drops. Nothing major."

"I'm in," Gemma said, and I smiled.

"Mira?" I looked at the blonde twin expectantly.

She was back to texting on her phone. "How long will it take?" she asked, barely looking up from the screen. "My boyfriend's on his way to pick me up. He'll be here in fifteen minutes."

"Just a few minutes." I strolled up to the bookshelf and grabbed the four different colored candles that sat right at eye level, along with the lighter to the side of them.

"Help yourself, why don't you," Rachael mumbled.

"Thanks." I glanced at her over my shoulder and smiled. Then I walked over to a spot of hardwood that wasn't covered by the rug and set up the candles in their required positions. "Where's the atlas?"

"I have one in my room," Gemma said. "I'll go grab it." She hurried out of the room and into hers, leaving the door wide open.

Mira finally looked up from her phone, and she focused on Julian and Reed. "Do the two of you even speak?" she asked. "Or do you just stand there and let Torrence and Selena handle everything?"

"Torrence is the one who needs to find the dragon," Reed said. "I'm just along for the ride."

"Male witches don't have much power," Rachael explained, and then she looked back at Julian and Reed. "If you do find this dragon, how do the two of you intend on protecting yourselves?"

Reed's eyes flashed black for a second. "We have our ways," he said.

"Whoa," Mira said. "That was cool."

Gemma rushed back in, holding a big book by her side. "What was cool?"

"Show her," Mira said.

Reed smiled wickedly, and his eyes flashed black again.

"That's not witch magic." Rachael walked over to stand with her daughters, as if she could protect them if we tried to attack.

"Each witch circle is different," Julian said smoothly. "Your circle—the Gemini Circle—is blessed with dragon magic."

"And his is blessed with what?" Mira asked. "Demon magic?"

"Mage magic." Reed smirked, clearly enjoying himself at their expense.

And reminding me that dark magic—*mage* magic—wasn't something I should be able to use. I unclasped my necklace and held onto the pendulum, as if the crystal could remove the unease coursing through my body.

"What's a mage?" Gemma asked.

"A super strong witch." I placed the atlas down in the center of the circle of candles and put my pendulum on top of it. "Anyway, I'm ready to go here. Julian—can you hand me the dagger?"

"Dagger?" Mira's eyes widened, and she stepped back.

"They need to get the blood somehow," Gemma said. "What'd you think they were gonna use? A safety pin?"

I smiled again, because I liked Gemma. She might have seemed quieter at first, but she had some serious spunk.

"It won't hurt," I promised Mira. "It's only a small prick on the pad of your finger. You'll be fine."

"Obviously I'll be fine." She scoffed. "I just wasn't expecting you all to be carrying a *dagger*."

Julian reached inside his jacket and pulled a silver dagger out of the ether. From the way he angled his body, it appeared like he'd grabbed it from an inside pocket.

He walked over and handed it to me.

"Thanks," I said, and I looked back to the twins. "Who wants to go first?"

Gemma held out her hand. "I'll do it."

I held her middle finger steady. "On three," I said, and then I counted off and pricked the pad of her finger. A large droplet of blood welled up on top of it.

She watched the entire time, and she didn't flinch.

I held the dagger under her hand, flat side up. "Squeeze out the blood and let it fall on the side of the blade," I told her. "Get as many drops out as you can."

She did as instructed, and the drops formed a pattern from the tip of the dagger to the hilt.

"I'll get a Band-Aid," Rachael said, and then she walked into the bathroom down the hall. She emerged a few seconds later with two Band-Aids, and handed one to Gemma.

Next up was Mira. She turned away, and flinched slightly when I pricked her finger.

"Done," I said, and I held the other side of the blade under her hand. "Do the same thing as Gemma."

She complied, and then quickly put on the Band-Aid.

I gripped the handle of the dagger, now splattered with drops of the twins' blood, and handed it to Gemma. "Hold on to this for a moment," I said. She held onto it carefully, and I reached for the lighter and lit the candles. With each one, a breeze that smelled like the candle's element blew gently through the room.

Once all four candles were lit, I placed the lighter down outside the circle. Then I picked up the pendulum, opened the atlas, and scanned the table of contents. I flipped through the pages until reaching the one for southeast Australia, and zeroed in as close to the Melbourne area as possible.

The dragons could technically be anywhere in the world. But with the Gemini Circle living here, and the dragon bones in Utopia, it seemed like as good of a place to start as any.

I held the pendulum over the map with my left hand and reached out to Gemma with my right. "The dagger," I said, and she gave it back to me.

The dagger pulsed with magic, like it was alive with it. *It's going to work.*

Excitement rushed through my veins, but I said

nothing. Instead, I focused on the objects in my hands, and the atlas spread out in front of me. I held the pendulum above the general location of the café, right near the start of John Astor Road.

Just like when I'd done the locating spell in the Otherworld, I didn't need to speak the words. Instead, my magic burst to life inside me, and the pendulum started to swing. It moved back and forth, going slightly to the west.

It stopped not too far away from where we were now.

I lowered the pendulum so the point of it rested on the place where it had stopped, and looked up to Rachael and the twins. "What's in this general area?" I asked.

"Ethan lives around there," Mira said. "My boyfriend. It's about a half hour away."

"We can work with that," I said. "What's his address?"

"I'm not giving you his address. But there's a restaurant nearby. McFly's Irish Pub."

"That'll work." I raised my watch, and told Siri to direct us to McFly's. Just like Mira had said, it was about thirty minutes away.

"What're you gonna do once you get there?" Gemma asked.

"Once we're in the general area, I can use a tracking

spell to find the dragon," I said. "I just need a bit of blood."

"Again?" Mira's face paled.

"Relax." I chuckled. "There's enough on the dagger for what I need to do." I dragged the pendulum across both sides of the dagger, smearing the twins' blood on the bottom of it. The blood absorbed into the crystal, and the pendulum ebbed with a small bit of light. "It worked," I said, staring down at the pendulum in amazement.

Rachael crossed her arms. "I thought you did this sort of thing all the time?" she asked.

"I do." I blew out the candles, stood up, and handed the dagger back to Julian. He placed it inside his jacket—back into the ether—and I clasped the pendulum's chain around my neck.

Gemma picked up the atlas, closed it, and hugged it to her chest. "After you find the dragon, do you think you could come back and teach us a bit of magic?" she asked. "If you have time, of course."

"I'm afraid that won't be possible," I said, and I looked to Selena.

My best friend gave me a single nod and took a deep breath. Then, she looked intensely at Rachael and the twins. "After we leave, you're going to forget you ever met us, and you're going to forget everything that happened since we arrived at the café," she said. Their eyes glazed over, instantly under her spell. "Do you understand?"

Guilt rushed through me at the sight of Gemma's slack, lifeless face. She was so excited about magic… and now she was going to forget all about it.

But maybe not. If the legend was true, she might be blessed with dragon magic at her next birthday.

I hoped she was.

"Yes," they said in unison, and then I glanced at the others, and the four of us blinked out.

41

TORRENCE

W E   R E A P P E A R E D in the parking lot next to the café. True to the café's name, two large pine trees towered at the far end of the lot.

With only a bit more than one hour to go, we couldn't risk trying to teleport to the pub and accidentally ending up in the middle of nowhere. A car was the surest bet, especially if we drove quickly.

"Your horseless carriages are fascinating," Julian said as he looked over the rows of cars. "They travel faster than pegasi."

"Yep." I looked over our options. Most of the cars were small—Australians apparently didn't drive big cars like Americans. Which was fine, since I wanted something *fast*.

I smiled at the sight of a red Mustang. "This one," I said, and I headed toward it.

"You don't think we should go for something a bit less... ostentatious?" Selena asked.

"What would be the point of that?" I smirked and placed my hand on the handle. Then I closed my eyes—I didn't want Selena to see them flash black—and called on my dark magic. It swirled up, ready to obey my command.

Unlock, I thought, and the doors clicked open.

I pulled on the handle, and sure enough, it was unlocked.

Reed put his hand on the top of the car, blocking me from getting closer to it. "You expect all four of us to fit in there?" he asked.

"There are four seats." I shrugged. "The ones in the back are just... compact."

"Not happening," he said. "Besides, even if we're able to fit, there are only two doors. What happens if we need to get out of the car quickly?"

"He's right," Julian said, and he pointed to the biggest car in the lot—a black Range Rover. "That one looks far more spacious."

"And more practical in case of an emergency," Selena added.

I huffed and slammed the Mustang's door shut, since

arguing would waste time we didn't have. Then I tossed my hair over my shoulder, strutted over to the Range Rover, and did the same thing to unlock it.

I settled into the driver's seat, Selena sat shotgun, and the guys took the back. I was the only one of us with a license, so the question of who would drive wasn't up for debate.

I quickly checked around for a key, but of course, there wasn't one.

"Your turn," I said to Selena.

She reached forward and pressed two fingers to the ignition. Spiderwebs of electricity lit up her hand, and the engine revved to life.

"Perfect." I removed my pendulum from my neck, my Apple Watch from my wrist, and handed both to Selena. The maps app was still open on the watch, waiting to direct us to McFly's Irish Pub. "You navigate," I said as I pulled out of the lot and turned left to head west. "And I'll see if this baby can do ninety."

The Range Rover could easily do ninety—kilometers per hour. Which wasn't very fast. I didn't know the conversion, but I put the petal to the metal and drove as quickly as I could along the meandering road. Driving on the opposite side of the road wasn't as difficult as anticipated, but it did take a minute or so to adjust.

As I drove, we devised a plan.

"No matter what, remember that this is a dragon," I finished. "He or she might be able to shift into human form, but dragons aren't like the shifters we know. They're not a natural species from Earth. They're monsters. We can't let ourselves forget that."

"Of course," Selena said, although she didn't sound totally convinced.

The pendulum's light brightened the closer we got to the pub. Finally, the sign for McFly's came into view. I pulled into the parking lot and glanced at the pendulum.

It still wasn't bright enough.

Good. Grabbing the dragon would be difficult in a public space. Given that it was Sunday night and the sun had already set, we were hoping the dragon shifter would already be home.

Selena moved the pendulum around in a circle. At the northernmost point, the light slowly pulsed. "That way," she said, and I kicked it into high gear and headed back onto the road, making the first right that I could.

We continued that way until turning down a long driveway and pulling up to a house on top of a hill. More than a house—a *mansion*. Since it was high up on the hill, it had a great view of the ocean.

"Damn," I said. "This dragon's living the good life."

Once we were close to the house, but not *too* close, I stopped the car. Selena handed the pendulum and watch back to me, and I quickly put them back on and checked the time.

7:15 AM Eastern Time, which was the only time zone I cared about now.

Twenty minutes to go.

We were cutting it close. *Too* close. But the pendulum glowed brightly and pulsed quickly. The dragon was in this house. It had to be.

Selena aimed some of her violet magic toward the pendulum. The magic soaked into the glowing crystal and disappeared.

"The glamour's working," she said. "We can see the crystal lighting up, but to anyone else it'll look totally normal."

"Good," I said, since we didn't want to put the dragon on the defense the moment it saw us.

I hopped out of the car and slammed the door shut behind me. Without pause, I hurried across the grass to the front of the house, not bothering to use the sidewalk. The others followed quickly behind. The pendulum's crystal brightened with each step.

We gathered in front of the door—Selena next to me, and the guys behind us.

I took a deep breath, and then I knocked.

After what felt like the slowest few seconds of my life, the door opened. A man in khaki pants and a t-shirt that said Hill Valley High stood in front of us. His topaz eyes looked more fae than anything else, and he had naturally tan skin. He looked around my mom's age, maybe slightly older.

And the pendulum was going *crazy*.

We had our dragon.

"Are you looking for Ethan?" he asked.

I stood there, shocked. Because Mira's boyfriend lived in this area. His name was Ethan. If this was his house, then was he…?

"We're not here for Ethan." Selena motioned to the car, interrupting my chain of thought. "We have a flat, and this was the only driveway nearby, so we were hoping you might be able to help us change it."

Dragons should be strong enough to fix a flat tire, right?

He paused, and I worried he was going to say no.

If he did, there was always Plan B.

Then, he smiled. "Four young, strong teens, and none of you know how to change a tire?"

"We're from the city." I shrugged. "It's not really something we do there."

Before he could reply, a young girl—maybe around seven years old—came halfway down the stairs. Her coloring matched his, down to the stunning topaz eyes. "Daddy?" she asked. "I thought we were gonna read before bed?"

"I'll be up in ten minutes, sweetheart," he said, and then a woman came down the stairs.

She wore a hooded robe, and her back was toward us. She stopped next to the girl and wrapped an arm around her shoulders. "Come on," she said. "Daddy has important business to take care of."

"But he'll be back?"

"I'll read to you while we wait," she said, and she ushered the girl back up the stairs.

Guilt panged in my chest.

I couldn't go through with this. There had to be another way…

He's a monster, I reminded myself. *I've killed plenty of monsters before. Don't be deceived by his human form. Besides, there's no more time. Either go through with this, or be trapped on Circe's island for all eternity.*

I reached for my dark magic and pushed down the guilt until it was gone.

The man—the *dragon*—waited until the woman and the girl turned into the hall. Then he looked back to us. "Right," he said in his bright Australian accent. "Let me grab my tools from the garage. I'll meet you at the car."

"No," I said, since I didn't want to let him out of our sight.

He turned around, surprised.

"We have tools in the trunk," I said quickly. "We just don't know how to use them."

"Hm." He glanced at the car. "All right, then. Let's go check out this tire of yours."

We walked over, and the sky rumbled with thunder, and lightning flashed overhead.

"The weather didn't call for a storm tonight." He stopped walking and looked up at the cloud-covered sky. "Looks like a nasty one. Hopefully we can get this tire fixed up before the rain comes."

"Hopefully," I agreed, and I headed toward the trunk and opened it up. "The tools are in here."

Selena looked at me, doubt shining in her violet eyes. I knew that look. She was having second thoughts.

Maybe we *should* stop.

This man had a family. And he was being kind to us.

Then Circe's face flashed in my mind, her lips curling slightly upward into a satisfied grin. Back on Aeaea, she'd looked at me so hungrily. And then there was the way she'd kissed me to seal the deal, like a promise of what she expected from me if I returned.

I won't let that be my future. I won't let an evil sorceress take advantage of me for all eternity because I let myself be deceived by a dragon. A monster.

My dark magic swirled angrily inside me, and I shook my head, silently begging Selena not to turn her back on me now.

We're doing this.

The man joined me and took a look. "Where are the tools?" he asked. "I don't see—"

Selena grabbed his arm, the three of us grabbed onto Selena, and a bolt of lightning struck us before he could finish his sentence.

TORRENCE

THE ELECTRICITY RIPPED me apart from the inside out. I would have screamed, if I wasn't reduced to tons of tiny particles zipping through the sky.

Piecing back together hurt even more.

My feet landed on the sand, and the pain stopped, although the memory of it remained. The light around us dimmed and went out.

We were in the same cove where we'd arrived. The one at the abandoned beach. With the sun down and no artificial light in sight, the cove felt haunted.

Technically, we could have teleported the dragon there, like normal. But we wanted to hurt him. Weaken him. Scare him.

Selena's lightning-travel was perfect for the job.

From the terrified expression on his face as he backed away from us, it had worked.

He held his hands up, palms out, and made no moves to attack. "I don't want to fight," he said, calm and serious.

"That's too bad." Reed's eyes flashed black. "Because you don't have a choice."

The man didn't flinch. "Why did you bring me here?" he asked. "And what type of magic was that?"

He waited calmly for our answer. Standing there, seemingly defenseless, he was a perfect target. And we were running out of time. I needed to take care of this—now.

I reached for my dark magic. It swirled inside me, ready for me to aim it toward this man, just like I'd aimed it at the cyclops.

But his daughter's voice echoed in my mind.

"He'll be back?" she'd asked the robed woman.

The woman hadn't said yes.

My entire body shook. But then I thought of Circe and called on more dark magic.

The smoky darkness smothered my guilt, and I stood strong.

The man slowly lowered his hands. "How did you find me?" he asked.

"Why aren't you flying away?" I asked in return.

"Fly?" He laughed. "What are you talking about?"

"Shift," I said. "Fly away."

Prove you're the monster we know you are.

"I'm not a shifter." He held a hand up at chest-level, palm to the sky, and a small bit of fire burst out from it. The flame danced over his skin, and the light flickered around the cove. "I'm a witch, like you. Or at least, like I think you are. I assume that's why you're wearing a pendulum?" He glanced at the crystal hanging around my neck.

It was still pulsing like a strobe light, although thanks to Selena's glamour, it would have looked like a plain pendulum to him.

But we were wasting time.

I reached for my magic again and shot it out at him. But not black, smoky magic.

Bright, purple magic.

He jumped above the beam of magic and *exploded* into a flying beast ten times his size. A giant, topaz, deadly-looking dragon. His head was taller than I was, and his slit, gemstone-like eyes glared down at me. His wings flapped as he hovered overhead.

The breeze stirred around me. I stared up at the monster he'd become, amazed by his majestic beauty.

But hesitation would kill me. So I raised my hands and released my dark, smoky magic toward his chest.

He snarled, opened his mouth, and blasted a laser beam of fire at my magic. The smoke and fire crashed together between us and boomed like thunder. The heat burned hot like a convection oven, but I forced my eyes to stay open and held strong onto my magic.

The fire inched closer to me.

Now that he was attacking in his dragon form, it was clear that I was right. He *was* a monster. And he was trying to kill me.

Die, I thought, and I pushed with all my might against his fire. Circe's face flashed in my mind again, and rage spread through me, strengthening my magic enough to stop the fire's progress.

Reed rushed to my side, held up his hands, and released his dark magic. It joined with mine, and together, we pushed the fire back farther.

Sweat beaded on my brow and dripped down the sides of my face. My arms shook from the strain of holding back the fire. I bent my knees to brace myself, but I didn't know how much longer I could keep this up.

Spears flew toward the dragon and embedded themselves into his scaly neck. Julian. But the weapons might as well have been toothpicks against the beast's thick, spiky hide.

Apparently realizing that he was getting nowhere, he threw one at the dragon's wings. It hit, leaving a small hole where it had pierced through. The next spear missed, and the one after it hit again.

But the dragon's wings were massive. The spears weren't taking him down quickly enough. The dragon's nostrils flared, each spear through its wings angering it further. The fire inched closer to me and Reed. The heat blazed against my skin, and it hurt to breathe.

We were going to burn to death.

I could try to teleport to another location in the cove and attack from a different angle. But then what would happen to Reed? And if we both teleported at the same time, what would happen when the fire hit the sand? Would it expand like a bomb and consume us all?

The risk was too big.

So I pushed out my magic harder. But it was no use.

We weren't going to win.

I glanced back at Selena.

She was standing there, staring up at the dragon, like she was helpless.

"Do something!" I yelled to her. "Now!"

She snapped back into focus and pulled the Holy Wand from the ether. The wand's crystals glowed, thunder boomed, and multiple bolts of lightning shot down from the sky. They hit the dragon and surrounded him with dancing webs of electricity that held him up in the air. He convulsed, and his fire stopped.

Reed's and my dark magic rushed forward and hit the dragon. But Selena's electricity acted like a shield, and the magic poofed into nothing.

No longer needing it to defend ourselves, we both let go of our magic. I released a long, exhausted breath, and wiped sweat off my forehead.

"Back up!" Selena hurried backward toward the ocean and stopped at the last of the dry sand before it turned wet from the waves.

The three of us followed, going backward as well so we could keep our eyes on the dragon.

Once the four of us stood in a row, the electricity around the dragon fizzled out and the beast crashed to the ground. Sand flew up around it in all directions.

That would have *really* hurt if it had gotten in our eyes.

The sand settled around the giant, collapsed heap of the dragon. Its wings were charred, and thin trails of gray smoke drifted up from them. The smoke traveled in the breeze, and the smell of burnt flesh assaulted my senses.

The dragon didn't move.

"Is it dead?" I asked, my voice only slightly louder than a whisper.

Selena's eyes were sad, and I knew what her answer

would be before she shook her head no. "I'm sorry," she said. "I couldn't."

I nodded, since I understood. It was the same reason why I'd originally attacked with light magic instead of dark. The dragon wasn't a monster. He had a teenage son, and a young daughter. The woman in the cloak was likely his wife. He was going to help four random teens fix their flat tire.

A disgusted pit formed in my stomach. Because he hadn't attacked first. He'd tried to make peace.

We were the bad guys here.

I walked slowly toward the dragon, and the others followed.

The tip of one of the dragon's wings twitched, and I stopped moving. The creature raised its head slightly, the air shimmered around it, and the space where the majority of the dragon had been was empty.

All that remained was the man in the center, curled in a ball on the beach. His skin was red and blistered. A few patches were charred black.

He groaned in pain, although the black patches were already starting to disappear. Accelerated healing.

How much longer until he was completely healed?

I glanced down at my watch.

7:24 AM Eastern Time.

A little more than ten minutes to go.

If I killed him right now and cut out his heart, would I have time to bring it back to King Devin, exchange it for the staff, and deliver the staff to Circe?

It would be tight, but yes. I'd just have to be quick about it. After all, it wasn't like we could let the dragon go. He'd gather more of his kind—*if* there were any more of his kind—and come for us.

So I didn't have much of a choice.

There's always a choice.

But sometimes—like when choosing between sailing closer to Scylla or Charybdis—neither option was a good one.

"Are you just going to stand there staring at it?" Reed asked.

I didn't answer.

"All right, then." His eyes flashed black, and he gathered a ball of dark magic in his hand. "I'll do it."

Before I could think twice, I blasted him with a beam of purple magic. His eyes widened right before it hit him. He flew back in an arch through the air and landed on his back in the sand.

He groaned and sat up, looking at me with murder in his eyes. "Fine," he said. "Wimp out and be imprisoned on Circe's island for all eternity. What do I care?"

His words stung, and I sucked in a sharp, pained breath. I wanted to sink into the sand and disappear.

Because despite everything, I'd always believed that Reed cared if I lived or died.

Now, I wasn't so sure.

Selena and Julian watched, waiting. I understood why. What we were doing was *murder*. They wouldn't interfere, but if someone was going to kill this man, it needed to be me.

I reached for my dark magic again, but stopped.

This wasn't me.

I can't do this.

There had to be another way out of this mess I'd gotten myself into. A way I'd be able to live with if I ever escaped Circe's island.

The man pushed himself onto his knees, although his breaths were labored, and he barely had the energy to sit up straight. He leaned back onto his heels and stared at me like I was the Devil incarnate. "If you're going to kill me, then do it already," he said. "But I know what you are. And I promise you that soon, my people will break free from their chains, and your kind will pay for what you've done to us."

His threat weighed heavily in the air. But I dropped my arms to my sides, because I knew I couldn't kill him. "My kind," I repeated. "Do you mean witches?"

"Witches." He chuckled. "Do you really expect me to believe you're—"

A woman appeared behind him and slashed a knife across the front of his throat before he could finish the sentence.

The life dimmed out of his eyes, he sagged forward, and the woman wrapped an arm around him to hold him up. His blood poured from the gash in his neck onto her pale, snow-white skin.

"This gift will please Lilith greatly." Lavinia flashed us a wicked grin and blinked out, taking the dead dragon shifter with her.

43

TORRENCE

I FELL to my knees and stared down at the bloodstained sand before me.

That was it.

We'd failed.

Reed blasted the bloodied sand with dark magic. "Dammit," he said. "We should have killed her when we had the chance."

"We needed that cure," I said. "We never had a chance."

"We could have figured something out."

I shrugged, because what did it matter? It was done. We couldn't change the past.

He blasted the sand again, then spun to face me. "How'd she even know we were here?"

"My blood." I held up my arms, showing the scratch

marks that went from my wrists to my elbows. "When we fought her, she clawed at my arms. She drew blood."

"But that was days ago."

"She wiped it on her dress," I said simply. "The same dress she portaled back to Earth in. She must have used the blood to track us."

Julian cursed.

Selena ran to my side and kneeled down next to me. "There has to be a way to track her and the dragon shifter," she said. "He's already dead. All we need to do is get his heart."

"We don't have time." I glanced at my watch. Two minutes to go.

Ice-cold fear flooded my veins.

I'd been so confident that I'd be able to get that staff back to Circe. Even after returning to Avalon to get the ingredients to make the cure and realizing how little time we had left, I was still convinced I could do it.

For my entire life, everyone had always admired my confidence.

But that very trait was what had gotten me into this mess. I'd overestimated myself, and now, I was going to pay the price.

No, I told myself. *Don't think that way. You did it for Selena. Even if you could go back, what could you have done differently?*

Nothing. Circe wanted to keep me on her island no matter what. At least this way, it would just be me who was stuck there. Sage was free.

But what was going to happen to me?

Fear of the unknown rattled me to the bones. Because I couldn't fight Circe before, and I wouldn't be able to fight her now.

Wait.

One big thing had changed for me since I'd left Aeaea.

I reached for my dark magic, and it rose inside me, filling me with power and suffocating the fear.

I'm going to escape Circe's island, I thought, and the magic danced through me, like it was telling me that yes, it could help me succeed.

So far, I'd resisted using it as much as I could. Despite how powerful it made me, the magic dug its claws into me each time I used it. It didn't want to let go. I'd only pulled back because of Reed.

But I was going to *need* that power to beat Circe. No more resisting. It was time to see how dangerous I could be.

I was going to take that witch down.

"Torrence." Selena gently shook my shoulder. "Stop."

"Stop what?"

"Your hands…"

I looked at where she was staring. My palms faced the night sky, and two balls of dark smoke swirled above them.

Power.

I smiled at the sight of it, but then let them evaporate away—for Selena's sake.

I didn't want her final memory of me to be of the person I was going to become. In the Otherworld, she'd made her opinion of dark magic clear. So no matter what, she couldn't know what I was planning.

"I've always been a survivor," I said, just as much to me as to her. "I'll get through this."

"You won't be there for long," Selena said. "Because I'm going to go there and rescue you. Just like you did for me."

"No." I twisted my head around to look at her straight on, and she jerked back, stunned. "You're the Queen of Wands. You have a responsibility to Avalon and the Otherworld. I didn't make this deal with Circe and chase you to a plague-infested realm just so you could risk your life trying to get me back."

Reed slowly walked forward and stopped when there were only a few feet between us. "You made the deal with her thinking you had three months to get her staff," he said. "Three months haven't passed for you yet."

"Maybe you can explain what happened," Selena said. "Maybe she'll give you more time."

"I'll try," I said, although I doubted it would work. "But no matter what, I'm going to escape. I can do this. I *will* do this."

"I'm not letting you fight her by yourself."

"No one *lets* me do anything," I said. "I make my own choices. And too many people are counting on you for you to risk yourself unnecessarily. Like the half-bloods in the Otherworld. Didn't you promise to return and free them?"

"I can do that after you're safe back home."

"But I don't want you to come after me." Maybe if I said it enough, I'd get through to her.

"Well, that's too bad, because I'm going after you anyway." She sounded as stubborn as me, and I was glad for it. Because she didn't need me anymore. She could handle whatever was coming next on her own.

No—not on her own.

With Julian.

"Don't you remember what Prince Devyn told you?" I asked, and she pressed her lips together, like she didn't want to be the one to say it. "He said you have to go straight to Avalon after returning to Earth. You've already gone against that by trying to help me get the staff. If you try rescuing me from that island, who knows what'll happen?"

"What'll happen is that you'll be safe."

"You can't know that."

She swallowed, since she must have known it was true. Prince Devyn's words had been more than clear.

"He said you need to put the greater good above your personal interests," I continued. "You need to put your duties as the Queen of Wands above our friendship."

"No," she said, as stubborn as ever.

Julian stood next to her, and he placed a hand lovingly on her shoulder. But she didn't notice. She was focused only on me.

"You're my best friend," she said. "I'm not going to abandon you. I'm going to bring you home."

I looked up to Julian, hoping he understood and would make sure she got to Avalon as soon as possible.

He gave me a small nod, and I relaxed slightly.

I glanced at my watch.

Less than a minute to go.

Reed lowered himself to his knees in front of me and took my hands in his. His hands were warm, and the intensity in his dark gaze took my breath away. "You're right—Selena has to return to Avalon," he said. "But I don't. And I'm going to get you off that island."

"I thought you didn't care."

"I didn't mean that." He squeezed my hands so tightly that it hurt. "I care more than you know."

I froze, speechless. Because I never knew what to think when it came to Reed.

Determination flashed in his eyes, and the next thing I knew, his lips were on mine and he was kissing me like his life depended on it. Warmth flooded through me, and my heart leaped. I sank into the kiss, blissfully unaware of anything but the fact that Reed was kissing me, and that unlike last time with Aphrodite's girdle, it was of his own free will.

For a moment, everything was perfect.

Then ice flooded through me, starting at my center and expanding outward. It pulled at me. Called to me.

Torrence, a voice I'd never wanted to hear again echoed through my mind. Circe. *Time's up.*

I gripped Reed's hands tighter and pulled him close, as if he could keep me anchored to the beach.

But it was no use.

Because one second, his lips were on mine.

The next, he was gone, and cold nothingness consumed me.

44

SELENA

My hand fell through the place where Torrence's shoulder had been.

No.

Reed sat right in front of me. Anger swirled in his eyes, and they flashed black. He spun around, ran to the opposite side of the cove, and threw smoky magic at the side of the cliff. Pieces of rock exploded loose with a bang and fell like an avalanche to the sand. He hit the side of the cliff again and again, until there was a giant mound of broken rock in front of him.

"Reed!" I screamed, and I ran toward him. "Stop."

He didn't stop.

So I grabbed his arm and jolted him with electricity. Not enough to do serious damage, but enough to shock him.

His body lit up with it, and he screamed, shaking from the force of my power. His magic disappeared, and his eyes turned back to normal.

I let go, and he collapsed down to his knees.

He cursed at me and shot black magic at me. But I held the wand in front of me and threw my magic into it. My tri-colored magic spread out like a shield and blocked his attack. Wind rushed around the two of us.

"Stop," I said again, still holding off his magic. He was surprisingly strong, but I was stronger. "We're going to go there and get her. Together. But we can't do that until you get ahold of yourself."

He shot another burst of black magic at the cliff.

Then, he stopped. The air around us stilled. He sat down on the sand, breathing heavily, and wiped at his cheek.

Is he crying?

He lowered his arm and stared blankly at the bloodied place in the sand where the dragon had been. "I failed her." He sounded so broken—so fragile.

"If anyone failed her, it was me," I said. "I could have killed him with my lightning." It would have been so easy. Except not. Because it would have been murder. And I knew even now, if I were back in that moment, I wouldn't have been able to kill that man in cold blood. "But I couldn't. And now, she's gone."

"It's not your fault," Julian said. He must have come over while I'd been holding off Reed. "Torrence made the decision to enter into the deal with Circe. She knew what the consequences would be if she failed. And she asked you not to come after her."

I waited for him to add something more—to say that obviously we were going after her anyway.

He didn't.

"What are you suggesting?" I stepped backward, feeling like I was talking to a stranger.

"I'm suggesting that you listen to Prince Devyn's final words," he said. "His actions led you to claiming your title of Queen of Wands. He made sure you got home. He had no reason to lie to you about what would happen if you went after Torrence."

"I don't care."

"But I do." He reached for my wrist and held it tightly. "Nothing good can happen from you going after her."

I glared at him. "You can't know that."

"Maybe I can't," he said. "But your father could."

"That man *wasn't* my father." My magic buzzed through me, and I yanked my hand out of his grip. No matter how angry I was at him, I still didn't want to electrocute him. "Prince Jacen of Avalon is my father."

"You're right," he said. "I'm sorry."

"Thank you."

"But I stand by what I said," he continued. "You should listen to Prince Devyn. Return to Avalon. Let the Nephilim army figure out how to help Torrence. If they're as strong as you claim, they should be able to do this."

Rage swirled inside me like a hurricane, and thunder rolled through the sky. "I have more power than anyone on Avalon," I said. "And we have no idea what Circe wants with Torrence. The longer she's there, the more danger she's in. So I'm going to Circe's island. I can either drop you off at the Vale first, or you can come with me and Reed. But I'm going, and you can't stop me."

Reed got up and stood next to me, facing Julian. "What's it gonna be?" he asked. "Are you coming or not?"

Julian watched me, like he was waiting for me to rethink my decision.

But my decision had been made long before Torrence had disappeared.

He must have realized that, because finally, he nodded. "Fine," he said. "If you're going to Circe's island, then I'm coming with you."

"Good," I said, and I turned to Reed. "You've been to Circe's island. Take us there, now."

"I can only take one of you at a time."

"Right." How could I have momentarily forgotten that teleporting didn't work like lightning-travel? "Take me first." I didn't want Julian to be alone on that island, not even for a second. "Then I'll come back for Julian."

"All right." He took a deep breath, then reached forward to take my hands.

"STOP!" someone yelled from behind us.

I lowered my hands and spun around to where the voice was coming from.

Two people were running toward us from the opposite end of the cove. One of them—a person in a cloak—stopped midway across the beach. The other met us where we were.

I stared, shocked at she got closer.

"Skylar?" I asked, since I'd recognize that bright red hair anywhere. The same red hair as the Queen of Swords, but Skylar was older. She was the Queen of Swords' mother—the prophetess of Avalon.

"Selena," she said, still catching her breath. "Julian. Reed."

"How do you know Julian's name?" I asked. "And how did you know we were here?"

"I'm a prophetess," she said with a small smile. "And I need to talk to you before you leave for Aeaea."

I studied the woman across the beach—presumably a witch who'd teleported Skylar here. Her hood covered her eyes, so I could only see the bottom half of her face. "Come closer," I said, curious who she was. I knew pretty much every witch on Avalon. "We won't hurt you."

"She's new to Avalon," Skylar said quickly. "She's powerful, but shy. But she's no matter. Because I had a vision, and I needed to stop you before it was too late."

"What type of vision?" My heart raced, worried about where this was headed.

"You can't go after Torrence," she said. "You have to go back home. Now."

Thunder cracked overhead. The wand's crystals glowed, casting their blue light on Skylar's face.

"Torrence is my best friend," I said, and the wind picked up, my hair blowing in the breeze. The waves crashed louder on the shore. "I would still be trapped in the Otherworld if it wasn't for her. Why's everyone trying to stop me from helping her?"

"I'm not stopping you," Reed said. "I'm going to Aeaea, with or without you."

"I know," I said. "I'm going with you."

"Then who cares what she says? Let's get out of here."

But I kept my gaze locked on Skylar's. Because her eyes were wide, and she looked… panicked.

Chills raced up my arms. Because the prophetess was always calm.

Something was seriously wrong.

"Tell us what you saw," I said.

"You and Julian can't go with Reed to save Torrence."

"Why not?"

"Because it has to be Reed—and *only* Reed—who goes after her."

"How do you know this?" I crossed my arms, since something wasn't adding up. "You don't have omniscient sight. You can only see the future as it's going to happen without any interference."

"Before I got here, you and Julian were going to go with Reed to Aeaea," she said. "I saw what was going to happen if the three of you followed through with that decision. Every terrible, awful bit of it. You see, to win the war against the demons, each Queen must fight in the final battle. But if you go to Aeaea, you'll die. Avalon will be no more. The people you love most will be gone."

"My parents?" I could barely get the words out.

She nodded, and watched me like the fate of the world depended on my decision.

Which it did. But I refused to believe it all came down to this.

"That's only one possible future," I said, desperate for another option. "There has to be another way. Tell me how I'll die. I can change it. I can do something differently once I get to Aeaea."

"If you go to Aeaea, you'll doom us all." Her voice was filled with so much certainty that it chilled me to the bone. "This moment is the turning point. And you need to go home with your soulmate."

"But *why?*"

"Because you're the Queen of Wands," she said simply. "Your duty is to your people. If you turn your back on them and go after Torrence, the war against the demons will be lost. The demons' power will grow, and Earth will be theirs."

Horror clung to my skin. I wanted to say she was wrong. I wanted to say that going after Torrence didn't mean I was turning my back on Avalon and the half-bloods in the Otherworld.

But I couldn't.

Because while cryptic, Skylar's vision matched up perfectly with Prince Devyn's warning. And I couldn't ignore that, no matter how badly I wanted to.

"So I can't go after Torrence," I said slowly, still trying to process the thought of *not* going after my best friend. "But Reed can?"

"Yes," she said. "However, teleporting to Aeaea with no plan or strategy won't be enough. Circe's an immortal sorceress—an extremely powerful one, at that. He'll need backup."

"What kind of backup?"

"He'll need the help of the Supreme Mages."

I tilted my head and studied her. Something wasn't right. Because I'd seen Skylar read the future before, and she always used her tarot cards.

"How did you know that so quickly?" I asked. "Now that we're on a path to a different future, wouldn't you have needed to look into your cards again to see what changed?"

She stilled, like she hadn't expected the question. "I'm not the only one who has insight into the future," she said simply. "I've spoken with others, and I'm speaking with you here and *now* for a reason."

"Is she your source?" I asked, and I looked to the hooded witch in the background.

Neither of them replied.

So I moved toward the witch to demand answers.

But with her vampire speed, Skylar was faster.

She took the witch's hands, and said, "Now."

"Wait!" I screamed, and a gust of wind rushed through the cove.

The two of them faded and flickered out like a faulty hologram, but not before the wind blew back the witch's hood.

A glowing crown of pointed, jagged, clear crystals sat on top of the girl's brown hair.

Gemma?

I stared absently at the place where they'd been standing. I'd only seen her profile, and only for less than a second, but I could have sworn...

"Did you guys see that?" I asked Julian and Reed.

"The crown?" Reed asked.

"No," I said. "I mean, yes, I saw the crown. But did you see who was *wearing* the crown?"

"Her hair was everywhere," Julian said. "But you were closer than we were."

"Why?" Reed asked. "Do you know her?"

"I'm not sure." I stared at the spot where they'd disappeared, unsure about what I'd seen. Because it didn't make sense. Gemma had barely any magic. Not anywhere close to the amount she'd need to teleport herself *and* another person. The witch who'd taken Skylar did seem to struggle with the teleporting—I'd never seen a witch fade and flicker out like a dying holo-gram before—but it was way more than Gemma would have been able to do.

Plus, I'd erased her memory of meeting us. I'd erased her memory of even knowing she had magic at all.

What were the chances that she'd have teleported to Avalon, picked up Skylar, and then teleported back here in time for Skylar to warn me?

Slim to none.

But I needed to check. Just to make sure.

"Wait here," I told them. "I'll be back in a second."

"Where are you—"

I teleported out before hearing the end of Julian's sentence, and landed in front of two tall pine trees at the edge of a parking lot that looked out to the ocean.

Twin Pines Café. Twinkling white Christmas lights lit up the outside of the building, the majority of them strung along the porch.

I hadn't noticed them before, since we'd gotten there before sunset. But Christmas was in a little more than a week. It was so strange to think that while Torrence, Reed, Julian, and I had been journeying through the Otherworld to find a cure to the plague, everyone on Earth was happily preparing for Christmas.

I walked across the parking lot and peeked through one of the windows.

Gemma stood behind the register, ringing up a customer. She was dressed the exact same as earlier. And while her hair was the same brown as the witch's who'd teleported Skylar to see us, it was shorter.

I breathed out in relief. I'd been imagining things.

Another girl worked behind the counter, and Mira was nowhere to be seen. Of course—Ethan would have already been by to pick her up.

Ethan, who was likely blissfully unaware of the fact that his father was dead.

Ethan, who was also, probably, a dragon.

Guilt weighed me down like a wet blanket, and I breathed slowly to get ahold of myself. We technically hadn't killed that man… but he'd still be alive if it weren't for us. I knew it deep in my soul.

I'd seen and caused too much death in the past few weeks to deal with. If I obsessed over it now, it would consume me.

I'd never be able to forgive myself for everything I'd done. I didn't *want* to forgive myself. I deserved to live with this guilt forever.

But there were still people I could help.

I could still free the half-bloods. So that was what I was going to do.

I teleported back to the beach, where Julian and Reed were pacing around, not-so-patiently waiting for me.

"What was that?" Rage burned in Julian's eyes. "You can't just teleport out like that without saying where you're going."

"I was only gone for a few seconds."

"And it was a few seconds too long."

He stared at me, and I knew I owed him an explanation.

"I thought the hooded witch might have been Gemma," I said. "So I teleported back to the café to see if she was there."

"And?"

"She was there," I said. "And her hair was shorter than the witch who'd teleported Skylar. Whoever the hooded witch was, it wasn't her."

Reed kicked at the sand near his feet and sent it flying toward the ocean. "Obviously it wasn't Gemma," he said. "Gemma doesn't have enough magic to cast a spell, let alone enough to teleport. Now, are we going, or what?" He held out his hands to me and Julian, just like he had earlier.

"To Aeaea?" I asked.

"No—to Disney World." He glared at me. "Of course I mean Aeaea."

Julian watched me just as curiously as Reed.

I shuffled my feet in the sand, thinking about what Skylar and Prince Devyn had said. I needed to put my duties as Queen of Wands before my personal interests.

Otherwise, you'll die, I remembered Skylar's warning. *The people you love most will be gone. The demons will win the war, and Earth will be theirs.*

I pressed my fingers to my temples, thinking. I needed to make a decision, and I needed to make it now.

Promise me you won't come after me, Torrence's voice echoed in my mind.

Maybe everyone kept telling me not to go to Aeaea for a reason. A bigger reason that I might not be aware of yet. Similar to how the Faerie Games had a larger reason behind them than I ever could have imagined.

I looked to Julian, who watched me, waiting. "What do you think I should do?" I asked.

"I think you should do what Prince Devyn told you to do before nominating you for the Games, and trust yourself and your instincts," he said. "He told you that your instincts would help you in the Games, and they did. There's no reason to think they won't help you now, too."

I nodded, and paused to think. Because before Skylar's visit, I would have gone after Torrence.

But now...

I turned to Reed. "What are the Supreme Mages?" I asked.

"They're the most powerful group of mages in Mystica," he said. "They're a task force, kind of like a magical version of the FBI. They seek out mages who've gone dark and lock them away."

"Gone dark?"

"Succumbed to dark magic," he explained. "None of us are born fully light or fully dark. Most mages are able to use both types of magic with no problems. But occasionally, mages are born who can harness an exceptional amount of dark magic. Power that strong can be overwhelming. It ends up controlling them. For the safety of the realm—for *all* realms—they have to be sent away."

"Where do they send them?" I ask.

"A prison realm that's impossible to escape," he said. "Ember."

"The same Ember where the fae send their prisoners?"

"Yep," he said. "The only way to create a realm strong enough to contain such dark magic was for the fae and the mages to work together. But besides that, the fae and the mages have an agreement. We don't bother them as long as they don't bother us—and we both send our worst criminals to Ember."

"Gods help anyone who gets sent to Ember," Julian said. "I can't imagine that the mages and fae there are living in harmony."

"Probably not," I said. "But Ember isn't our concern right now. The Supreme Mages are. If they take care of Circe, Torrence will be free. Reed—do you think you can convince them to help you?"

"So it's just me now," he said. "You're not coming anymore?"

"You didn't answer my question."

"Fine," he said. "Circe's a sorceress, and a dark one at that. She's stronger than a mage. So yes, it's possible that the Supreme Mages might see her as a threat, and be willing to go after her. They'll likely be intrigued when I tell them about Torrence—enough that they might be willing to free her from Aeaea, so they can learn how she's able to use mage magic."

I nodded, since I was interested in learning the answer to that, too.

"And the Supreme Mages are strong enough to take on Circe?" I asked.

"They're the most powerful mages in the Universe. If anyone can take on Circe, it's them."

"All right," I said. "But I have one more question."

He looked at me to continue.

"Before Torrence was taken away, you said you cared about her more than she knew. So if I'm going to trust you with my best friend's life, then I need to know—do you love her?"

"Yes," he said without a second thought. "And I'm going to do everything in my power to save her, so I can tell her myself."

"Then I expect you to do just that," I said, and then I looked to Julian. "What do you think?"

"This plan is exactly what Avalon's prophetess recommended," he said. "I believe that should speak for itself."

I straightened my shoulders, feeling much more confident with the decision—especially now that I knew

Reed cared about Torrence as much as I did. "It's settled, then," I said. "We'll bring Julian to the Vale, and see him and his family off on Avalon's trials. Then, the two of us will go straight back to Avalon. Because we have a lot to do, and not much time to do it."

45

SELENA

JULIAN and his family were in excellent hands at the Vale. King Alexander himself saw them down the steps that would lead them to the portal. Once through the portal, they'd land on an anchor island that served as the starting point of the trials. What happened during the trials was secret, and as someone who was born on Avalon, I didn't know what he was supposed to expect. Reed knew, but like everyone else who'd gone through the trials, he said nothing.

All I knew was that I was positive Julian and his family would pass.

And the moment Reed and I were back home, he was going to go to his sisters so they could get him an audience with the Supreme Mages.

"We've got this," I said to Reed after leaving the boundary of the Vale.

Situated between the snow-covered peaks of the Canadian Rocky Mountains, the kingdom was stunning. I wouldn't have thought it possible for such tall, majestic mountains to exist without seeing them myself.

But I didn't have time to get distracted by the kingdom's beauty. Besides, it was freezing—a bone-chilling cold I hadn't felt since trekking through Hypernia.

So Reed and I nodded at each other, took each other's hands, and teleported out.

I arrived in the middle of my bedroom, facing the fireplace. Fresh logs sat inside of it. Everything in my room was clean and perfect, like it was waiting for me to come back. Even my desk was perfectly arranged with my books for school.

The only thing that felt out of place was me.

Electricity hummed over my skin, and I shot a small bolt of lightning into the hearth. It burst with flames that danced across the logs.

I stared emptily into the fire, and then turned to look at my four-poster bed, remembering standing there with Torrence all those weeks ago when she'd given me the transformation potion.

It felt like a lifetime ago.

Grief for my best friend exploded in my chest.

Thunder rolled overhead so loudly that the castle walls shook, and lightning brightened the sky. I walked over to my large window and placed my hands on the sill. Avalon's mountains were as green and beautiful as ever. But while it was mid-day, the cloud cover made it look like night.

The people milling around outside stopped and looked up at the lightning-filled sky, their mouths open in shock.

Because it never stormed on Avalon. The island always had perfect weather. It was lush and green because of magic—not because of rain.

Something banged behind me—the door being pushed open so forcefully that it slammed into the wall —and I jumped and spun around.

My mom and dad rushed inside and enveloped me in a hug.

I sank into their embrace. Then the floodgates burst open, and suddenly I was crying so much that it seemed impossible to stop. My mom cried, too, and my dad hugged me tighter. They kept repeating my name and repeating that I was back home, like they were afraid if they stopped saying it, it wouldn't be true.

"How'd you know I was back?" I asked after we eventually pulled away.

Both of them looked thinner and more gaunt than I'd ever seen them.

"Skylar told us we'd find you in your room after the sky filled with lightning. We rushed here the moment we saw the storm." My mom smiled at me so much that I didn't think she'd ever stop. She still held onto my hand, and her cheeks were flushed red with excitement.

My dad, on the other hand, was paler than ever. His skin was thin and transparent, and he looked like he'd aged ten years, even though vampires were immortal.

"Did the fae give you blood while you were trapped at the Crossroads?" I asked him.

"They provided food and water, but no blood," he said simply.

"But they said they'd given you everything you needed. And they can't lie."

Then I realized that they technically hadn't lied. Because without blood, a vampire didn't die. They simply shut down until someone trickled blood down their throat to revive them. The process of a vampire shutting down was supposed to be more excruciating than anyone could imagine. It supposedly felt like burning alive from the inside out.

Like what I'd nearly done to myself when I'd tried creating the portal from the Otherworld to Avalon.

Anger buzzed through me at the thought of my dad going through that. I pulled away from both him and my mom, not wanting to accidentally electrocute them with my magic.

"I was there with Bella." My dad glanced at the door, where Bella stood in the frame. Sage and Thomas were behind her. "She voluntarily provided me with the minimal amount of blood I needed to function."

I looked to the witch and lowered my eyes in respect. Witch blood supposedly tasted awful to vampires, but it would still do the trick. "Thank you." The words slipped out, as natural as ever.

"Don't mention it," she said. "Anyone else would have done the same."

"They wouldn't have, and you know it," said Sage.

Bella didn't refute it. Instead, she stepped inside my room, looked around, and asked, "Where's Torrence?"

The words were a punch to my gut.

"How much did you tell them?" I asked Sage and Thomas, who'd also joined us inside.

"Everything," Sage said. "At least, everything that the four of us knew."

Which meant Bella knew about the deal Torrence had made with Circe. And from the worried—yet still hopeful—look in her eyes, she was waiting for me to say anything *but* what had ended up happening.

I wished I could.

But as it was, I might as well be out with it.

"We went to King Devin, and he offered us a trade," I said. "But we couldn't get him what he wanted in time. I'm sorry."

"So Torrence…"

"Disappeared the moment time was up."

Bella cursed and turned away from me. "How am I supposed to tell Amber?" she asked. "She already thought she lost her once. She can't go through this again."

"Torrence isn't dead," I said, and tendrils of electricity buzzed between my fingers.

My mom glanced at it, and horror splashed across her face. Only for a second, but I saw it before she hid it.

Was she disgusted by my magic, or by my scars?

Maybe both.

I looked away from her, refocused on Bella, and reined in my magic. "Reed's going to get her off that island," I said. "He's with his sisters now, filling them in on our plan."

"I want in," she said, and then, she disappeared. Teleported out, presumably to find the mages.

Thomas looked to me. "What did King Devin want?" he asked.

"A dragon heart," I said simply.

My mom gasped, and my dad froze. But neither of them said a word.

"I assume you went straight to Utopia?" Sage asked.

"Yep. Torrence put together the connection, too." From there, we sat down on my bed and I told them everything that had happened in Utopia, and in Australia.

"Maybe I should have killed him with my lightning," I said once I'd finished. "He died anyway. At least that way, maybe Torrence would be back home, too."

"It sounds like Lavinia was on your trail no matter what." Sage snarled. "*She's* the one you should have killed."

"She came out of nowhere, and it happened so quickly. I don't think any of us fully processed it until she was gone." The memory of the dragon's blood spurting from his neck flashed through my mind, and I tried to shake it away, but I couldn't.

It wasn't just his death that had happened so fast. *Everything* since returning to Earth felt like it had happened in the blink of an eye.

I was hungry, and exhausted, and I just wanted this to be over.

But it would never be over.

This was my life now. I'd wanted magic, and now I had it.

I supposed that no wish granted ever came without consequences.

"The question is, what does Lilith want with a dragon heart?" Thomas asked, pulling me out of my spiraling thoughts.

No one said a word. Because as far as I knew, none of us had known that dragons existed until today. We'd also never been able to locate Lilith, no matter how many supernaturals we put on the task.

She was just as hidden wherever she was as we were on Avalon.

"I don't know, but we'll have to return to this later." My mom reached for my hand, not pausing at the sight of my scars. "Because right now, my husband and I would like time alone with our daughter."

46

SELENA

WE WENT BACK TO MY PARENTS' room, and all day and well into the night, I told them everything that had happened while I'd been in the Otherworld. Well, *most* everything. I kept the more intimate moments between me and Julian to myself.

My parents didn't pipe in with judgments about my decisions. Instead, they listened patiently and respect-fully, not commenting one way or the other.

I supposed they were holding back their opinions until they knew everything. But also, as the Queen of Wands, I was considered an equal with my mom now, and a higher rank than my dad. While I was still their daughter, and the worry they expressed during the more troubling parts of the tale were apparent, the dynamics between us had changed.

It was near dawn when I finished. I kept yawning, and could barely keep my eyes open.

Unable to gather the energy to walk or teleport back to my room, I slept on their couch. Although it wasn't completely because I couldn't teleport to my room. It had been a while since I'd slept alone—minus when Sorcha was keeping me prisoner—and I felt safer with my parents close by.

The sun was already shining brightly through the windows when I awoke the next morning. I glanced at the clock on the mantle—2:04 PM.

My parents were nowhere to be found. So I sent my mom a fire message to let her know where I'd gone, and teleported to my bathroom to wash up.

After only being able to take baths in the Other-world, a shower felt amazing. I must have stayed in the shower for an hour, at least. But my thoughts were stuck on Torrence's last moments, and I kept playing out any other possible ways yesterday could have gone differently.

Where *exactly* had we gone wrong?

I didn't know. Maybe I'd never know. All I could do was pray that Reed and the Supreme Mages were successful in their mission to get her back.

In the meantime, I needed to focus on the people who were counting on me. The half-bloods in the

Otherworld. At least, the ones who'd survived the plague. I needed to free them, and then, I needed to get them the cure.

I needed to get *all* of the fae a cure. Yes, they had holy weapons to defend themselves and the domes I'd fortified to keep them safe, but it wasn't enough. The longer I waited, the more of them would get infected.

Realizing that I was wasting time, I turned off the water and dried off. I'd expected the jeans and sweatshirt I'd picked out to feel comforting—like home. Instead, the material felt coarse in comparison to the soft dresses and cloaks of the Otherworld. So I switched to lightweight shorts and a tank top instead. It wasn't perfect, but it was better. More freeing.

A look in the mirror showed that my skin had retained the soft, smooth glow it had taken on when I'd entered the Otherworld. And while fae wings were always hidden on Earth, Avalon was technically on a separate plane, anchored to Earth. I successfully removed the glamour, revealing my tri-colored wings. They sparkled with magic and hummed with tiny currents of electricity.

Feeling more like myself, I removed the Holy Wand from the ether again (I'd shown it to my parents last night), and stared at my reflection, readying myself for everything to come.

Even though I was home, things would never be like they were before. I was no longer Selena Pearce, the powerless daughter of Queen Annika and Prince Jacen, who needed to remain on Avalon to stay safe.

I was the Queen of Wands, and the chosen champion of Jupiter.

It was going to take time to discover my new place on Avalon. But I was ready to start— today.

My parents sent a fire message to my room that they'd had a late lunch delivered to their quarters, and were ready to continue our discussion whenever I was. So I teleported back to the hall outside their door, knocked, and they let me back in.

The small table was set, and a platter of round white fruit—mana—and a pitcher of Holy Water sat in the center. It looked bland and boring compared to the lavish meals in the Otherworld.

Why do I keep thinking about the Otherworld as if I miss it there?

Maybe I needed to stop comparing it to Avalon, and appreciate each for what it was. After all, like Prince Devyn had always told me, I was half-fae. The Otherworld was part of me, whether I liked it or not.

My parents must have spent a solid five minutes complimenting and examining my wings. Then we sat down, and we each took a piece of mana, cut into it, and started to eat.

Mine tasted like the finger sandwiches from the delicious platter that Princess Ryanne had served me and Julian the first time we were guests in her villa.

Aunt Ryanne.

It was going to take a while to get used to that.

"Your father and I met with the Queen of Swords and debriefed her on what's going on," my mom started. "We all agree that the half-blood slaves in the Otherworld must be freed."

"I didn't realize it was up for debate." I pressed my lips together, surprised at myself. Not because of *what* I'd said—it was the truth—but because of how easy it had been to talk back to my mom.

"Your decision to free them wasn't up for debate," she said. "As the Queen of Wands, it's your responsibility to do as you must for your people. Just like I have to do what's best for my people—the citizens of Avalon—and the Queen of Swords must do what's best for the Nephilim army."

"So you're going to help me?"

"Usually, the interests of the Queens align," she said, and my heart dropped with worry that she was going to say this was an exception to the rule. "And it's in all of our best interests to free the half-bloods."

My father took a sip of his water, then set down the glass. "We've been in a stalemate with the demons for over sixteen years," he said. "We don't know the extent of what Lilith is capable of, especially now that she has the dragon heart. And the longer the demons continue to work with the dark witch circles, the more dangerous they become. That was evident with the plague Lavinia created."

I nodded, although there was no way for my parents to fully understand how devastating the plague was without seeing it for themselves.

"Like I mentioned last night, the free half-bloods have powerful magic," I said. "They can help us against the demons."

"We agree," my mom said. "Especially because once the half-bloods are free, they'll likely want the option to leave the realm that's kept them oppressed for over a thousand years. I'm happy to open Avalon's doors to any half-bloods who pass the island's trials—and to any full fae who wish to join us, too."

"Great." I sat straighter, ready to move forward. "To launch the sort of large scale attack necessary to free an entire group of people and lead them to Avalon, we're going to need portal tokens. Lots and lots of portal tokens. From there, we'll need to defend ourselves against the fae while I free the half-bloods and bring them to the portal locations. I'm going to need the Queen of Swords' help—and help from the Nephilim army—to pull this off. Should we bring her in and start discussing a plan?"

My parents gave each other a long look, and neither of them said a word.

I shifted uncomfortably in my seat.

Had I said something wrong? I hoped not. It felt good to have a purpose again. To feel like I could *do something* to help people, instead of obsessing about what I could have done differently to get Torrence that staff.

My mom spoke first. "If we invade the Otherworld, it won't help anyone, especially if the realm is in as bad of a condition as you described," she said. "There will be casualties—many of them the half-bloods you're trying to help. They won't be of use to anyone if they're dead."

"But how else am I supposed to free them?" I asked. "The fae aren't going to stand back as I free their slaves, and they're certainly not going to lend us their portal tokens so I can whisk the half-bloods off to Avalon."

"I never said they would. But you told us the Empress is ready to meet at the Crossroads, to discuss a deal so she can provide the cure to her people. And while I have my fair share of issues with the Empress after all you've told me about her, she doesn't sound completely unreasonable."

"But the Empress was in charge of binding the half-bloods in the first place," I sputtered, shocked by what my mom seemed to be suggesting. "She's not just going to—"

I paused mid-sentence, realizing my mom's point. Sorcha desperately needed our help. And she was always open to deals. So why not try going the diplomatic route first?

If it worked, a huge number of lives would be saved.

If it didn't, then I had the support of my mom and the Queen of Swords for whatever needed to come next.

"The half-bloods in the Sanctuary called you Queen Gloriana returned." My mom smiled, looking at me like she was seeing me in an entirely new light. "Do you feel this is true?"

"No," I said. "But I *am* the Queen of Wands. I'm the only one who can free the half-bloods. As a half-blood myself, I'm *their* queen, and I'm not going to fail them."

47

SELENA

JULIAN and his family passed Avalon's trials, as I knew they would. My parents welcomed them like family and set them up in the castle with quarters fit for royalty.

Despite being soulmates, my parents insisted that Julian live with his family. Once I was eighteen, I could live with whomever I chose. Until then, I was to follow their rules.

As if that would stop Julian from teleporting into my room each night.

At dinner, we discovered that holy water neutralized Vita's stomach condition. But the witches had already set to work on developing a more permanent solution. It was going to take time, but the holy water could hold her over while she waited.

The next day, Julian and I said goodbye to our families, and we teleported to the Crossroads. The shimmering pond, flowering bushes and trees, and colorful birds chirping all around reminded me of the Otherworld.

It was so pristine and tranquil that it was hard to imagine that for the past three months, this place had been a prison for my dad and Bella. Not even a single blade of grass looked like it had been trampled upon. And the grass made it clear where the Crossroads began, because inside the circle it was a darker, lusher shade of green that glimmered with magic.

There was no reason to wait for the full moon, since Julian and I could defend ourselves if Sorcha tried anything against us. There would also be no purpose in Sorcha trying anything against us. And if there was anything good I could say about the Empress, it was that she didn't do anything without purpose.

"Ready?" Julian asked.

"Yes." I stepped over the line in the grass. Inside the Crossroads, the sweet smell of honey wine lingered in the air.

During our many conversations in Vesta's Villa, Bridget had taught me how the ancient fae who had lived on Earth had used the Crossroads as a peaceful meeting place between realms. The Crossroads inherently relied on blood magic to connect Earth to the

Otherworld, but it was far easier for a fae to make the connection than for other supernatural creatures.

I kneeled down next to the lake. The water was so clear that I could see straight to the bottom. I cupped my hands together, dipped them into the water, brought them up to my mouth, and drank. The water was surprisingly sweet, like honey. I sipped it all down, and my head tingled, like I'd just drank an entire glass of wine.

"You okay?" Julian asked.

I blinked a few times, and the buzz subsided. "I'm good," I said, and I stood up slowly, glad when the ground remained steady beneath my feet. Then I held my hand out toward Julian with my palm to the sky.

He pulled a small knife from the ether and pricked the pad of my index finger. I bit the inside of my cheek to stop from grimacing. Pain was always worse when you knew it was coming, even if it was something as small as a pricked finger.

A drop of blood popped out in a bubble over my skin. I held my hand over the pond, turned it over, and squeezed my finger so three drops fell into the water.

Liquid taken from the Crossroads, and liquid given to it.

"I invite Empress Sorcha and one half-blood ambassador of her choosing to meet me, Selena Pearce, and my soulmate, Julian Kane, at the Crossroads of their own free will."

For a moment, I worried it hadn't worked.

Then the Empress and her half-blood advisor, Aeliana, shimmered into existence ahead of us. They stood on top of the water, like it was a clear sheet of ice.

Sorcha wore a long, white dress threaded with gold silk. Her blonde hair flowed freely down her back, and of course, her tall, sparkly crown sat on her head. Aeliana wore a gold dress threaded with silver, and she smiled slightly when her gray eyes met mine.

Sorcha's diamond wings sparkled in the sunlight. She took a deep breath and looked around. "Ancient Ireland," she said as she gazed past the Crossroads, out to the rolling green hills that spread out in every direction. "The Earthly reflection of the Otherworld. Or the Otherworld's reflection of Earth. No one quite knows which came first."

"What?" I asked, momentarily sidetracked from the reason why we were there.

"Surely you notice how similar this area looks to the Central Plainlands?"

"I do. But what do you mean that it's a 'reflection?'"

"Each supernatural realm reflects an area on Earth," she explained. "There are slight differences, but think of it like two places occupying the same space, one layered on top of the other. The supernatural realms in one universe, and Earth in another."

"So the supernatural realms are all on the same planet? A reflection planet of Earth?"

"That's the simplest way to describe it," she said. "However, our realms are all separated from one another, whereas you can travel freely between your countries and continents."

I nodded as I worked through the implications of what she was saying. "How many other realms are there?" I asked.

"That's a question that not even the fae have an answer to," she said. "And it's certainly of no importance now. Because I trust you called for me with a proposition in mind?"

"Yes." I pulled the Holy Wand from the ether, and its crystals glowed blue. "Avalon is interested in an alliance with the Otherworld. We'll help you rid your realm of the afflicted by supplying you with as much of the cure as we can, and by sending one-fourth of the Nephilim army to the Otherworld to slay the zombies until they're gone. In return, you'll allow me to free the half-bloods from bondage, and you'll allow them to come to Earth if they please."

"Why are you so interested in the half-bloods?" she asked.

"I'm a half-blood," I said. "So is my soulmate."

Julian's face was a deadly mask of calm.

"You're half-fae, half-witch, the chosen champion of Jupiter, and the Queen of Wands," she said. "Julian is the chosen champion of Mars. Both of you have far more magic than a simple half-blood—even a freed one— could ever dream of."

She sounded so convinced that I would have believed her—if I didn't know better.

"You can drop the act," I said.

Confusion passed over her face. "What act?"

"We know that free half-bloods have as much magic as full fae. You may have hid it from the rest of the Otherworld, but we know the truth."

"I'm afraid I have no idea what you're talking about."

I opened my mouth to accuse her of lying. Then I shut it, since she couldn't lie.

Sorcha turned to Aeliana. "Do you know what she speaks of?" she asked her advisor.

"The Queen of Wands speaks the truth," Aeliana said simply. "I recommend listening to her."

Excitement flooded my body, but I took a deep breath to squash it. Because this wasn't over yet.

"Very well." Sorcha was a master of hiding her emotions, so whatever she thought about what I'd just said remained hidden. "You say the half-bloods have as much magic as the fae. But half-bloods aren't immortal. As far as I—and everyone else I know in the Otherworld —are aware, they only have a small bit of magic."

"That may be what you believe," I said. "But you're the Empress. How is it possible that you don't know the truth?"

"I might be the Empress, but I'm not all-knowing," she said. "Between Queen Gloriana's time and my own, most information about life during and before the First Queen's reign was lost."

"How could that happen?" I asked.

"It's a long story, but the basics are this. After Queen Gloriana was murdered, her younger sister—Queen Norah—took the throne. Queen Norah invented the process of using royal fae blood to bind the half-bloods' magic. She ruled for centuries, and she hated the half-bloods, since a half-blood killed her sister. The half-bloods of her time lived in far worse conditions than the half-bloods do now.

"Queen Norah ruled until the start of the Century of Fifty Queens, when she was killed by the first of the fifty queens to seize power—Queen Brielle," she continued. "But Queen Brielle didn't maintain her power for long. She was killed by another usurper, that queen was killed by another, then she by another, and so forth. The Otherworld divided into multiple opposing factions.

War raged throughout the realm. Most of our books were burned, and the majority of fae in the Otherworld were killed. Our society regressed thousands of years during that single century."

"It sounds similar to Earth's Dark Ages," I said.

"Very similar," she agreed. "The Dark Ages actually started when the fae on Earth were cursed by dark witches to be allergic to iron, and were forced to retreat back to the Otherworld. We returned to a realm that had been at war for a century. Our kind had nearly driven ourselves to extinction, and those still alive lived like barbarians. And so, with the support of the gods, I named myself the Empress and formed the Empire. The Otherworld would be a very different place if I hadn't stepped in. It might not even exist at all. I shaped the Otherworld into the civil society it is today."

"'Civil' isn't a word I'd used to describe the Other-world," I said bitterly.

"Than you wouldn't have wanted to see it during the Century of Fifty Queens."

"Most definitely not," I agreed. "But if you wanted to create a civil Empire, why keep the half-bloods in bondage?"

"Because the tattoos remind the half-bloods that one of their own murdered the First Queen, Gloriana. Her murder resulted in the downfall of the realm. The tattoos remind the half-bloods of their place in society, and that we can control what little magic they have."

Electricity buzzed over my scars and up over the Holy Wand, and a breeze blew around me. "An entire race isn't responsible for the actions of one person," I said.

"Perhaps not," she said. "But it stops them from trying to rise up against us again."

Fury swelled inside of me.

But I reminded myself of my goal, and forced myself to focus. "If you want the cure, and if you want Avalon's help against the afflicted, then you *will* allow me to free the half-bloods," I said. "And you'll allow them to leave the Otherworld—to go to *any* realm they choose."

"Calm yourself," she said. "We're here for a diplomatic conversation. I don't like being threatened."

I nodded, focused on breathing steadily, and pulled my magic inward.

The air around me stilled, the last bit of electricity disappeared, and the Empress nodded. "I want both of those things," she said slowly. "But what makes you so convinced that the half-bloods have magic as strong as full fae?"

"Because I've seen it for myself," I said. "Julian—show her your arm."

Julian removed his leather jacket, pushed up the

sleeve of his t-shirt, and showed Sorcha his bicep. As I already knew, there was no tattoo around it.

She narrowed her eyes, as if trying to see through glamour. She gave up after a few seconds. "How is this possible?" she asked.

"I removed his tattoo with the Holy Wand," I said, and then I looked to Aeliana. "Would you like me to remove yours, too?"

"Yes." She gave me a knowing smile. "I most certainly would."

"Kneel before me."

She did as I asked, and I pushed my multi-colored magic through the wand and out toward her. It surrounded her in a brilliant, sparkly orb. Tendrils of it entered her skin, and she pressed her lips together to muffle her screams.

Sorcha stepped toward me, as if she was going to try to stop me. "You're hurting her," she said.

"I'm freeing her."

I reversed the flow of my magic, and the tendrils sucked the red dots of poison out from Aeliana's body. The poison came out quickly at first, and then it slowed. Once there was none left, I let go.

The orb of light surrounding Aeliana shattered and disappeared.

She gasped and fell forward onto her palms. She

took a few quick breaths, and looked up to me, her gray eyes wide. "Did it work?" she asked.

"Take a look and see for yourself."

Aeliana forced herself to her feet. Then she reached for her sleeve and pulled it up to her elbow.

The tattoo was gone—as I knew it would be.

She stared at the unmarked skin for a few seconds, stunned.

"Test your magic," I told her. "Create fae light."

She let her sleeve fall back down, cupped her hands in front of herself, and focused.

An orb of golden light appeared in her palms, and her lips widened into a circle of surprise. Then she giggled like a young girl and released bubbles of golden light up to the sky, her eyes following them upward until they popped out above the trees.

The Empress cleared her throat.

Aeliana dropped her arms to her sides and stood straight, like a soldier.

"Is it true?" Sorcha asked. "Is your magic as powerful as a full fae's?"

"I can't say for sure, since I've never experienced what it feels like to have the magic of a full fae. But the magic inside of me feels strong." She turned to face me. "Strong enough to join Avalon's army and help you fight the demons, as payment for you granting me my freedom."

I opened my mouth to say she didn't have to pay me back, but then I closed it. Because Avalon needed the half-bloods' help.

There was too much at stake for me to free them and not accept their loyalty in return.

We all stared silently at Sorcha.

"You and the people of Avalon will help the Otherworld until all traces of the plague are gone from the realm?" she asked.

"We'll help until everyone infected is cured, and until everyone fully succumbed is turned to ash." I assumed that was what she meant, but with the fae, it never hurt to be careful of wording. "In return, you'll permit me to free the half-bloods. You'll do everything in your power to stop the fae from rebelling against me as I do so. You won't bind their magic ever again. And you'll allow them to leave the Otherworld to go to *any* realm of their choosing."

"I don't see why that won't be possible," she said. "However, you seem to think that all of the half-bloods will choose to go to Avalon. You're forgetting that the Otherworld has been their home for thousands of years. I believe many will choose to stay."

"They may," I said. "And those who stay will be angry.

But the fae are far more experienced fighters than the half-bloods, and I have no interest in seeing my people slain, especially so soon after they're freed."

"And I have no interest in having a civil war break out in the Otherworld."

"For once, we agree on something."

"I wouldn't say it's the first time," she said. "But you call the half-bloods 'your people.' Do you mean all of the half-bloods? Or only those who choose to go to Avalon?"

"I mean all of them," I said, ready to present the final part of my proposition. "And once they're free, the half-bloods will need a queen they can trust. A queen they know is powerful, and has their best interests at heart. A queen they'll be quick to follow."

Any traces of friendliness vanished from her face. "Are you threatening to try taking my place as ruler of the realm?"

"Not at all. You're the Empress of the Fae, and I have no interest in taking that title from you." She relaxed slightly, and I continued, "But the Otherworld is in ruins. Much like when you brought order back to the realm after the Century of Fifty Queens, a new political system—one where *all* citizens are free—will need to be established."

"There will be much to change," she agreed. "I

assume you have some thoughts on the method of approach?"

"I do," I said. "It won't happen overnight, but I believe that if we work together, we can prevent civil unrest and rebuild the Otherworld. So I'd like to rule by your side—as not only the Queen of Wands, but also as the Queen of the Half-Bloods."

She pursed her lips and stared at me.

She's going to say no.

My heart raced, and I tightened my grip around the wand. This had been going so well. I'd really thought it was going to work.

We had other options, but they were mainly violent. So many innocents would die.

Please, say yes.

"I won't step on your toes," I said, hoping to find the words that would convince her to agree. "In fact, I want to learn from you. I fully believe that if we work together, we can bring the Otherworld into a new Golden Age. One that Queen Gloriana would be proud of. I think that's what Prince Devyn wanted, too. I think it's why he went to such great lengths to ensure I stepped into my position as Queen of Wands, and to ensure that we met at the Crossroads like this today. Whatever we decide here will determine the fate of the Otherworld. And I want that fate to be a good one."

Julian's intense energy radiated from his spot beside me. If necessary, he was ready to fight.

I was, too.

But I hoped it wouldn't come down to that.

"If you try anything against me, I *will* turn on you," the Empress finally said.

"As you should," I replied. "But as long as you work with me, and as long as you don't turn against me and my people, I intend to work *with* you—not against you."

"And you promise that Avalon won't turn against me, either?"

"Avalon wants peace with the Otherworld so we can fight as allies against the demons," I said. "I'm a half-blood fae who was born and raised on Avalon, and whose soulmate is a half-blood born and raised in the Otherworld. I'm tied to both worlds. If you agree to the deal, I'll be the chain that links our kingdoms together."

The wand's crystals glowed, their light soft and steady. I'd said everything there was to say.

Now, it all came down to the Empress.

"Very well, Selena Pearce—chosen champion of Jupiter, Queen of Wands, and Queen of the Half-Bloods," she said with a genuine smile. "You have a deal."

48

SELENA

I STOOD outside the door that led to the small dining hall used for more intimate occasions, fiddling with the skirt of my gown with one hand and holding the Holy Wand with the other.

Vita stood next to me, radiant and happy. Her golden hair gleamed, as did her ice-blue eyes that matched Julian's. And while she was still thin, she no longer looked like she could be blown over by a bit of wind.

It was amazing what a few meals of mana and holy water could do for someone.

"Just wait until you see the inside," she gushed, seemingly oblivious to my nerves. "I helped Iris with the color palette—blue, violet, and silver, of course. And I was in charge of the flower arrangements. They bring a bit of the Otherworld to Avalon. You're going to love it."

"So you officially accepted her offer to become her apprentice?" I asked.

"Yes." She beamed. "I feel like I've finally found a place where I can be useful. You see, I've never been much of a fighter, which is funny considering my brother is the chosen champion of Mars. But while *he* might disagree, celebrations are important. They keep up our spirits and bring people together. We need events to look forward to while we're home—like celebrating the coronation of the Queen of Wands."

That was what tonight was about—my coronation. But after the Faerie Games, I'd had enough with official ceremonies for the next century. So my mom and Iris had settled on a small dinner in my honor with the leaders of Avalon.

A fire message appeared in Vita's hand. She unrolled it and smiled. "It's time," she all but squealed. "Are you ready?"

"Yes," I said, although really, I was ready to get this dinner over with and move on to more important matters, like the meeting with Sorcha, my mom, and the Queen of Swords tomorrow where we were going to discuss the details of our strategy for helping the Otherworld.

But after everything my mom and dad had been

through these past few weeks—not knowing if I'd ever come home, or if I was alive at all—I'd agreed to this one night to celebrate my return home.

Then, tomorrow, I had serious work to get started on.

Vita opened the door slightly, so we could hear everyone inside.

"And now, it's my honor to welcome our special guest for the evening," Iris said brightly. "The Queen of Wands, Selena Pearce!"

Vita flung open the door, and I zeroed in on the four most important people in the small group. My mom, my dad, Julian's mom, and Julian. They watched me with pride from the center of the room.

But before walking toward them, I glanced at Vita, who was watching me expectantly. "The room looks amazing," I told her, and she smiled again.

"You mean it?" she asked.

"Yes. I mean it."

And I did.

There were light blue, violet, and silver flowers *everywhere*. Petals were placed perfectly over the tables, the bouquet centerpieces overflowed with life, and flowering vines twisted along every piece of decor, including the chandeliers.

I glanced around, happy to see so many familiar faces. Thomas, Sage, the Queen of Swords, her mate Noah, Skylar, Bella, the three mages, and more. They were all dressed for the occasion, in everything from a tight black leather dress (Bella), to wide, colorful gowns (the mages.)

If only Torrence were here, I thought. *She'd love this.*

But she was going to be here—soon. With support from his sisters, Reed left for Mystica yesterday to speak with the Supreme Mages. He'd sworn not to return to Avalon unless Torrence was by his side.

And once Torrence was back on Avalon, we were going to have a party that would blow this one away. Because she *was* going to get back to Avalon. I refused to accept anything else.

"What are you waiting for?" Vita said, quietly and quickly. "Go inside."

Right. Of course.

I stepped inside, and petals representing each color of my magic drifted down from the ceiling and fluttered around me. Julian clapped, and the others followed suit, until applause sounded throughout the room. But this applause was tempered and quiet—a far cry from the raucous cries in the arena.

Now that I was a co-ruler of the Otherworld, I was going to make sure no one died in that arena ever again.

The applause died down, and all eyes were on me. "Thank you," I said, looking around at each of them. I needed to say something.

But what?

Nothing could truly encompass everything I'd been through in the past few weeks, and everything I'd discovered about myself along the journey.

So, short and sweet was going to have to work.

"The entire time I was in the Otherworld, I was fighting to get back to Avalon," I said, and the wand's crystals glowed, like it enjoyed the spotlight more than I did. "Back to my *home*. But while I was in the Otherworld, I found the Holy Wand and unlocked my magic as a half-blood fae. I realized I'm tied to the Otherworld as much as I'm tied to Avalon. So, as your Queen of Wands, and as the new Queen of the Half-Bloods, I'm going to be returning to the Otherworld to free the half-bloods from over a millennium of slavery. With our new alliance in place, I'm going to lead any fae from the Otherworld—whether half-blood or full fae—to Avalon. Together, we'll join forces and win the war against the demons once and for all."

At first, silence.

They hated that I was returning to the Otherworld.

Then my dad stepped forward and smiled. "To our Queen of Wands and the Queen of the Half-Bloods—my daughter, Selena Pearce," he said.

"To the Queen of Wands and the Queen of the Half-Bloods," everyone else repeated, then the champagne was poured, and the celebration began.

SELENA

As the guest of honor, I had to do my round of the room and speak to everyone in attendance.

"I think it's important that you resume your studies," Tari—the Headmaster at Avalon Academy—said. I rarely saw her in anything but her Avalon uniform, but tonight she wore a bright yellow, patterned dress that was striking against her dark skin. "You're still only sixteen, and have much more to learn about your witch magic."

"I definitely want to learn more about how to use my witch magic," I told her. "But as you know, the Other-world needs me. I'm going to have my hands full there for quite a while. However, I plan on taking a class or two next fall, once I hopefully have a small bit of extra time to devote to studying."

"I'm glad to hear it." She smiled. "But I'm thinking

that private tutoring might be in order, given how different your magic is from the other witches. And we'll have to condense everything into a shorter amount of time to fit with your schedule."

"That makes sense." I gazed around, since while I *did* intend on eventually resuming my studies, it was far from the first thing on my mind.

Finally, I located the person I was searching for in the far corner of the room. Skylar had pulled the hood of her silk cloak over her head, but the bright red hair sticking out from the sides of it made her impossible to miss.

"If you'll excuse me," I said to Tari. "I just saw someone I still need to thank."

"Of course." She sipped her champagne, and I picked up my glass to head toward Skylar.

She picked at a platter of grapes on the buffet, so her back was toward me as I approached.

"Skylar," I said softly, not wanting to startle her.

She spun slowly around, looking everywhere *except* at me. "Selena." She lowered her eyes and clasped her hands together in front of her waist. "I'm so grateful for your safe return."

"Thank you," I said.

"Is there something you wanted to speak with me about?" Her eyes darted around the room, like she wanted to escape this conversation at the first possible moment.

"I've been wanting to thank you for coming to me on the beach," I said, and she stilled, and swallowed. "As hard as it was to make that decision, so many people were saved by my returning to Avalon and meeting with the Empress of the Otherworld. We've already been getting as many vials of the cure to her as possible. Our alliance is going to change the lives of so many for the better."

"It will," she agreed.

"I was too wrapped up in my emotions to see it clearly before, but I can now. And I'm grateful to have your assurance that with Reed working with the Supreme Mages, they'll get Torrence off Circe's island."

"It was my pleasure." She glanced over my shoulder. "Now, if you'll excuse me—"

"Wait," I cut her off, and finally, she looked straight at me.

She seemed worried. Or uncomfortable? Maybe a bit of both.

"The witch who was with you on the beach," I continued. "You never told me who she was. And I'd like to personally thank her, too."

"I'm afraid you won't be able to do that," she said. "At least, not any time soon."

"Why not?"

"Because she's not from Avalon. She'll come here eventually, but not for some time. Once she does, I'm sure she'll be more than happy to see you again."

"Again?" I asked. "But I still haven't met her."

"Yes, you have," she said quickly. "On the beach."

"Right." I nodded slowly, since I'd hardly call that an official meeting.

Skylar wasn't telling me something. I couldn't pinpoint what it was, but it was there.

Then again, all prophetesses were odd and mysterious. They tended to keep their visions to themselves until the time was right to act on them. Which was frustrating, but it was their way. And I wanted to be a kind queen like Gloriana—not the type that forced information from innocent people. Whatever Skylar was hiding would become clear eventually.

Until then, I needed to be patient.

Skylar returned her focus to the grapes, examining them like she was searching for the perfect one.

"I'm glad we got to talk," I said, since she clearly didn't want to continue this conversation. "I'll see you around, I guess."

I spun around and hurried away. That was awkward. But luckily, it didn't take me long to find Julian. He was standing with his mom and sister, listening as Vita explained every detail of what she'd helped Iris design in the room.

I walked straight into his open arms. "Hi," I said, brushing my lips softly against his.

"Hi, yourself." He smiled. "Vita did an incredible job with all of this, didn't she?"

Vita straightened and beamed at her brother.

"She did," I said. "It's perfect."

Vita and her mom went to refill their drinks, leaving me and Julian alone. A heavy silence hung over us.

"Are you sure you don't want to stay here with them while I'm in the Otherworld?" I asked. "Vita looks up to you so much. And you haven't seen them in so long..." I glanced over at them, surprised to see that Vita had marched off on her own to chat with the Queen of Swords's mate, Noah.

From the way Vita was looking at him, she was clearly interested. But of course, the Queen of Swords—Raven, as she'd asked me to call her—rushed to his side to stake her territory.

Vita frowned and stepped backward. Then she quickly scanned the room, stopped on the leader of one of the other packs, pulled down the neckline of her pink dress, and strutted over to him.

He faced Vita straight on, seeming open to her advances.

She's a bigger flirt than Torrence.

My heart dropped, like it always did when I thought about my best friend.

Trust Skylar, trust Reed, and trust the Supreme Mages, I reminded myself. *Torrence will be home soon.*

"You can't get rid of me that easily," Julian said, pulling me out of my looping thoughts about Torrence. "I'm going wherever you go. Even the Queen of Wands isn't indestructible. Who knows when she'll need a chosen champion of Mars to keep her safe?"

"You certainly did your fair share of that in the Otherworld." I smiled. Because if it weren't for Julian, there was no way I'd be here—alive—right now. He was the anchor that held me steady in rough seas, and the lighthouse that illuminated my path in a storm. He'd pulled me out of my lowest lows and believed in me when I didn't have faith in myself. "Even though we're both strong individually, we're always stronger together."

"You know it," he said. "Which is why I'm staying by your side, even if you venture into Hell itself."

My heart raced like it had the first time I'd laid eyes on him. "I love you," I said.

"And I love you."

We moved closer to kiss again, but then someone screamed, and glass shattered on the hardwood floor.

I spun around to see what had happened, ready to strike at the first sight of a threat.

A woman in a purple dress who hadn't been there when I'd entered stood in the center of the room. Her brown, wavy hair that reached her waist blew around her, and a colorful flower crown sat on her head. The flower petals in the room moved toward her feet like a magnet and bloomed into a small garden around her.

She stood at human height, but I could feel the godly essence pouring off her in waves. "Selena Pearce." She smiled, her earth-green eyes warm and welcoming. "I've heard quite a lot about you."

I stood there, dumbstruck. Everyone else in the room had quieted, too.

Which god is she?

Ceres, perhaps? The flowers and earthly presence would make sense.

Or else, maybe…

"I'm sorry," she said with a warm smile. "I suppose I should have introduced myself. I'm Persephone. The Queen of the Underworld."

SELENA

THE QUEEN of the Underworld was here. In Avalon. In *our dining room.*

She was Ceres's daughter, so my guess of her identity hadn't been too far off. And I had a hope about why she'd dropped by... but I immediately squelched it. Because she was alone.

So what was she doing here?

"Don't you mean Proserpina?" Julian was the first to speak.

She smiled again, like she found him amusing. A few more flowers bloomed at her feet. "Proserpina is the name I go by while in my Roman form," she said. "But different aspects of our personalities are stronger depending on the realm we're in. In the Otherworld, I'm Proserpina. On Earth, I go by my Greek name.

Persephone."

Realizing that I was still on guard, I relaxed my grip around the Holy Wand. No need to look like I was about to attack a goddess. "So you're two different people in one body?" I asked.

"No." Her laugh was musical, like chirping birds. "Our Roman sides are strong in the Otherworld because that's what the majority of that realm knows us as. On Earth, our Greek forms are more well known, so that side of us is stronger while we're here."

My mother was instantly by my side, and she lowered herself into a curtsy. "Your Highness," she said. "Thank you for joining our celebration."

"Please, rise," Persephone said, and my mom did as requested. "And call me Persephone. Gods don't need nor require formal titles of address."

I'd definitely told my mom that when I'd recounted everything that had happened in the Otherworld. But after all of my etiquette lessons on Avalon, I knew it took some time to get used to it.

"How did you get here?" someone asked from my mom's other side. The Queen of Swords, Raven. She had her hand wrapped around the handle of the Holy Sword, Excalibur, although luckily, she didn't draw the weapon. "Did you go through the Trials?"

I watched the goddess and waited for her response, since I was curious as well.

"I did go through the Trials," she said. "And, as you can see, I passed."

People shuffled around and whispered to one another, apparently more comfortable now that they knew Persephone wasn't a threat. If she wished us harm, she wouldn't have gotten through the Trials.

Their questions filled the room.

Why's she here?

Is she really a goddess?

What type of magic does she have?

"What brings you to Avalon?" I asked, and everyone quieted once again.

"I can't stay for long, but I've stopped by to surprise you," she said, and hope took hold once again.

I held my breath, waiting and praying that I might be right. "Surprise me with what?" I asked, and then I cursed inwardly. Persephone was a goddess. The surprise could simply be her presence at my party.

But I hoped it was more than that.

"After you left the Underworld, I received an invitation to dine with Gloriana," the goddess continued. "I accepted, of course. I do love spending time in Elysium. When I'm there, I can sometimes even pretend I'm back in the realm of the living." She glanced out the nearest window and smiled, as if thinking of a happy memory. Then, she refocused on me. "During the meal, Gloriana had a request. And I've come here to grant it."

I reached for Julian's hand and squeezed it so tightly that I was probably cutting off his circulation.

Persephone stepped out of the garden blooming at her feet. She held out her hand, and green magic poured out of her palm, toward the flowers.

A floral, earthy scent filled the room. It felt like breathing in the essence of life itself. From the deep breaths and sighs of pleasure sounding all around me, everyone else was having a similar experience, too.

The flowers sparkled, and they grew and grew, until they were around the same height as me. The magic glowed brighter—so bright that I nearly had to look away. But I didn't. Instead, I watched as the vines swirled around each other, shimmering and sparkling as they settled into the form of a person.

The light disappeared, and I looked into forest green eyes I didn't think I'd ever see again.

"Cassia?" I said her name, as if that would be enough to prove I wasn't imagining she were here.

She looked like a goddess in a purple dress the same color as Persephone's, and she had a dainty flower crown on her head. She touched her face and ran her fingers through her hair, as if checking to see if she were real. "Selena." Her voice cracked—like she hadn't used it for a long time—and her eyes filled with tears as she gazed around the dining hall. "Where are we?"

I returned the Holy Wand to the ether, ran toward her, and smothered her in a hug.

My fingers didn't slip through her, like they had in the Underworld.

She was real.

"This is Avalon," I said after finally pulling away. "My home."

My mom and dad were by my side in an instant. Julian, too. My heart felt fuller than it had since returning to Earth, and I couldn't stop smiling.

I looked back at Persephone to ask if this was permanent. But the goddess was gone.

And she hadn't taken Cassia with her.

"Cassia," my mom said her name warmly, and she placed her hand on my friend's forearm. "We've heard so many wonderful things about you. I'm Annika—the Earth Angel, the Queen of Cups, and, most importantly, Selena's mom. And it's my pleasure to welcome you to Avalon."

EPILOGUE: TORRENCE

A FEW WEEKS LATER

SUNLIGHT SPILLED THROUGH THE WINDOWS, warming my face and waking me up. All of the bedrooms in Circe's house faced east, since she insisted on rising with the sun.

I groaned and pulled the covers over my head. They didn't help much, but I rolled over and closed my eyes anyway to try going back to sleep.

"Torrence," Circe chirped from outside my door. "Are you dressed?"

"Do you care?"

"Of course I care." She flung the door open and smirked down at me. "I hope the answer is no."

Anger boiled deep within me, and my dark magic filled me, protecting me. My magic was the only thing that kept me sane. It was crazy to think about how help-less I'd been before embracing it. How *weak* I'd been.

The person I'd been before coming here was a distant memory, and I never wanted to be that vulner-able ever again. Nothing hurt me anymore. Anger, yes. But hurt? I had ghost-like memories of feeling that way, especially around Reed. But I didn't remember the actual feeling itself.

I preferred it this way.

"Then you're going to be disappointed." I threw off the blanket and stretched, my strappy pink silk night-gown rising to the top of my thighs. It didn't cover much, but it was better than nothing.

Not that I cared if Circe saw me naked or not. But I *did* care if I angered her. I loved angering her. Every time I did, victory rushed through me, strengthening my magic.

"That's no fun." She walked forward to stand at the end of my bed, and her hungry eyes stared down at me like I was a feast she was ready to enjoy.

I stared right back, although I was sure my gaze was as dark as the magic swirling in my soul.

"You've been here for weeks," she said. "And even though I'm immortal, I'm beginning to get impatient."

"Impatient for what?"

"You." She lowered herself down onto her knees at the edge of my bed.

"Not gonna happen.'" I sat up and leaned against the headboard. "Now, what's on the breakfast menu this morning? Bacon? Sausage? Ham? All of the above?"

"I'm going to have to lure more men here to keep up with your voracious appetite." She grinned.

"What can I say?" I shrugged. "It's far better than the bland porridge we'd have otherwise."

"That it is," she agreed. "But I'm hungry for something other than breakfast." She crawled closer to me, like a cat, and stopped when she was right in front of me.

"And what's that?" I challenged.

"Your submission to me." She pulled one arm out of her strappy dress, then the other. It slid off her, into a small pile at her knees.

She wore nothing underneath it.

I narrowed my eyes, and shadows darkened the room. "Never."

"You're so tempting when your eyes turn black like that," she purred. "It makes me want you even more."

"How'd you guess? That's exactly my intent." Sarcasm dripped off me nearly as much as dark magic.

She recoiled, snarled, then quickly recovered. "You look

tough and talk tough, but you're forgetting one important thing." She smiled like she'd already won. "I'm a sorceress. This is my island. I'm in control here. I've been waiting for you to come to me willingly, but I've grown impatient."

"What're you going to do?" I sat up on my knees, so I was at the same level as her. "Force yourself on me?"

"That's exactly what I'm going to do." She twirled a strand of her hair, and then ran her finger down along her breast. "And you're going to enjoy it."

"Like hell I am."

I reached for my magic, but she blasted me with hers first, freezing me in place. I tried to move, but my body wouldn't listen to me.

Panic squeezed my lungs.

I was trapped.

She tilted her head and studied me like I was an expensive piece of art she was considering purchasing. "That's better." She reached for one of the straps of my nightgown and pulled it down, like she had with hers. She did the same with the other strap, and my nightgown fell to my knees.

We faced each other like mirror images, both of us stripped down to nothing.

I tried to move again, but I couldn't.

Anger surged through me like a volcano about to

erupt, and I stared her down, daring her to try anything further.

If she did, she'd burn for it. I was going to *destroy* her. I might have been powerless to say it, but my magic was still there. And every moment she held me down, my magic pushed harder outward, like a balloon ready to pop.

"You're perfect," she said. "And you're mine."

She flicked her wrist, and her magic jerked at me. One moment I was on my knees, and then I was laying flat on the bed.

I tried to scream, but I couldn't move. Instead, the scream joined with my magic, fueling the storm raging inside me.

You took away my life, I thought, and I hoped my eyes got across my fury. *I'm not letting you take my dignity, too.*

She crawled over me and hovered there, her gaze roaming up and down my body. The corner of her lip curled up into a small smile. "You're going to come crawling to my bed every night after this," she said. "Just wait and see."

She slowly lowered herself down, pressed her lips to mine, and slipped her tongue inside my mouth.

Die, you crazy bitch, I thought, and then my magic blasted out of me and into her like a bomb, surrounding us in a suffocating explosion of thick black smoke.

The smoke blew around like a hurricane, blinding me. It was like white noise everywhere. I breathed in, and it filled my lungs, pushing its way inside of me. The power was all consuming. I needed *more* of it. So I opened my mouth and sucked it down, until the last bits of it entered my body and my magic was back where it belonged.

Instead of the ceiling, I looked up at the clear blue sky. I tried to move my fingers, and they obeyed my command.

I was free from Circe's magic.

I sat up and looked around in shock.

Because I was no longer in the palace. I was still on the island, but all that remained was scorched rubble. It was like someone had dropped an atomic bomb. Except I felt no pain, whatsoever.

I glanced down at my body.

Ash covered me. I studied my palms, which were coated with it.

What had I done?

"Torrence Devereux," a voice boomed from in front of me.

Four men and three women in black clothes that I could only describe as medieval stood about ten feet away. They all had silver hair and glowing silver eyes, except for one of them.

"Reed." I pushed myself up, stumbled slightly, and hurried toward him.

I was only halfway there when two of the men appeared by my side. Before I could blink, they snapped a cuff around each of my wrists.

They burned like they'd come straight out of a fire, and I screamed.

A person behind me pulled my wrists behind my back. The cuffs must have welded together, because I couldn't move my arms.

The man who'd snapped on the first cuff pushed down on my shoulders, and I fell to my knees in the rubble. The pebbles dug into my skin. But the cuffs cooled down to normal temperature, so they no longer seared my skin.

The six of them surrounded me in a semi-circle and stared down at me with their creepy silver eyes. They looked so alike that they had to be siblings.

"You're indecent," said the woman with the longest hair. She removed her cloak, moved toward me, and wrapped it around my shoulders. "There. That's better."

I reached for my magic, and the cuffs burned again. I screamed, and sweat gathered on my skin. Tears ran down my face.

I tried to teleport away, and it hurt even worse. Red, hot, scorching, agonizing pain.

Reed pushed through the silver-haired people and crouched beside me. "You can't use your magic with the cuffs on," he said. "You have to stop trying."

I glared at him and reached harder.

Pain sliced through me so intensely that I collapsed into his arms. He held me tightly as I tried to breathe, and just like he'd promised, the burning stopped when I stopped trying to fight.

"Why are you doing this?" I pulled away to look at him. "Who *are* these people?"

"Do you promise not to try fighting again?" he asked.

"Are you going to answer my questions?"

"I see you haven't changed much," he said with a small smile.

"Wrong." Shadows covered my sight, then more pain from the cuffs, and I screamed again. The pain only disappeared when my vision returned to normal.

Reed reached for me, steadying me as I breathed through it. "You said you wouldn't try to fight."

"I didn't do that on purpose," I said. "Besides, I never said I wouldn't try to fight. I just asked if you were going to answer my questions." I looked back at the mysterious silver-haired people, who'd been silent since pushing me to the ground.

The man in the center—the tallest of the group—stepped forward. "We're six of the twelve Supreme Mages," he said. "Reed came to us three months ago and told us about your situation. We've been trying to free you since. After several unsuccessful attempts to locate Circe's staff to offer her a trade, we've been discussing other options with her for the past two weeks. We'd nearly reached an agreement, but then…" He pressed his thin lips together and looked around disapprovingly at the destruction surrounding us.

"I saved myself," I said darkly, trying with every last bit of effort to push down the magic trying to rise up within me.

"That you did," said a harsh-looking woman with short hair that brushed the tops of her shoulders. "And in the process, you killed a sorceress and hundreds of helpless men."

"You mean the pigs?"

"Those weren't their natural forms," she said. "They were human men. All of them murdered by your dark magic."

"I did what I had to do to free myself from Circe," I said. "And it worked."

"You killed hundreds of innocents."

Six pairs of disapproving silver eyes stared down at me. None of them looked like they were going to budge.

In their eyes, I was a stone-cold killer.

Maybe I was. Maybe I should have felt guilty about killing those pigs. Those *men*.

But I didn't.

I straightened my shoulders and glared right back at them. "They were necessary casualties for ridding the world of Circe," I said. "I'd do it again in a heartbeat."

The woman who'd given me her cloak frowned. "You've gone dark," she said simply.

"Hey." Reed scooted closer to me, although from the way he looked up at the mages, he looked *scared*. "We don't know what Circe was doing to her in there. She's been through a lot. Give her some time to process. I'm sure there's an explanation."

"There's only one explanation for this." The tall man motioned around the scorched island. "And it's exactly as we feared. She's followed in the footsteps of her father, and succumbed to darkness."

Reed stiffened next to me. "No," he said. "You don't know—"

"Hold on," I cut him off, focused on tall mage. "My father barely had any magic, like most male witches."

"Wrong." He smiled, although his smile was more evil than anything else. "Do you truly think you could access so much magic if your father was a mere *witch?*"

"I can access so much magic because Reed and I did

spells together." The moment the words were out of my mouth, I glanced over at him.

But he stared straight ahead.

"Mages—and witches—can't *share* their magic with each other." The short-haired woman laughed and looked to Reed. "Is that what you've been telling her?"

"I haven't told her anything." He still refused to look at me.

"Interesting," she said, and she looked back down at me. "Your father is a mage. He's one of the most dangerous criminals in the history of Mystica."

"No." I shook my head, since my mom wouldn't have lied to me about something so huge. "That's not true."

"About eighteen years ago, he succumbed to dark magic," she continued. "He tried to hide on Earth, but we found him. And it appears he had a bit of fun while on the run, too." She paused to eye me. "When Reed told us about you and showed us your picture, we suspected this might be the case. You look just like him."

I swallowed, since I looked nothing like my blonde-haired, blue-eyed mom.

She'd always told me I'd gotten my looks from my dad.

"What happened to him?" I asked.

"We captured him and sent him where we send all mages who go dark," she said. "To Ember."

Fear prickled down my spine at the name of the prison world Selena had told me about.

A fiery hellscape full of monstrous, flying beasts.

"You've heard of it?" the tall man—the one who seemed to be their leader—asked, and I nodded. "Good. Because you'll be joining him there."

My body numbed.

"What?" Reed stood up, and his eyes flashed black. "You were helping me find her so we could bring her back to Avalon."

"Change of plans," the short-haired woman said. "Her bloodline is tainted with an addiction to dark magic. There was a chance she could fight it, but she's given in, just like her father."

Rage built inside me.

How dare these people act like they know my mind?

"You're wrong." I stood up, but the cuffs jolted me, and I fell back down to my knees.

"You killed one of the most powerful sorceresses in known history," the man said. "Some go as far as saying Circe was a goddess. Nothing but pure, dark magic could have done this."

"She deserves a trial," Reed said. "At least give her that."

A man with a long silver beard who'd been quiet so far stepped forward. "She's going to Ember," he said.

"You can't fight us on this, boy."

"Watch me." Reed's eyes flashed black, and he raised his hands to shoot dark magic at the bearded mage.

The mage easily held off Reed's magic with his own, at the same time as the tall mage and the long-haired woman snapped cuffs around Reed's wrists.

Reed's magic stopped, and he screamed. The mages forced his hands behind his back and pushed him down onto his knees next to me.

"You shouldn't have done that," I told him. "They're obviously stronger than you."

"That's not why I did it."

"Then what were you trying to do?"

His eyes were back to their normal dark brown, saddened as he looked at me. But he said nothing.

"She asks a good question," the short-haired woman said. "What *were* you trying to do?"

"I'm not letting her go to Ember alone," he said, and then he turned back to me. "I'm going with you."

"Don't be ridiculous," I snapped.

"I'm not being ridiculous," he said. "I promised Selena I was going to get you home. If that means going with you to Ember, then that's what I'm going to do."

"No."

"You can't fight me on this."

We sat there, staring at each other, locked in a stand-off. "I don't want you there," I finally said. "I can handle myself. I don't need a knight in shining armor to save me."

"Then it's a good thing I'm not a knight in shining armor."

The tall man cleared his throat loudly, and we both looked to him. "Are you sure about this?" he asked Reed. "You're from an aristocratic family in Mystica. You're able to control your dark magic. You owe this illegitimate, half-breed girl nothing."

"Wrong," Reed said. "I owe her everything."

"Very well."

The two quietest mages who'd been standing on the sides pulled matching syringes out of their pockets and disappeared.

Their feet crunched in the rubble as they teleported to stand behind us. Then there was a sharp prick on the back of my neck, my vision blurred, and everything went dark.

THANK YOU FOR READING!

I hope you enjoyed the conclusion to Selena's story! If so, I'd love if you left a review. Reviews help new readers find the books, and I read each and every one of them :)

A review for the first book in the series is the most helpful. Here's the link on Amazon where you can go to leave your review → mybook.to/faeriegames

Torrence's ending was pretty intense, but don't worry—her story will continue in the next series in the Dark World universe, The Dragon Twins, coming September 2020!

In the meantime, I've written a BONUS SCENE that happens when Torrence and Reed wake up in the place the mages sent them. (Ember? Mystica? Somewhere else entirely?)

How will Torrence react when Reed finally confesses his feelings to her?

To find out, visit michellemadow.com/faerie-plague-bonus-scene to grab the bonus scene!

Go to michellemadow.com/subscribe to get an email from me when The Dragon Twins releases!

ARE YOU NEW TO THE DARK WORLD UNIVERSE?

Then you'll want to check out the two other series' in this world—The Vampire Wish and The Angel Trials. These series' are about the Queen of Cups and the Queen of Swords.

Turn the page to learn more about them!

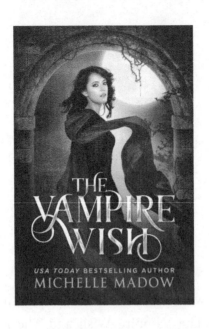

Meet Annika: The Queen of Cups

Annika never thought of herself as weak—until vampires kidnapped her to their hidden kingdom of the Vale.

As a brand new blood slave, Annika must survive her dangerous new circumstances—or face death from the wolves prowling the Vale's enchanted walls. But sparks fly when she meets the vampire prince Jacen. She hates the idea of falling for the enemy, but her connection with the mysterious prince could be the key to her freedom.

Because if she can convince him to turn her into a vampire, she'll finally have the strength she needs to escape the Vale.

Get it now at:

mybook.to/vampirewish

Meet Raven: The Queen of Swords

Raven Danvers is a typical student… until a demon attacks her on the night of her birthday. Luckily, she's saved by Noah—a mysterious, sexy wolf shifter who appears and disappears before she can ask him any questions.

Then Raven's mom is abducted by the same demon who came after her. And who turns up at the scene of the crime again? Noah. He's hunting the demons who are taking humans, and he's ultimately heading where

Raven needs to go to save her mom—the mystical island of Avalon.

Now Raven's joining Noah's demon hunting mission whether he wants her there or not. Which he doesn't. But nothing stops Raven, so she and Noah will have to learn to work together—if they don't kill each other first.

More importantly, she has to survive his crazy demon hunt. Because surviving is the only way to get to Avalon and save her mom's life.

Get it now at:
mybook.to/angeltrials

ABOUT THE AUTHOR

Michelle Madow is a USA Today bestselling author of fast paced fantasy novels that will leave you turning the pages wanting more! Her books are full of magic, adventure, romance, and twists you'll never see coming.

Michelle grew up in Maryland, and now lives in Florida. She's loved reading for as long as she can remember. She wrote her first book in her junior year of college and hasn't stopped writing since! She also loves traveling, and has been to all seven continents. Someday, she hopes to travel the world for a year on a cruise ship.

Click here or visit author.to/MichelleMadow to view a full list of Michelle's novels on Amazon.

To get free books, exclusive content, and instant updates from Michelle, visit www.michellemadow.com/subscribe and subscribe to her newsletter now!

THE FAERIE PLAGUE

Published by Dreamscape Publishing

Copyright © 2020 Michelle Madow

ISBN: 9798654269249

This book is a work of fiction. Though some actual towns, cities, and locations may be mentioned, they are used in a fictitious manner and the events and occurrences were invented in the mind and imagination of the author. Any similarities of characters or names used within to any person past, present, or future is coincidental.

✽ Created with Vellum

Made in the USA
Coppell, TX
03 July 2020